AF422087

ERICA M. REILLY

The Shallows of Avalon

First published by Bover Publishing 2026

Copyright © 2026 by Erica M. Reilly

All rights reserved. No part of this publication may be reproduced, stored, or transmitted in any form or by any means, electronic, mechanical, photocopying, recording, scanning, or otherwise without written permission from the publisher. It is illegal to copy this book, post it to a website, or distribute it by any other means without permission.

This novel is entirely a work of fiction. The names, characters, and incidents portrayed in it are the work of the author's imagination. Any resemblance to actual persons, living or dead, events, or localities is entirely coincidental.

This book was not written with AI, and the author is firmly committed to writing and editing by humans only.

First edition

ISBN: 979-8-9906258-3-9

Editing by Ria Cooper

This book was professionally typeset on Reedsy. Find out more at reedsy.com

This one is for my husband, Brett.
You know all the reasons why.

Contents

Acknowledgments

It takes a village. Thank you to my childhood best friend, Ria Cooper, for all the texts, calls, and edits. This would simply not have been possible without you. Also, to Jennifer Pooley for your insights and feedback. You have such a gift with words!

Thanks to my sister Colleen for giving me the Emmy idea; Jim Talone for all the advice, edits and support; Kenny Pollack for explaining how the Ocean City Police Department works (it's a shame we had to cut the bridge scene); Gail Guterl for reading and offering advice; and Marisa Hamrah for reviewing all the details of the Newport, Rhode Island venues. Anything I have missing or incorrect is my own fault.

Bonnie Raley always helps with designing and formatting my covers. You are such a talented photographer and supportive friend.

Fellow author Kimberly Brighton is a wonderful author and one of the funniest people I know. Read all of her books about Cape May, and her new one set in Sea Isle!

To my kids, Bowe, Samantha, Parker, and Tori; my parents, Mary Jane and Jere; all of my wonderful Reilly/Lawton in-laws; the OG Melanie Kalantari; my Ohio U. roommates; Del Val HS friends; the D-Town Posse; ACAC girls Lauren Stauffer and Heather Coyle; and the West Chester/St. Max mom crew. You all are simply the best.

The lifeguard on the cover is a real person named Markus from Duck Surf Rescue, who greeted my family every morning on the beach. Thank you for agreeing to let me use your photo. Markus, you should be the official mascot of the Outer Banks.

I

The Cast of The Shallows TV Series, 2012-2016

Eve Mattson .... *Josie Remington*

Shea Maisal .... *Paige DeBello*

Francesca Giordano .... *Valerie Worth*

Jack Tucker .... *Tate Masters*

Chase Stattler .... *Mason Stauffer*

Hazel Mattson .... *Rebecca Radcliffe*

Mrs. Mattson .... *Elise DeLonghi*

Mr. Mattson .... *Marty Lawson*

Liam Tucker .... *Scotty Redcross*

Chapter 1

"What? We're moving to California?
Who's even heard of Duffy Beach?"
- Eve and Hazel, Pilot Episode

Josie, April 19

Josie stands in front of the processed meat section in the deli area, trying to decide between smoked and roasted, when she hears low murmurs of conversation close to her.

There's a tingle at the back of her neck. Someone is staring. Whispering.

Instantly, Josie knows she's the topic they're talking about.

She's been caught. Tagged, bagged, and identified. At a ShopRite grocery store in Clinton, New Jersey.

She really doesn't have time for this today.

She slips her sunglasses off the top of her head and pulls them down over her eyes. It might keep more people from identifying her as she makes a break for the exit.

Damn it. She wishes she had a hat.

Abandoning her careful review of multiple brands of sausage, Josie pushes her cart away from the two girls gawking at her and makes one last-ditch attempt to sneak out by making a right turn down the paper products aisle. She might still be able to pull off a quick dash through self-checkout.

But she's not fast enough. They're on her before she passes the massive stacks of toilet paper rolls.

"Excuse me?"

She walks faster, picking up the pace. Trying to get some distance between them.

"Hello?" Josie hears over her shoulder. "Miss?"

They're getting closer.

"We just want to ask you something."

They are just steps behind her. They look so eager. And *young*.

It's going to be impossible to get out of this one without making a public scene or coming off like a total bitch to a couple of young teens. You can't get away with having a bad day in public. These days, someone always has a phone handy to record it. She accepts defeat.

Time to grin and bear it, Josie. Say hi.

She turns around and forces a polite smile that's friendly but not *too* friendly. The game is up. She may as well give them what they want.

"I'm just trying to get some grocery shopping done," Josie explains. "And I'm in a hurry." She neither verifies nor denies her identity. There's no use arguing with them. They already know who she is.

Now that they're up close, Josie can see the excitement beam across their faces as they confirm it *is* her. In person!

They know who Josie Remington is, but they'll probably call her by her character's name, Eve Mattson. Everyone does.

She waits for them to tell her that they're her biggest fans.

"I can't believe it!" The smaller one squeals and claps her hands together. "I watched every episode of *The Shallows.*"

Her braid is swinging back and forth as she hops on the speckled tile floor. "I wanted you to end up with Chase. He's *so* dreamy." She's probably 12 or 13 years old, with a pattern of freckles across her nose.

"A lot of people did, but it wasn't up to me. The writers wanted it to be Jack." It's an automatic answer. Josie has said the same thing a thousand times. Her character's love triangle with the two male leads, Jack and Chase, had caused global speculation over who Eve would choose. Eve also had a fling with a reality TV star named Zad at the end of the first season.

"I loved the senior prom episode. I've watched it over and over."

"That was one of my favorites, too."

How could it not be? Eve and Jack had split during their junior year and gone their separate ways. The following year, after she lost out on prom queen, he found her crying in the science room. They had an epic, steamy reunion on one of the lab tables with the song "They Can't Take That Away From Me" playing in the background. The episode was so widely watched that it made the song hugely popular again.

Households across the country tuned in to watch the season finale. It broke the 2016 Nielsen Media record for the highest number of viewers in the coveted demographic of 18 to 44 and held that top spot for years. Ironically, that episode ended up being the finale of the entire series, although the cast and crew didn't know it while they were filming it.

The plot of *The Shallows* was a classic TV drama, based on similar shows like *The OC, 90210, Dawson's Creek,* and *Gossip Girl.* Young and beautiful teenagers navigating the grade school and college years.

They lived in a fictional beach town called Duffy Beach (which was actually Avalon, New Jersey). It shot from 2010 to 2015, over four seasons that conveniently mirrored their freshmen to senior year of high school.

Even though it's over, it's still very much a part of Josie's life. Like now, she can anticipate the questions she knows are coming. She can even count down to them ... three ... two ... one ...

"Can we get a selfie with you?" the older girl asks.

Josie nods her head. "Of course." Maybe she'll get out of there faster if she's agreeable.

Squealing, they gather around each side of her and take a few photos.

Click. Click. Click. The one holding the bright yellow phone pulls it back toward her to check the last shot on her screen, satisfied with their impromptu photo shoot.

"Got it. This is amazing." She's a few years older than her friend. Josie pegs her at maybe 15 or 16. A young teen, fresh-faced and social media savvy.

They couldn't be nicer, but Josie wishes she'd been able to get some basic groceries without being recognized. She knows it will be up on Snapchat, TikTok, and Instagram within seconds.

Letting everyone know she's at the local grocery store. Buying meat snacks.

"Thank you so much, Eve," the younger girl gushes. Josie doesn't bother to correct her. Most people consider her and her character interchangeable.

Now that she's been in their company a little longer, she can tell they're sisters. Two young girls getting groceries who were lucky enough to spot a celebrity.

Big sis is already uploading the photos. It didn't take long.

"No problem." Honestly, they're super sweet. And they don't mean any harm. But she wishes they hadn't noticed her.

They're making enough noise for people to catch on that someone famous is there. A few customers pause at the end of the aisle, trying to figure out who it could be. A singer? Celebrity? Professional athlete?

The man working behind the deli counter has stopped slicing meat to see what's happening. Did he miss something big? He pulls his phone out of his apron and starts scrolling, trying to figure out where he knows her from.

Other shoppers begin to approach cautiously. They're not sure exactly what's happening, but they don't want to miss out on passing up something that could be important. A newsworthy moment. And, honestly, most people are just naturally nosy. They want to see what all the fuss is about.

A familiar flicker of panic begins to flutter in Josie's throat. She decides to abandon her cart without checking out the items. She doesn't want to risk dealing with a growing crowd.

"I really do have to run," Josie says with a tinge of apology. "It was nice meeting you." She shoots a last look of regret at her grocery cart. She'd been so excited to try that new key lime pie Greek yogurt. Zero sugar, too. But it's too late. She has to get out of there.

If she stands in the aisle any longer, more people are going to start approaching her for autographs. She's learned that it only takes one person to notice before a crowd begins to form.

She ought to know better by now. But she'd just ducked in for some groceries. She was *hangry*!

There would be nothing in her fridge when she got home. She'd just landed from a long week away on a work trip and had a ton of things to do. But she needed to grab food and supplies first, so she'd pulled off Route 78 at Exit 15 on her way from the Newark airport.

She should have picked a different exit when the sign said Pittstown.

"This is so fire," the older one says without looking up as she watches the likes coming in on her phone. "No one at school is going to believe we ran into you at the grocery store."

She looks at her little sister, who chimes in. "You know, Eve, we're your biggest fans."

Josie just smiles as she walks away. They always were.

Chapter 2

"Regret is a terrible thing. A hell of a waste."
- Chase, Season 3, Episode 5

Paige, April 22

"Miss DeBello? They're ready for you now."

Paige nods, flipping the papers in her hands back in order. "I'm ready." She rises from her seat in the waiting room and grabs the canvas bag hanging off the empty chair next to hers.

The fresh-faced assistant offers a hesitant smile, her back propping the door open. Paige walks over to meet her. She turns and waves her hand, gesturing for Paige to follow while she leads her down a narrow, threadbare hallway.

"I was so excited to see your name on the callbacks," the assistant confides, lowering her voice so no one overhears her. "You were my favorite character on *The Shallows.*"

Paige might have heard it a million times, but it never gets old. "That means the world. It was a special show," she responds graciously. It can't hurt to get on the young woman's good side.

"The *best.* I watched every episode at least five times. Especially the last ones. I was so happy when you were voted prom queen!"

She was younger than Paige, somewhere between 22 and 25 years old. Fresh out of college, working her first job for a casting agent. Bursting with excitement about getting a job in show business, and all the famous people she's going to meet.

Paige had felt like that once. Full of hope and excitement.

"It was quite an experience," she says honestly. She had been so grateful to the writers for putting in the prom queen twist. Eve was always the more popular character, the lead, while Paige's character Shea was the sidekick. But in that scene, she was the star. The one everyone voted for.

The Shallows lasted for four seasons, from freshman to senior year. Life lessons were taught, from surviving heartbreak to the dangers of taking illegal drugs. Even when it ended, the teen drama retained its cult status. Ten years later, people are still obsessed with it.

Val's character, Francesca, played the bad girl who was always getting into trouble. She was frenemies with Eve, played by Josie, who had just moved into town from the Midwest. Eve's parents, Marty and Elise, were relatable characters–the sympathetic but strict parents who wanted only the best for their daughters Eve and Hazel.

The high school hero Jack (played by Tate) was best friends with Chase (played by Mason) and had a younger brother, Scotty (played by Max Rodriguez). Jack and Chase were friendly rivals who both had a thing for Eve. Paige played Eve's best friend Shea, a bubbly sidekick who Chase dated in the final season.

Her character Francesca also had a story arc about dealing with an unexpected pregnancy over spring break. The writers were able to sidestep her character needing to make a polarizing decision by writing in a miscarriage. The father was never announced–it was supposedly a surfer boy–but there were rumors it was Jack or Chase, too, especially after Jack was caught making out with Francesca.

There were other scandals, too. Shea suffered an overdose after doing too many Jell-O shots at a party, allowing the writers to write about alcohol abuse and teenage drinking.

Jack dated a girl from another town that was not as wealthy as Duffy Beach, creating a storyline about the tensions and differences between affluent and poor neighborhoods. Hazel ran off after a fight with her parents, and Eve found her younger sister before she was taken advantage of in the big city.

There's no doubt the show had been cheesy. There's also no arguing that it had been wildly successful.

"Do you all still stay in touch?"

"Of course we do," Paige answers diplomatically.

"It's just like the cast of *Friends*. Or *Gossip Girl*. All of you, still so close. Hanging out." The assistant sighs happily. "Amazing."

"It really is." They're approaching the audition room. Paige's nerves begin to rise. She needs to cut this conversation short so she can focus. "We were all so lucky," Paige tells her, a tinge of finality in her voice.

"I heard they're having a reunion at the Jersey shore in August. Are you going?"

This woman is persistent, if anything. "Of course." She tilts her head to the door, a more obvious cue to end the conversation. "I'm so glad you're a fan. But I'm excited to try out for *this* show now." Even if it is about zombie penguins.

Her companion still doesn't take the hint. "I already bought tickets with my friends. We can't wait to go back to Duffy Beach."

"Then hopefully I'll see you there." Paige is done waiting. She opens the door herself, striding into the room with enough confidence to say *I'm here!* without looking like she's thinking *I'm the shit.*

It's a strategic balancing act, and one she grew up learning. She's paid her dues.

This isn't her first rodeo. Paige DeBello was born to be a star (according to her mother, Jean). From the moment she offered up her first toothy smile paired with long ginger curls, she was getting booked for diaper and baby food commercials.

In the coming years, her easygoing nature and trademark freckles helped secure larger, more lucrative endorsements from national brands. Her fame kept rising until she hit the height of her fame as Shea Maisel, the sweet and supportive best friend of Eve Mattson, on *The Shallows.*

She knows she was lucky to be plucked out of thousands who auditioned. But this is Hollywood, and fame is fleeting. Ten years later, Paige is still auditioning for roles in a damp waiting room with other struggling actors.

It's so depressing.

The casting director looks up from the sheet he's been studying. "Paige DeBello, second callback for Mae Armstrong, supporting actress?"

"That's me." Always the supporting actor, never the lead. She's gotten used to it. She's *had* to get used to it.

"Could you start from Act 5? When you're attacked by one of the male penguin zombies?"

She nods. "Of course."

An hour and a half later, Paige returns home to her studio apartment in Jersey City. It's a little bit of a hike from New York City, but it's a much more affordable option than living in Manhattan. She's still close enough to the city without paying the jaw-dropping rents.

In her opinion, the audition went well. The character she auditioned for dies in the first half of the movie, sliced open by the flipper of a penguin zombie. It's not much of a role, but she'll take it. Maybe it will become a beloved quirky flick, like *The Meg* or *Rocky Horror Picture Show.* Or maybe not. She's never even heard of the director.

I'm doing my best. Paige tries to quiet the nagging voice inside her. The one she's had since she was a little girl and lost out on an important audition.

And things aren't so bad. She's been able to book a few guest appearances on popular shows and several lucrative commercials, giving her enough padding to make the rent and keep up with the grooming needed to look good on camera. She has a new film coming out that wrapped last year, which, oddly enough, was also about destructive animals.

But she's worried it's not enough. If her career doesn't pick up soon, she's going to need to look into an OnlyFans account.

Paige enters the lobby of her apartment building. It's late, but she checks her mailbox automatically. She never knows when a royalty check will pop up out of nowhere, especially from her early days.

Every little bit helps.

There's a thick cream envelope with her name scrawled across the front in distinguished calligraphy: *Ms. Paige DeBello.*

This is unusual. Her mailbox is mostly full of junk: ads from one-day shower replacement companies, lawn care, and discount mailers for local grocery stores.

It must be something special. Ripping it open, she slides out the thick cards to scan the handwritten invitation: *You are cordially invited to a celebration of Sage Domingo and Simon Hartwick, Saturday, the first of June. Newport, Rhode Island. Black tie only.*

Well, this came out of the blue. Sage Domingo and Simon Hartwick. She wouldn't have expected an invitation to their wedding. They're not exactly close anymore. When was the last time she even talked to either of them?

It's been years. The golden days of her career, when she was making headlines and starting trends, not chasing after them.

Ironically, she was just talking about *The Shallows* today. The show may have ended, but it never went away. It's a part of her, just as much as her trademark curly red hair or her painful experience as a child actor.

Sage and Simon both worked on the set of the show. Sage was in the art department, and Simon was the head writer. Paige was there when they started dating and fell in love. And now, the two of them were getting married.

She draws a shuddering sigh as she looks down at the invitation once more. After all these years, was it time to finally own up to what she'd done? To see everyone face-to-face and tell them the truth? Ask for their forgiveness and see where they end up?

Paige doesn't know if she's ready.

Chapter 3

"Do you really think you're that big of a deal? Because I don't."
- Eve to her boyfriend Zad, Season 1, Episode 7

Tate, April 23

Tate grabs another can of Diet Coke from the drink fridge. It's nearly 2 am, and they've been at it for more than ten hours straight, but he needs to make sure they've got it locked down.

Squeaks, his business partner and sound engineer, shoots him an angry look. "We have to wrap this up soon," she says. "If we keep pushing, we're going to start making mistakes."

He knows Squeaks is right, but they're almost there. This album is going to be one of the best they've ever produced–he can *feel* it. They just need to make sure it's absolutely perfect.

"Can you give me one more set? Ease off the bass in 'Changing Standards' but add some more vocals to 'If You Wait'?"

Squeaks rolls her eyes but goes along with his request. She knows exactly what he's asking her for. Her instincts are perfect.

She remixes the two songs for another 20 minutes and plays them back. They're good. *Really good.* This is exactly what he's been looking for.

Tate grabs her out of the chair and pulls her up for a hug. "We nailed it! I adore you."

"Not my type, but appreciate the look," Squeaks smirks, her dark brown eyes dancing.

She reaches up and pulls her headphones down so they're resting around her neck, against her thick braids. Her eyes are tired, equal parts exhaustion and excitement bundled together. "I can't believe it's this late."

"You're the best." He knows he pushed them, maybe too hard, but it was worth it. They finally got it right.

It's how they always work together, driving each other to perfection. One more take, then just one more, until they get it right. Until it *works.*

Tate and Squeaks have been working together for several years now, developing a solid partnership in their recording studio. They trust each other's judgment and respect their opinions. Most of the time. When they don't agree, she usually wins the argument anyway.

"I'm sorry," Tate says guiltily. "We were on such a great roll. I wanted to knock it out."

Now that they nailed it, she relents a little. "You're a pain in my ass, but you were right. These guys are going places."

"I know."

Squeaks smacks his arm. "Although right now, I'm beat. I'm out."

"I'll get you a car. Leave yours here. There's no way we should be driving home this late. One of us will end up passing out." Tate pulls out his phone and requests one.

She nods in agreement. "I'll come get it tomorrow."

A few minutes later, they walk out of the studio. It's dark, cold, and quiet. He can barely make out the stars above the street lights.

No one in their right mind is still up working in this part of town. Maybe partying, but not still working.

Tate knows it's a shared insanity. He and Squeaks both will keep going until they get it right.

It's a crazy business, but he can't help but love it. There's no other feeling like knowing you crushed your goals. Achieved something no one else even knew about yet, and had the opportunity to show it to the world. Taking someone's rough creativity and polishing it until it sparkles.

Just wait until they release the album. It's going to be huge.

A long, black sedan pulls up. His partner gets in the back and flashes him a peace sign. "Don't even think of calling me before tomorrow afternoon. I need some sleep."

Tate salutes. "Aye, aye, Captain." He goes back inside to lock up the studio.

After *The Shallows* ended, Tate Masters bounced around. He did the typical teen heartthrob bullshit: bounced around Bali and Thailand, partied at nightclubs in Greece and Miami, made stupid decisions and passed out on couches.

Eventually, he got tired of that life and started to seriously think about what he wanted to do for the next five years–and not just as the answer to an interview question. Where he honestly wanted to live and what kind of person he actually wanted to be.

He invested in a few start-ups: a liquor brand that did okay, a private plane charter service that didn't, and a Bitcoin stake that was still up in the air. Does anyone really know how Bitcoin works anyway?

Tate found himself at loose ends. Not sure what to do or where to go. He'd missed out on the whole college experience.

Sure, he got his bachelor's degree online. Even earned it from a decent school. But was it the same as actually going to college? Living in a small, dingy dorm room with a pack of friends? Trying to sneak into bars with terrible fake IDs? Tailgating at sweaty football games?

Probably not.

Tate can't complain, though. *The Shallows* was a once-in-a-lifetime experience. It gave him the freedom of having enough savings to do what he wanted, without the burden of any debt to repay or big expenses to worry about. And working on the show is what sparked his interest in audio production.

Which is why he's in the parking lot of a recording studio in Philadelphia at 2:30 in the morning, finalizing a new album for a promising band.

He loves every minute.

When Tate was still on *The Shallows*, he used to hang out in the editing booth after a day of filming. He liked seeing how the production sound mixer took the raw audio and added background noise or buffered the sound to make it sound cleaner. Cut the dialogue so it blended seamlessly without the audience even realizing some scenes were filmed on different days or multiple takes.

The sound crew was cool with him, a young teen asking a lot of questions. Poking his nose into the studio while they were trying to get real work done. They took the time to explain how the process worked and talk about new software that was coming out.

He learned from the ground up, and he knew he was extremely lucky to rub shoulders with some of the best in the business. He caught on quickly.

Tate absorbed enough to realize that what he was doing for fun on the side had turned into something he might be able to use as a career. Something that he was good at.

Still, it was tough. It was a continually evolving industry. So much of the technology was outdated just a few years after launching. He needed to constantly learn new software or streaming platforms. No one knew what was going to happen with the advance of AI. Tate lumps AI in with Bitcoin, something he reads articles about but still can't wrap his head around.

He loves every aspect of producing music, though. It's the only time he completely lets go, so wrapped up in what he's doing that he loses track of time.

Tate was brought up surrounded by live music.

Tate's parents are famous. Ridiculously famous. His mom and dad met when they were young and glamorous, going out to clubs and partying in New York. They were the "It" couple of their generation, their photos splashed across magazines around the world.

Kate Noble is the founding member of The Peacocks, an all-female band that ruled in the 80s. His mom was a pretty big deal. No one could rip a guitar chord like her.

His father is Crew Masters, the leader of the Maverick Pack. They were a group of young actors considered some of the "hottest upcoming stars" of the 90s.

Kate and Crew. Tate was their only child. From the crib, he heard live music played throughout his house. It was woven into his childhood memories.

Crew didn't push his son into acting, but it was natural that he met some casting directors as a result of his father being in the industry. He booked a few shows and television ads before joining the cast of *The Shallows*.

When he was a kid, his mother, Kate, tried making him a musician: piano, guitar, ukulele, drums… Tate did it all. When they both realized he wasn't a natural, his mother finally agreed to let that door close. No one was more surprised when Tate opened it back up again with a career in music production.

Turns out, Tate had an ear for music all along. He might not have been able to play the ukulele that well, but Tate could recognize a good harmony when he heard it. For that, he could credit his mom.

Tate met Squeaks at a party for a music label, and they clicked right away. She grew up in the music business, too. Her aunt Izzy was part of a famous R&B group called Gemini.

Squeaks brought extensive experience with folk rock and soul. Tate was into more alternative and classic rock. They blend both styles together harmoniously.

The Covington Five, the current band they're working with, has a mashup of different styles. Lots of remixes, some nostalgic riffs, and a husky-voiced singer named Vicky with ridiculous vocals and a Dua Lipa vibe.

Tate loves their style and energy. After seeing them perform at a club in Chicago's Wicker Park neighborhood, he knew he had to be their producer. They came to Philly to record in the studio and knocked out all of their recordings in just a few weeks.

He and Squeaks will both take the day off tomorrow to let their minds clear before going back over what they produced. Have a break before they go back and catch any mistakes they made or sounds they missed. They'll meet with the band's manager and record label to share what they've got. Fingers crossed, the label will love it.

From there, it's out of his hands. Once the label takes over marketing and touring, Tate will be out of the loop. On to the next band.

He flicks off the last light and locks the door. He's usually the last to leave. There's no one waiting for him at home. There hasn't been anyone special since he and Josie broke up, which is pathetic, since it's been ten years.

There's never been anyone he cared about as much as Josie Remington. From the first moment that Tate laid eyes on her, he was struck down. Flattened. In all this time, he's never had that feeling again.

It's too bad she hates his guts.

Chapter 4

Mason, April 27

"I said I wanted the one with the blue flowers on it! Give me that piece!"

"Okay, honey, just calm down. Mommy's going to get it for you. We need to be patient."

"I don't want to be patient! I want the cake!"

"You'll get it. I promise."

"I WANT THAT PIECE NOW!!"

Mason slides past the screaming child standing on the chair wailing for sheet cake and makes his way across the room, stepping over a crawling toddler, dodging a parent handing out juice boxes, and bypassing two moms he recognizes from the car line, huddled together whispering secrets.

Their voices are too low to catch anything. He wishes he could hear what they're talking about, but he has no doubt he'll find out soon enough. These two love to gossip. It won't take much to get it out of them at school next week.

He finally makes his way to his destination, handing over a slice of cheese pizza on a plastic party plate. "Here you go," Mason says gallantly. "One of the last pieces left. I got it just in time."

The pies had been devoured by a swarm of second graders clamoring for the pizza as soon as it was brought into the "Fun Zone" party room.

Maeve grants him one of her super-watt smiles, the one where every missing tooth is on display. "Thanks, Daddy-O." She takes the pizza from his hands and sets it gently on the table.

He can't help it. One more piece of his frozen heart cracks off and melts. "Anything for you, kid."

How could he have ever known how wonderful kids could be? No one told him. He must have missed the memo. Because it's simply amazing.

Well, not other people's kids. They're *terrible*. Absolutely irredeemable. Especially that freckly-faced brat screaming for the slice of cake with the biggest amount of artificially-colored icing. Someone needs to slip that kid a Xanax.

But his girls? Maeve and Ivy? They were the absolute *best*. Thoughtful, generous, smart, and entertaining. Even though they're technically his stepkids, he still takes pride in how special they are. Ivy is ten and Maeve is eight, hence this birthday party, where everyone from her class is invited. Including the heathens from another planet.

He's smiling down at Maeve when he's hit on the back of the head by a foam bullet from a Nerf gun.

"Gotcha!" A little kid brags, waving the bright yellow toy.

Who lets their kid bring a gun to a birthday party? "Nice one," he tells the kid. "Can I borrow that for a sec?" He's reaching over to grab it when he's stopped by a hand on his arm by his partner, Kit.

"Don't do it," Kit warns, laughing. "He's just a kid."

"Who I'm doomed to spend the next hour with in this fun zone circle of hell."

"Just ignore him. He's having fun."

Mason sighs. "The things I do for you." But he drops his arm.

After *The Shallows* ended, Mason Stauffer knew he didn't want to return to acting. He knew there was no way he was going behind a desk. He'd always liked working in the soil, spending time outside, so he took a leap and started a landscape and design firm, Stauffer Designs. And met Kit, the love of his life.

He's lucky to enjoy what he does, and it shows. Over the past few years, he's built his company into a team of 20 full and part-time employees: landscape designers, experienced stonemasons, and skilled workers.

Mason and Kit live in the suburbs of Philadelphia, less than two hours from New York City or Washington, DC, but a world away from the big city. West Chester is a hamlet of Revolutionary-era homes and horse farms on large properties that line the Brandywine Creek.

The town is perfect for them. They share a house in the borough that's within walking distance of everything they need: a farmer's market, gym, coffee shops, and even a liquor store. His business is just outside of town, housed in an old farmhouse that Kit, who's an architect, converted into an office building.

Mason has changed enough in the past ten years—he's gone from being a baby-faced teen to a young man—that he can usually go out without being recognized. It doesn't hurt that he had long, golden surfer hair during the show, and it's now shorter and darker as a 32-year-old.

And then there's the 'stache. Kit's favorite actor is Glen Powell, so Mason has decided to grow out a thick moustache, too. He's leaning into the look of a 70s porn star in his prime.

Still, if a fan realizes he's one of the former leads of *The Shallows,* he doesn't mind signing an autograph or two. He still gets sentimental about the show–he just doesn't want to be part of the acting scene anymore. He's happy being here. Well, not *here*, in this birthday party room. But this area. In general.

"How much longer do we have?" he asks Kit.

"It's almost over. They already sang Happy Birthday. Fifteen minutes tops."

"Is there a piñata? Someone save us."

"Fifteen minutes, and I'll make you the driest martini around."

Mason rolls his eyes, but nods in agreement. "With blue cheese olives?"

"Of course."

"Fifteen minutes. You owe me."

An open cup of fruit punch falls, spilling all over his tan Ferragamo loafer. "Oops," a kid says. "Sorry."

Mason watches the bright red punch spread across his brand-new shoes. This stain isn't coming out. Really? Hundreds of dollars, down the drain.

"Where did that Nerf gun go?" he asks.

Chapter 5

"You can't control who you are, at the core. No matter what you promise yourself, the real you isn't really going to change."
- Francesca, Season 2, Episode 8

Val, April 30

An hour ago, Josie texted, *Are you going to the wedding?*

What wedding? Val replied. And then vaguely remembers seeing a thick envelope weeks ago.

Josie texts back immediately. *Sage and Simon's! Jeez, Val.*

She must have completely forgotten about the invite as soon as she opened it. She definitely dropped it, and now it's lost somewhere in the deep abyss of her apartment.

I'll find it! Val responds and then starts looking, but things don't look promising. There are piles of take-out containers, shopping bags, laundry, and who knows what else all over her counters.

How did this place become such a mess? No wonder she forgot to respond. It's like a tornado landed right in the middle of her living room.

Val is always doing things like this. Messing up. Missing details or important dates. Screwing someone over. It's never on purpose—she doesn't MEAN to be an asshole—but it still happens. ALL the time.

Since she was a little girl, she would leave her lunch box at school every single day. Then, when she'd focus on remembering the lunch box, she'd forget her coat.

Even now, after seeing a psychiatrist years ago and being officially diagnosed with ADHD, learning how to make lists and build her time management skills, she can't stop herself from dropping the ball on important things. Like wedding invitations.

Val can't help being unreliable. She can only focus on what's immediately in front of her. Ask her to pick someone up from the airport or help with moving that day, and she's more than happy to do it. But ask her to commit to an event that's weeks away?

Forget about it.

It's caused a lot of headaches and heartache with friends and family, colleagues, and acquaintances. Some people have dropped her completely. And with jobs? Please. She's been fired more times than she can count.

Every time it happens, she vows to do better ... but she never does. Just like her drinking. She always expects that the tomorrow Valerie will be stronger than today's Valerie. It doesn't happen. And then Val feels the familiar clench in her stomach that she's screwed up once again.

This time, there is a valid reason why she's been avoiding going through her mail. Honestly. A very good one.

She walks over to the mound of paper piled on her counter to find the invite for the wedding. It has to be in there.

As soon as she touches it, the stack of mail comes crashing down, scattering all over her kitchen floor. Magazines, flyers, junk mail, and bills go flying in all directions.

And there it is. The piece of mail she's been dreading. The reason she's been avoiding checking her mailbox.

If she doesn't acknowledge it, did it even happen?

Unfortunately, it's staring her right in the face. There's the same familiar block print they always use. The same bright white, A4 envelope. The same fake return address that she's looked up, over and over, desperate for clues as to who sent it.

Val crouches down to pick up the envelope. It's small, and easy to overlook.

She knows the letter inside will be exactly the same. It always is. Timed a couple of months apart, so she just begins to relax, thinking maybe they've forgotten her. The tension in her shoulders will start to ease. She'll stop looking over her shoulder. And then another letter arrives.

It's a special kind of torture that Val knows she absolutely deserves. Payment for what she did so long ago. They won't let her forget.

The first time she got the letter asking for five grand, she thought it was a joke. They even called her Francesca Giordano, the name of her character on the show.

"If you don't pay in two weeks, we'll let the world know what you did in LA," it said.

She thought it was a joke.

Then they sent pictures. And she realized they knew. So, she paid.

Val knows the blackmail is never going to end. Asking for just enough money that she can dig up by selling something she kept from the show on eBay, or working an extra shift at the bar.

She even had to give them an heirloom diamond pendant her mother had gifted her before passing away. It was an Art Deco piece that had been in her family for generations. Val wore it all the time on the set of the show. The scariest part was that the blackmailer specifically asked for it. She thinks they may have seen it after she wore it for some of the episodes.

The asshole takes everything and then gives her a break until they reach out again. Just enough time to make sure she doesn't forget that they know. That they're never going away.

Fuck it. Val puts the envelope back on her counter unopened. She'll deal with it later. What's one more day at this point?

She opens the wedding invitation and quickly scans it. This time, Val is *not* going to get sidetracked.

Shit. Yesterday was the last day to RSVP for the wedding, and Val still hasn't sent the response card back. She pulls out her phone to RSVP on the couple's wedding website, anyway.

Valerie Worth will be attending solo. One person. She'll have the fish entree.

Val is going to do everything she can to make sure she's there for Sage and Simon. She puts a huge X on the date in her wall calendar (that her sister passive-aggressively bought for Val after she missed her niece's piano recital two years in a row) and puts three alerts in her phone: one a week before, one a day before, and one on the morning of the wedding.

June 1st, at 6 PM. Newport, Rhode Island. Rosecliff Mansion and Grounds. A Friday night welcome reception at Belle Mer, followed by a sunset wedding on the lawn on Saturday.

This was going to be a true black tie, sophisticated wedding. Multiple hundreds of dollars a plate. Maybe a thousand. And she hadn't even had the decency to reply.

"I just responded. I'm coming!" Val texts Josie.

She can do this.

It's been ten years since *The Shallows.* Time for them all to grow up. Val feels like she must have missed the memo. Almost everyone from the original cast has gone on to lead real lives. Met someone special. Found solid jobs. Discovered absurd hobbies.

As for Val? She's been bartending at O'Donoghue's, a crowded dive bar, for more than five years. It keeps her busy. She does better when she's busy, and the job makes just enough to cover her rent and car payments. The royalties from past acting jobs supplement bigger-ticket items like medical bills or unexpected car repairs.

She dates infrequently, depending more on easy, no-fuss one-night stands from dating apps or guys she meets at local bars. It's easier that way, not having to see them again. She's learned the hard way she can't trust anyone. Especially men.

When Val goes home to Virginia, her extended family always wants to know what she's doing. Her latest audition. How many famous people she has met. What the latest gossip is.

She used to be honest, but now she just tells lies. Says she's starring in some indie movie. *It's coming out soon.* That Netflix just passed on her latest project. Anything other than admitting that she's a washed-up, 35-year-old actress with a blackmailer and a drinking problem. That she hasn't been paid to act in almost ten years.

Val grabs a bottle of wine out of her fridge. She tells herself she's only going to have one glass. Once again, lying to herself. But after receiving yet another blackmail note she can't pay, she can't handle facing the truth.

Chapter 6

"The only thing you're actually consistent about,
is the ability to continually disappoint me."
- Eve to her ex-boyfriend Zad, Season 1, Episode 8

Josie, May 3

Josie finally caved, as her former agent Justin had said she would. "I've thought about it long and hard, and I'll attend the reunion convention," she emails the event organizers.

Checking another item off her to-do list, she RSVP's to Sage and Simon that, yes, she will be there for their wedding. She can't wait. She's going to have the steak. And, no, there isn't going to be a plus one.

It will be the second event in less than six months where she'll be mingling with her former castmates. She hasn't seen many of them in years, and now she'll be with all of them twice in one summer.

Is that exciting or absolutely terrifying? Jo can't decide. Instead, she grabs her overnight bag and hops in her car. She has plans to reunite with Paige and Val in Hoboken. Catch up on their lives and get tipsy.

Josie owns a condo in Lambertville, New Jersey, a quirky, artistic community along the Delaware River. It's less than an hour and a half from New York City and two hours from Washington, DC, two major hubs for her clients.

As long as she's close enough to an airport and she has her equipment, she's good to go. She practically lives out of her suitcase.

The one-hour drive to Hoboken stretches ahead of her, navigating the winding roads of routes 202 and 78 as she sheds the quieter countryside for the busier city highways. She has time to make the call she's been avoiding.

Josie braces herself as she dials her former agent. They're past due for a recap.

Justin picks up right away. "I told you, didn't I?" he says before she can even get a greeting out.

"Of course, you did." He won't notice her sarcasm. Justin is blunt to the point of pain, and he's never going to change. He has a reputation for telling people what he thinks, regardless of who it affects or how much it hurts.

"So, I take it you already heard?" Josie asks. "I just sent the email."

"Within seconds."

"You're always right."

"Funny," Justin answers. "But you do realize that it wouldn't have been the same without you. Baby girl, you're the *star.* Everyone wants a piece."

"I'm not a star anymore, Justin. And I don't feel like giving any more of myself away."

When will it end? She hasn't acted in ten years, since the show ended. And it still doesn't matter. Josie can't stop attracting attention whenever she goes out in public. They even find her in the grocery store, even though she's nothing like the character she played.

Damn it, she's never going to get the chance to try that key lime pie Greek yogurt.

"It will be good for you. Trust me. I know best." Justin is smug.

"You know how to always be an asshole, too." Josie isn't sure if Justin is happier that he won their bet or that she's going to the reunion. He's been trying to get her to commit to the reunion for nearly a year. Because the event will most likely make the cover of *People* magazine, she has a feeling it's the latter.

The insult rolls right off his back. "The PR team has been calling me daily. They need to know the lineup for the breakout panels and what you're going to talk about. Hot topics only."

"Do I really need to do a panel?"

"Of course. People are paying hundreds of dollars a ticket to hear you guys talk. And sign autographs. We're going to announce you as the secret last-minute guest. VIP all the way."

Ugh. Hasn't she committed to going? And now she has to talk, too! She hates being on stage. "When do I have to decide?"

"Yesterday."

"Seriously, when?"

"Seriously, yesterday." Justin won't let up. "Also, are you willing to do a session with Tate about your love triangle? Talk about it with Mason and Val? They said they would."

"I don't know. It seems so cheesy."

"Just think of the money you'll make on meet and greets alone."

"All you think about is money," Josie tells Justin.

"Botox isn't cheap."

She stifles a laugh. The reunion is going to be held in early August in Avalon and Stone Harbor. Together, the towns make up Seven Mile Island, an elite coastal playground in southern New Jersey.

Thousands of fans are expected to descend on the town for photo opps and autographs from their favorite teen actors. They'll be waiting around every corner for any opportunity to snap a selfie with the stars.

And then there will be the really serious fans. The ones who still live for the show.

The actors have had real stalkers in the past, people who just couldn't let go of the fantasy of Duffy Beach. Josie doesn't like to think about some of the messages she's received over the years. Creeps who thought they were the answer to their problems or the key to their fantasies.

The producers and executives had done their best to protect them, hiring security on set. But mistakes happened. Screaming teen girls and obsessive fans were hard to keep away from. She doesn't miss the big crowds that have thinned over the years to smaller, more manageable ones. Why try to get them back?

How is it that one small slice of her life is still managing to affect nearly every single moment following it? No matter how hard she tries, she can't escape the past. It's like she's stuck in an endless loop of TV series hell. Trapped in a role she didn't create. Tied to a person who never existed.

Eve Mattson was just a character in a teen drama. And yet, every person Josie meets thinks she has the same personality as someone who was created by a team of writers. The truth is nearly the exact opposite. She's really just a low key girl from upstate New York.

"I'm taking it one day at a time," Josie finally answers. "I'll let you know when I decide who I want to be paired up with and what topics we should get into."

She isn't going to agree to pair up with Tate before seeing what happens at the wedding first. They still have so much unresolved conflict between them. Things that were never explained.

Attending the wedding was a no-brainer. Has Josie ever really had the option to say no to Sage?

She can't miss it. She had been there for the early stages of Sage and Simon's love story, from their first side glances to their first date in Ocean City. Josie was lucky enough to see their relationship grow into something solid. Something real.

There's no doubt that it's going to be the dreamiest event that Josie has ever attended. Sage creates magical settings. When they were filming, she came up with some of the most iconic ideas for the show: group dance montages, sand dune backdrops, beach bonfires against streaks of pink sunsets.

Her phone starts beeping with another call. "I've gotta run." Josie cuts Justin off and disconnects. One of the advantages of being a first-rate tyrant is that he doesn't take much personally. He's used to people hanging up on him.

"Jo Jo?" Val says sweetly. "Honey, you're going to kill me."

The always incredibly unreliable Val. You might as well have written it in a script.

Josie sighs out loud. "Seriously? I'm already driving more than an hour to meet you, and now you cancel on me?"

They'd planned to meet for brunch and then go dress shopping along Hoboken's Washington Street. Paige lives in the next town over, Jersey City, and Val is a couple of hours away in DC. Since Josie also lives in New Jersey, it made sense to meet in Hoboken.

Perched directly across the Hudson River from Manhattan, Hoboken's brownstones line cobblestone streets filled with bars, restaurants, and boutiques. Perfect for the three of them to reconnect after a long stretch of not seeing each other.

And now it's ruined.

"Something came up," Val says vaguely. No explanation. She's always like this. Quitting, canceling, swapping jobs. Never giving a reason why.

"Something *always* comes up," Josie says with frustration. It's so hard not to lose her temper with Val when her friend is always disappointing her.

"You know I can't keep track of my schedule," Val answers. "I have a big audition today that I can't miss." She sounds completely insincere.

"Did you tell Paige?"

Silence. Then, Val admits, "I was hoping you would."

"Whatever, Val," Josie answers. "See you." She has to hang up anyway. She's approaching the Pulaski Skyway, and traffic is picking up. Cars whiz past her as she navigates the narrow lanes. She always forgets how scary driving in the New York area can be.

She really needed to see her friends today. Get reassurances that everything would be okay the next time she saw everyone from the show. Reconnect in person after months of not talking, just sharing memes back and forth on Instagram.

Josie narrowly dodges a car that cuts her off, making her brake within inches of the guardrail on the elevated highway.

"Asshole!" She gives him the finger, but he shrugs it off and keeps driving.

The trip will be worth it. At least she has Paige.

Paige never lets her down.

Chapter 7

"High school is like a riptide. The more you fight it,
the harder it is to escape."
- Shea, Season 3, Episode 7

Paige, May 3

"Bzzz!" Paige's intercom loudly announces Jo's arrival.

"I'm here!"

Paige pushes the button to let her into her building, then looks around her small space, feeling a momentary flicker of panic. How long has it been since she's seen Josie? It seems like forever. Time slips past so quickly that months go by without them even realizing they haven't talked or made plans to meet up.

It isn't great timing for her now, either. Paige was just rejected after the final round of callbacks for the zombie penguin series.

"Are you kidding me?" she asked when she got the call. "I got turned down for a part where I'm sliced open by a *flipper?*"

It's a new low. There are no other prospects on the horizon. She already wrapped up filming the pilot for a new series she was hoping would get picked up by a streaming channel. That show, *Zootopular,* was centered around a zoo in Northern California. Paige played the sexy lion trainer in love with a vet from the reptile house. Ridiculous, but fans will probably eat it up with a spoon.

But she had received a small stipend up front, so of course, she'd said yes.

When the first cuts had been released, Paige had been mortified. It was so *amateur*. All the bigger studios had quickly passed on the project, so now the director was shopping it around to various film festivals.

No bites yet. Paige is just hoping that the publicity from the reunion will give her career the boost it needs.

She couldn't even tell her mom about *Zootopular*. She lied to Jean to make her character's part sound bigger and more glamorous than it was. Because she was pretty sure she didn't want to be known for training lions that were actually CGI.

Paige was brought up as a child star. "Put on a brave face," Jean would say to her daughter. "No one wants to see a sullen kid."

For Jean, every day was a competition. She didn't allow tears. Only successful auditions were celebrated. Paige's school years consisted of a long line of different tutors, with each subject chosen to help advance her acting career.

Nothing else mattered to Jean. Friends were carefully screened before coming over for playdates. Most didn't like her anyway. "Too snotty," the mothers would say. "Who does she think she is?"

Paige could withstand cutting rejections and subjective criticism with ease. She'd been told she was too old, too young, too skinny, too fat, too *anything* for the part. Even with all the negative feedback, though, Paige continued booking jobs. She made a name for herself.

She changed her natural auburn hair to blonde, then dark brown, and back to her natural red. Anything for a gig.

Her mother was relentless. Jean DeBello didn't raise a loser. Paige was going to be a star. Jean did everything in her power to make her one, divorcing her disapproving husband and moving them from the suburbs of Chicago to sunny California. She took a job as a receptionist at a production company and spent every free minute taking her daughter to auditions.

It worked. Paige was featured in countless magazines and TV shows, splashed across celebrity news sites and social media from TMZ to Perez Hilton.

By the time she was nine, scores of delighted fans were regularly asking for her autograph.

At the age of 11, Paige experienced her first panic attack. When she was 13, she developed an eating disorder. At 16, she started to experiment with drugs and alcohol.

Paige experienced every single celebrity cliche that could happen to a child star: the climb to fame and the devastating fall from grace. Public scandals that quickly and embarrassingly appeared in gossip rags and on news sites.

She learned, when she was 14 and her first serious boyfriend sold her out to the press about her bulimia, not to trust anyone too much. Or confide her biggest secrets. A silly crush or a lame joke could end up on the front page of a celebrity magazine the next day.

Luckily, the scandals never lasted too long. Her issues were usually forgotten when it was someone else's turn for their existential crisis.

At 19, after a brief stint in rehab for drugs (her second), Paige auditioned for the role of sweet and supportive Shea Maisel, the best friend on an upcoming TV show.

To Paige's complete and utter surprise, she won the part. *The Shallows* officially began production six months later.

Filming *The Shallows* had been one of the best times in Paige's life. She was clean and sober, taking part in a successful TV show that was already generating lots of buzz, and she had a healthy and dependable paycheck. She was also a safe distance across the country from Jean, who gave her space once her dream of her daughter making it to the big leagues finally came true.

The majority of the cast were new to acting. They looked to Paige for guidance, asking, "Can you help me run lines?" "What's the best way to film this scene?" "How should I respond to my publicist?"

Paige loved every second of it. The writers, well aware of her troubled past, capitalized on Paige's natural vulnerability and shaky confidence for the part of Shea. Her thin frame and long, straight hair helped solidify the image of a sweet but shy teen girl.

She relished her role as America's Sweetheart. For once, Paige finally felt confident in her own skin. She wore little to no makeup on set, letting her natural freckles shine.

Paige stopped constantly twirling and tugging on her hair, a habit she couldn't stop doing when she was nervous. Constantly pulling at it over the years had made sections of her auburn hair fall out, exposing patches of her scalp. Now, with less anxiety, it's growing back, and the salty Avalon air gave her healthy, natural waves. She never looked better.

Shea was billed as the next girl next door, a cross between Jennifer Grey's Baby in *Dirty Dancing* and Mischa Barton's Marissa Cooper in *The OC*: earnest, yet vulnerable.

The target audience of teens and young adults loved her. The people *outside* their target audience, seniors and middle-aged viewers, loved her. Shea was one of the most beloved characters on the show. She got some of the biggest plotlines and story arcs out of everyone in the cast: love triangles, parental marriage problems, and school drama.

Paige finally had the love, attention, and affection she'd always craved.

Okay, so maybe some of the fame got to her head. She slipped up with her sobriety. A few times … maybe more. First it was a sip, then a glass, then a bottle, and finally back to recreational drugs. Her favorite was cocaine. She kept telling herself it wasn't a habit, yet she kept going back to it. If only to blur the lines and ease the stress for a few hours.

And now so many of the same people are all coming back into her life. What is Jo going to think of where she's living and what she's doing with acting? She doesn't have a whole hell of a lot to show for it.

There's a knock on her door. Paige shoves her concerns aside and puts on her happy face. She'll worry about the state of her career later.

She swings it open, shouting, "Jo Jo!"

Josie blows in like the whirlwind she's always been. She sucks up all the air in the room, carrying an energy – the It Factor – that's made her a natural star.

Everyone wants to be near Josie. They always have. But even with all the people who want a piece of her friend's attention, Jo has driven all this way to see *her*. Paige.

So much has changed since they used to live in each other's pockets for months at a time, eating all their meals together, getting their hair and makeup done, filming scenes, and waiting around for further direction.

Sure, they keep up with quick texts or sending funny memes to each other's Instagram accounts. But nothing beats catching up in person.

"Come in! I know it's not much," Paige says, her eyes sliding around the one-bedroom apartment. "But it's just temporary. I never know which coast I'm going to be needed on."

"It's beautiful," Josie responds with a dazzling smile. She pulls Paige in for a hug. "I'm just so glad to see you."

Paige hopes Jo is telling the truth. She's worked hard to make her apartment a comfy spot to recharge from the never-ending cycle of rejections in audition life. It's not a penthouse apartment or a beachfront mansion, like some of the actors she's worked with who have gone on to be huge successes. But it's home.

"I wish Val could have made it, too. Let me give you a tour."

It's a quick one. The oversized sectional takes up most of the space. It's the best spot for lounging under the tall picture windows. For color, she added pillows and throw rugs in bright patterns that she picked up at flea markets and discount stores. Paige can't do much about the narrow galley kitchen, but the counters are clutter-free.

The entranceway has a gallery of photos filled top to bottom with actors and friends she's worked with over the years, interspersed with cinema memorabilia.

"Look at us," Josie says. She's staring at a black and white shot of the five of them at the beach: Josie, Paige, Val, Tate, and Mason. "We were so young."

"And so hot."

Josie bumps her. "We still are."

"At least some of us," Paige says with a laugh. She turns, and Josie follows. "And this is my bedroom." That space is small, too, and she sacrificed the idea of bedside tables to fit the queen mattress. She hung lights and candles and called it a day.

Jersey City doesn't have the same prestige as the square-mile yuppie town of Hoboken next door, but it's accessible to New York by the PATH, New Jersey's train system, as well as the bus system. And if you squinted hard enough, you could just make out a view of the water from her apartment building. The Hudson River and New York skyline make it worth the price of rent.

Her mother has never seen it. She doesn't visit the suburbs. Jean DeBello prefers to meet her daughter at a swanky hotel in New York City. Paige has given up trying to change her.

She shakes her head, clearing her thoughts of her mother. Better not to go there. Today is about old friendships, even if one of them is missing.

"Are you ready?" she asks Jo after she drops her bags.

"Can't wait."

They have the best day together. Mimosas for brunch at Elysian Cafe, shopping at Alba and Brooke & Bel. Espresso martinis at Metropolis, then late-night dancing at Green Rock Tap & Grill.

At one point in the night, Paige has her arm slung around Josie's shoulder. They're singing at the top of their lungs to "Don't Stop Believing."

A crowd of guys gathers around them, which is the norm when you take Josie out in public. She's like a light bulb attracting moths. And then there's Paige. The perpetual sidekick.

She had gone into the bathroom a few minutes earlier to do a bump of coke. Obviously, she knows it's not a great idea, but she needs it, doesn't she? Just to take the edge off. It's not going to become a problem. She knows how to manage it.

Full of energy, Paige smacks a kiss on Josie's cheek. She's off balance, making it land closer to her ear. It doesn't faze Josie, who's also tipsy.

"I love you, girl," Jo says boozily.

Paige grips her hand. "You've always been there for me. I wish I had done the same for you."

Josie turns, puzzled. "What do you mean?"

'The things I did. I didn't mean to."

Paige is about to say more when she's cut off by a couple of guys trying to buy them drinks.

"Hey, gorgeous!" the leader of the pack shouts in her ear. "Want a shot?"

"No thanks." She tries to hold on to Josie, but her hand slips out of their grip as one of the other guys leans in to talk to her friend. "Jo!"

But it's too late. He's already caught her attention. Josie's head is turned towards him and away from Paige. She's laughing at something he's telling her.

What was she thinking, trying to talk to her now? It's too hard to hear anything in the crowded bar without yelling. And Josie always gets attention. It's impossible to be in public with her. Even if they don't recognize her from acting, she's still getting hit on.

Paige gives up and accepts the free drinks. "Why not?" She says to her new drinking buddy. "I'll have an Elaine." It's a vodka, soda, and orange juice that one of the regulars from Fred's Tavern in Stone Harbor introduced them to.

By the time they grab a slice of pizza to soak up all the booze and get a cab ride home, it's four in the morning. They wash their faces in a half-assed way and stumble into bed before passing out immediately.

Paige never has the chance to explain more, and the next morning over coffee, Josie thankfully doesn't bring it up. Paige wishes she had never said anything in the first place. What would it help at this point anyway? It was so many years ago. There was no point in bringing it back up again.

Paige tells herself the same lies she's told herself for the past ten years. And when she hugs her friend goodbye and goes back to bed to sleep off the hangover, she tells herself once more that it was okay. That she wasn't that bad of a person. And that no one will ever find out what she did such a long time ago.

Chapter 8

Tate, May 13

"I told you I didn't like Clay," Squeaks reminds Tate as they lounge in chairs at their studio. "He was always trying to look down my shirt when I leaned over."

"You were right," Tate acknowledges. "You usually are."

Squeaks likes this answer. "Damn right." She shakes her head. "What a moron. Everyone knows you don't cheat in the same building."

"But it's okay to cheat in separate locations?" Tate's not sure exactly how to take that piece of advice.

Squeaks shrugs. She's always lived by her own set of rules.

Clay, one of the guitarists of "The Covington Five," was found in his bathroom with a 19-year-old neighbor by his current girlfriend, Vicky. They were also naked. And really high.

The music executives are in a full-scale meltdown. A PR firm dealing in crisis management is retained. The publicity team is on high alert.

Their album was just about to drop. A team of publicists has been promoting it for months across social media, in print, online, and on the radio stations.

The other problem the band is facing is that, in addition to being his girlfriend, Vicky is also their lead singer. The main person on vocals. And as of now, she's flat out refusing to tour with Clay.

Rightfully so. Until their management can convince her otherwise, everything is on hold.

"It really doesn't look great for them, though," Squeaks says. "I don't see how they'll be able to play all the places they booked."

"Sucks for us." Tate *knows* it's destined to be a hit. He's worked with more than a hundred artists by now, and has learned when something was going to be big. You can just feel the energy behind it.

The album has such a wide range of genres that will appeal to multiple audiences: lovers of rock, soul, punk, hip hop, and even country. And Vicky's vocals are incredible. There are also some major guest artists lending their vocals to a few of the bangers.

This is going to be one of those game-changing albums. Tate has personally seen it evolve over the past six months as the band laid tracks, and he has never been more excited for an album to come out.

The release party was set for May, followed by an eight-month tour across the country. Hell, they'd even booked Red Rocks. That legendary venue was notoriously hard to get into.

If only Clay hadn't decided to snort blow off a teen girl's neck.

The first single was primed for release. Right now, it's on hold until the music execs figure out what to do in the face of the crisis. There's a particularly damaging TikTok going around of the band's reaction to the scandal that someone must have filmed when all hell was breaking loose.

It doesn't help that Vicky cut the girl's ponytail off when she found them together. The photos were instantly all over social media.

Tate and Squeaks have already done their jobs producing the album, so they take the hit with a "what can you do" approach. It's out of their hands, and all they can do now is wait.

It looks like they have some unexpected downtime, though. "What should we do?" Tate asks Squeaks.

"Let's get away. Someplace warm."

"Agreed. Do we need a beach? Or just a pool?"

"I'm fine with either. You're paying?"

"I guess I am now."

Tate's mom is on tour, so he knows they can use her house (and guest house) in LA. Hang by the pool, drink some good tequila, and visit some iconic places. He offers it to his partner as an option.

"That's exactly what we need," Squeaks tells him. "A week with nothing to do but relax."

Two days later, they're landing in sunny California.

As soon as they get off the plane, Tate realizes that he and Squeaks need to change their clothes. They look completely out of place, with their black leather jackets and torn jeans. Everyone else is in white sundresses and pastel board shorts. Luckily, it doesn't seem like anyone recognizes him.

A long black car picks them up at arrivals and whisks them to the Hollywood Hills. They drive the legendary winding roads made famous in the movies until they get to their destination.

"This is your *house*?" Squeaks' mouth gapes open as their driver maneuvers the car through the front gates, past tall green hedges, and up a long, winding drive.

"Yeah." It's a lot to take in.

"I know your parents are famous, but I guess I didn't realize you were THIS loaded. This place is crazy."

Tate shrugs. "It's not my money, it's theirs." He pauses, then adds honestly, "But it is nice to take advantage of the perks every once in a while."

"Tell me about it," she says under her breath. "We didn't exactly have this growing up in Chicago."

Tate knows that Squeaks put herself through college by working night jobs and taking on a ton of loans, which she's still paying for. Whenever he asks her about her childhood, she brushes him off, but he has a feeling she spent a lot of time working or helping out with her siblings.

Growing up, Tate was in a bubble. He didn't know it at the time. Now that he's older, he feels guilty that he had so much and always took it for granted.

He honestly thought everyone had famous parents and personal assistants, too. His classmates at his expensive private school were all driven to class by chauffeurs. And, yes, he now realizes that makes him sound like even more of an asshole. What can he say? It's what he was used to.

Even so, being celebrities doesn't mean that things have always been rosy. Years ago, someone stole several of his parents' awards: his mom's Grammy, his dad's Emmy, and other trophies they'd collected over the years from recording and film academies. Just plucked them right out of their house.

It was devastating, to say the least. Some of them could be replaced, but they weren't the originals. The ones Kate and Crew had each clutched as they gave their acceptance speeches at the podiums, shining in their special moment of fame and recognition.

Worse, the safety of their home had been violated. The thief must have been someone they knew personally, because the trophies had been stolen without any alarms being triggered. The police saw no evidence of any locks being picked.

After that, his parents couldn't stop fighting. His mom blamed his dad for hosting lavish parties and showing off what they'd earned. Crew blamed Kate for opening the door to anyone in the music industry who needed help or a place to stay.

At least he had the filming of *The Shallows* as an escape. And Josie Remington, his first love. His only love.

They became close after spending a lot of time on the beach. Josie had grown up near the Finger Lakes and wasn't used to the Atlantic Ocean. Tate taught her to surf, to recognize the rhythm of the waves and react to them. The first time she'd stood up on her board, it had been magic.

She helped him make it through the dark days, when he didn't want to go home. They'd sit on their blankets for hours, just talking. Sharing stories.

It helped him forget all the fighting, the petty snipes at each other.

Tate remembers the arguments his parents were having. It had gotten so bad that he never wanted to come home on breaks from filming. The house was so heavy with tension that any conversation was a ticking time bomb. Finally, one day, both his parents sat him down and told him their family was ending. He didn't tell them, but at that point, it was nearly a relief, just so they'd stop arguing.

Kate kept the house, and his father bought a pad a few miles away that Tate never visited. It was just too sad, seeing the empty cupboards in the kitchen that his dad never tried to fill. Crew still lived that same lifestyle, flopping in places that he never bothered to decorate, much less make his home.

"I know this is a lot," Tate says as he opens a side door into the glass atrium. "I'm not trying to show off. Like I said, it's my mom's house, not mine."

"It's a lot of house for one person," Squeaks tells him. "But I can help with that."

The home is filled with light. Fresh flowers are everywhere, even without anyone living there at the moment. There's a full staff of housekeepers and gardeners.

Tate shows her around the grounds, offering one of a dozen guestrooms for her to choose from. Squeaks picks one overlooking the pool house and citrus trees.

"Baby, just let me know if you feel like a trophy wife. I'd be happy to fill in," Squeaks teases. "This place is sick."

"Just name the venue, and I'm yours." Tate knows she's not serious. Squeaks is one of the only people who doesn't take him seriously or ask for anything in return. That's what she does—accepts people where they are, without asking them to change.

They spend the next week exploring Malibu and the tourist traps of Hollywood, dining out in Melrose, and swimming in Santa Barbara. It's the perfect week, aside from a few times when they're spotted by paparazzi.

"Is that Tate Masters?"

"Look here!"

"Tate, where are your parents? Is your mom dating Harry Styles?"

They're relentless. He does his best to ignore it. Tate isn't a big fish now, but he *is* a former heartthrob. The former crush of teenagers across the country. He's always a good subject for a "Stars: Where Are They Now?" feature.

Once they spot them, the cameras continue to follow them. They try figuring out who he's with and if they're an item, taking photos of their time together.

They try to make an outing to Venice Beach, but Tate turns around as soon as he spots a few paparazzi. "I'm sorry, Squeaks. We should probably go."

"It's okay. Let's get out of here."

It's intrusive and annoying, but there's not much they can do about it if they're out in public. He never gets to show Squeaks all the sights. They end up spending a lot of time at the house, just to avoid the press.

One night, Tate shows Squeaks the awards room, now sitting empty, and tells her the story of what happened.

"It was when I was here with a bunch of my friends from the show," Tate says. Two couches and a couple of chairs flank a two-story fireplace flanked by shelves of rock memorabilia. Abstract artwork and framed paintings of his mom playing guitar line the walls.

"This is incredible," Squeaks says as she turns around to take it all in. "So much stuff."

"Yeah. We had so many parties. The doors were constantly open with people coming and going. Someone could have just walked in." He doesn't add that he felt like it was his fault.

Squeaks is baffled. "So, you never found out what happened? Ever?"

Tate shrugs. "We didn't have cameras back then. Just security alarms."

"And they never got them back. Damn." She looks around. "How many were stolen?"

"Four of them. The biggest ones were my mom's Grammy and my dad's Oscar. The ones here are reproductions."

"Your parents must have known who did it. Even if they never found out who it was."

He looks around the room, lost in memories. "I think that's the hardest part. That someone close to them took their biggest accomplishment and made off with it. Someone they trusted. Once that was broken, they stopped trusting each other."

"It could also have been a stalker," Squeaks responds, as she looks around at the shelves. "Your mom is a rock icon, and your dad is a movie star. They must have had a lot of crazy fans."

"True. I remember getting weird presents left at our front gates. Like really strange shit."

When his parents announced they were separating, Tate told himself his mom was touring and his dad was shooting on location, then closed that part of his life. That's how he coped, even though it wasn't healthy.

Later, when he got older, he realized he used denial as a way of dealing with disappointment. Shoving it away in a corner, trying not to think about it.

It's weird to think about it. Later, looking back, he realized what they really lost that night: their family.

"I wonder what they're worth now," Squeaks says. "The awards have their names on them. I can't imagine how you would even hide them."

"Probably some wacky collector who has a thing for one of them. Or both." Tate closes the double-panel doors to the room. "Let's go." Thinking about the theft takes him back to those terrible days he doesn't want to revisit.

He badly wants to ask their old crew if they know if Josie is coming, but he doesn't want to make too big of a deal about it. It's been nearly a decade since he last saw her. He's sure she's moved on with some asshole he's going to hate.

Without his work to focus on, Tate feels at loose ends. It makes him start thinking about their time together, filming *The Shallows*.

Ten years later, Josie is still the only woman he's ever loved. No one else has ever come close. He wonders if it's because they left things unresolved. He still doesn't understand what went wrong or why she turned on him so quickly. Or why she ended things without an explanation.

Maybe one day, Josie will tell him what happened. Why she ignored him during the last few weeks of filming, and then the day after shooting wrapped, dumped him without any reason. Just coldly told him it was over.

There was no longer any need to be together on set, so he didn't get to see Jo. And she never responded to his calls. Hell, Tate had even shown up at her rental, desperate for a chance to change her mind. But Josie was stubborn when she wanted to be. She wouldn't see him. Wouldn't answer her phone or the door.

Maybe that's why Tate still can't get her out of his head.

51

Maybe that's why Tate still can't get her out of his head.

Chapter 9

Mason, May 24

Mason didn't think much could surprise him anymore. But hell, you learn something new every day if you were lucky to live long enough, right?

They're about to sit down for dinner when Kit's ex-wife Alex calls, and of course, Kit picks up and puts her on speaker.

Their conversation goes from civil to threatening in seconds when she threatens to torpedo their custody agreement if he doesn't come to a family reunion with their kids, Maeve and Ivy.

"I'm not kidding, I will tie you up in court for months and deny you access to them," Alex yells over the phone.

"But why should I go? I'm not part of your family anymore," Kit answers. "We got divorced more than five years ago."

Alex won't listen to reason. "You're the reason for my shitty relationship with my parents," she tells him.

"How is that possible?"

Mason is waving his hands wildly, trying not to make noise but make it clear that this is insane.

"Because of the divorce! They said we destroyed our family. Broke up our home. And you need to make up for it."

Kit sighs, pinching the bridge of his nose with his fingers. "We both agreed to do it," he says reluctantly. Mason can *tell* by the look on his face that Alex got to him. "We weren't happy."

"And now you are, and I'm not," Alex snaps.

Kit sighs again. "When's the reunion?" He puts the phone to his ear. Mason can't hear Alex's response now, but he does hear Kit's. "The first weekend of June?"

That's next week. Are you kidding me?

Mason almost can't believe his ears. Almost. Kit is the biggest pushover. Obviously, Mason loves this trait when it helps him win an argument or choose the next spot for their getaway trips, but not when they're dealing with Alex.

"She's an evil witch intent on destroying our happiness," Mason tells him after Kit hangs up the phone.

"I know that. But she's the mother of my children."

It's all Mason can do not to roll his eyes.

Kit and Alex had been just friends in college, until one night they drank too much and slept together. What was a simple mistake turned into an unexpected pregnancy. They decided to work through it and try raising the baby together.

They'd been married for a few years when Kit had enough and asked for a divorce, but by that time they had two girls–the sweetest, most adorable girls–who Alex is happy to use ruthlessly whenever it suits her needs. She's constantly trying to pull Kit back into her life. To make him feel guilty for moving on.

Kit and Mason met when Stauffer Designs was installing the landscaping and patio at one of the houses that Kit's architectural firm was remodeling. It was one of his biggest jobs.

Mason enjoys designing projects but *hates* billing and financial paperwork. That's why he has Ida. His 80-year-old assistant actually enjoys spreadsheets. And vintage items. "I like everything old but my men," she always tells Mason.

She's always auditioning candidates for a pool boy. "But you don't have a pool?" Mason asks after he heard her flirting with one of them. She ignored him.

Ida loves finding old teen magazine articles of Mason at estate sales and hanging them up around the office. The crew gives him shit about his gelled hair and coordinated track outfits. He was just glad they didn't have to pretend to be vampires or werewolves on the show.

To say that Mason and Alex don't get along is an understatement. She blames Mason for "turning her husband gay" (as if that's a thing). He retaliates by commenting on "how tired she looks" every time he sees her. Petty, but effective.

Alex has the upper hand, though. The girls. Maeve and Ivy. The most darling, lovable girls ever.

He simply adores them. They refused to call him Mason when he and Kit got married, nicknaming him "Daddy-O" instead. They share equal custody of the girls with Alex.

Ivy is a preteen in love with Taylor Swift, soccer, and any kind of gummy candy she can find. Maeve is quieter and more introspective. She loves listening to "classic" music from the 90s and 2000s, which Mason can still hardly fathom is now considered ancient.

Even though Mason is the one he's married to, Alex will always be an integral part of their family. It's something Mason can't change, no matter how much he wishes he could. She's the girls' mom, and he understands and respects that. He never tries to override any of her rules. But he wishes she would stop interfering in his relationship with Kit.

Mason tries to stay neutral most of the time. Really, he does. But the family reunion is the *exact same weekend* as the wedding.

And he knows Alex knows that, too.

She's such a bitch.

But there's no changing Kit's mind when Alex applies her passive-aggressive guilt tactics. He's such a pushover.

"She told me the girls specifically asked for me to go," Kit says, arms folded across his chest. He's leaning against the kitchen island. Kit gives off leading man vibes: brown shaggy hair, beefy biceps, and a square jawline.

Kit is so cute that Mason usually can't even stay mad at him for long. Usually.

"I realize that, but can't you go with them next year? Or take them somewhere this weekend?" Mason answers. "You know what a big deal this wedding is to me." It will be the first time he gets to introduce Kit to all of his former castmates.

"Of course it is, but these are my daughters. I can't say no to them. They need me."

"*I* need you," Mason shoots back.

"You're a grown man. You'll be okay."

There are times you keep fighting and other times you just leave and sulk. Mason decides to go with the latter.

"I'm not taking you to the reunion now," Mason threatens Kit as he strides out of the kitchen in a huff.

This really is bullshit. They had the wedding on the calendar for months since they got the Save the Date card. And now Mason has to show up alone, standing around awkwardly as everyone pairs up for dancing. Relegated to sitting by himself at the singles table.

Mason used to show up solo at big premieres and industry events, or attend with a girl who knew he only wanted to be friends. He hid who he was for so long that it was the biggest relief when he finally told the truth about who he loved.

Since then, many young actors have publicly thanked him for coming out and helping them do the same. Now, it seems like it's so much more accepted to be gay or bisexual, non-binary, or gender fluid. He likes to think he had a part in that.

Kit, on the other hand, doesn't think of himself as gay. He's just in love with Mason, who happens to be a guy.

But Mason has always been attracted to men. Never women. When the show was filming, he'd travel the half hour from Stone Harbor or Avalon to go on dates at bars in Atlantic City.

He's been flooded by so many old memories of *The Shallows* lately. It's not surprising, with their reunion and the wedding coming up. The cast and crew shared so much in such an intense time. Good memories and bad ones. Constant drama.

Mason isn't the same person he was ten years ago. He's happy. At peace with himself and his career, where he's living, and who he's spending his time with. He's never looked back.

He still isn't sure why he committed to the ten-year reunion, but he is a sucker for nostalgia. He told the event planners that he'd do it. Come back, sign autographs, and do meet-and-greets with fans. It'll be fun. Kit promised he'd come, too. After missing the wedding, he'd better.

Ivy walks into the kitchen while he's standing there, stewing in resentment. "Daddy-O? Are you mad at us?" He realizes she must have overheard their conversation. Kids are always listening.

"Never, baby girl. I could never be mad at you." Mason walks over and squats down so they're eye level.

Ivy smiles. "I just don't want you and Dad to fight." She wraps her arms around him in a hug.

Damn it, he really hates Alex. She won this round.

Chapter 10

"She's the kind of girl who looks good on the surface.
But underneath it all, there's nothing there."
- Francesca, Season 2, Episode 4

Sage, May 30

"You're sure the content creators know to use the right filters for the church?" Sage asks Heather. "There's a lot of different lighting with the stained glass windows."

Her wedding planner nods. "We did a run through on Tuesday."

"And what about the sound levels?"

"Well, it is a church. They have great acoustics."

Sage is certain Heather thinks she's a bridezilla. But she doesn't understand what this means for Sage. Everything has to be absolutely and completely *perfect.*

Her wedding is going to be the ultimate display of her talent. The perfect showcase for her creativity in art and set design. Nothing can go wrong.

"Show me again where everyone's going to be standing when we walk out of Trinity Church."

Heather's eyes are probably rolling inside her head, but she opens her portfolio obligingly and finds the document. Reaching over, she hands it to Sage, who scans it briefly.

"Good. This works."

"I still can't believe the entire cast of *The Shallows* is coming to your wedding," Heather gushes. "It must be the first time they've all been together in years."

"I guess it is." It's one of the reasons she hopes her wedding gets covered by the major bridal magazines. Her guest list is strictly A-listers.

There's a knock on the door. "Can you get that?" Sage asks while she ducks into the bathroom. This early in the morning, she's still wearing her robe while she waits for the hair and makeup team to arrive.

She learned early on in the movie business that it's better to leave it to the professionals. It might be expensive, but having someone else apply makeup and style her hair makes her look much better than she could ever accomplish on her own.

"Sage? It's just Simon," Heather calls out. "Can I let him in?"

"Of course." She didn't expect her fiancé to be at her hotel room this early, but she can't exactly tell him not to come in. Even if she has a million things on her checklist to accomplish before everyone arrives on Friday.

Dabbing on some perfume, she splashes water on her face and goes to greet him. "Heather, can you give us a few minutes?"

"Absolutely." Heather grabs her binder and ducks out of their suite, shutting the door behind her.

"Hi, darling." Simon leans in for a kiss.

"I wasn't expecting you. Anything wrong?"

"Can't a man want to see his bride? I feel like I haven't had a chance to talk with you for days."

"I'm sorry, babe. There's just so much to do." She feels a tinge of guilt that she's been so wrapped up in planning that she hasn't even thought about him. Sage rests her head on his shoulder. "I missed you, too."

"Do you have time to get something to eat?"

"I wish I could, but I still have to go over our food selections for the rehearsal brunch."

Simon smiles indulgently, displaying his crooked canines. His smile was one of the first things she noticed about him on the set. He has an open friendliness that draws you in, making everyone feel welcome. And his understanding of people—she guesses it comes from being a writer, examining human traits. He sees the good, the bad, and the ugly, and takes it all in.

"I did want to ask you one thing."

"Yeah?"

"Are you sure you don't want me to fly your family in? We're already way over budget. What's a few last-minute flight tickets?"

Her stomach drops. "No, Simon. I told you. They can't make it, even if we paid." She's told him that her family is from a small town in Oregon. He's never even met her parents, who she's been estranged from for years. Simon, being Simon, doesn't push. But he gently nudges.

"I just don't want you to regret not having them here on your big day."

"Trust me, you don't want them here."

He looks at her intently. "You're sure? This is the last time I'll bring it up."

"Yes, I'm sure. As I'll ever be. I'm not going to change my mind."

He kisses her forehead. "Okay, then I'll leave you be. Do you need anything? I can grab you some coffee in the lobby."

Sage shakes her head. "Thanks, babe. I'm good. I love you."

"Love you, too." He leaves, and she feels a sense of dread. She's been hiding her background for years. Inventing a life and upbringing that is far from the one she was born into.

She just hopes, with all the attention her wedding is generating, that no one back home will notice. That none of them will realize the fabulous Sage Domingo is actually the small town, dirt poor Sarah Lopez she spent the first 18 years of her life being.

Chapter 11

"Never wear more than one showstopper."
- Shea, Season 2, Episode 5

Josie, May 31

Josie finishes applying her mascara and steps back from the mirror. "Ready in five minutes," she calls out to Paige, who's getting dressed in the bathroom.

"I need at least fifteen."

"We're going to be late!" Jo hates running behind. She always has.

"What else is new?" Paige does not.

Since they're both solo, they decided to get ready together in Jo's hotel room at the Gardiner House before heading downstairs to the rehearsal dinner. It helps to have a buddy at events like this. They have no idea what kind of situation they're walking into.

The opening night dinner is being held at Belle Mer, a stunning mansion on the edge of Narragansett Bay in Newport, Rhode Island. It's one of the most exclusive venues along the East Coast. Black tie only.

Josie has been in hair and makeup chairs long enough to know what colors work best with her blonde hair and hazel eyes. Her cocktail dress is a one-shoulder lavender gown that falls to her ankles.

She pairs the dress with gold hoops and thick stacks of bracelets, adding thick, strappy heels to give her 5'6" frame a lift. She hopes she looks good, but not that she's trying too hard.

Is she ready for this? Seeing everyone in one place, at one time? It hasn't happened in so long. The nerves in her stomach won't subside.

Fame is a slippery slope. All of a sudden, hundreds of thousands of people think they know what it's like to be in your shoes. You become someone to pick apart. Fans love to comment on every aspect of your face, your body, and your hair. What you wore that day and who you interacted with.

And it was nearly always wrong.

Josie loved acting, but the fame that came with it shredded her self-esteem, caused her to doubt her work, and ruined her self-worth. The attention essentially destroyed her ability to go out in public without creating a commotion.

It has improved over the years. She's no longer in the limelight like she was before. But she can never shake it.

When they started filming, Josie was just as naive as her character, Eve. She'd also never been in love. She experienced it the same way Eve did, falling quickly and totally for Tate Masters.

The only child of Hollywood and rock star royalty, he was blessed with the square jawline of his movie star father and the wide eyes and golden skin of his musician mother. It was 2010, and sexy surfer types were the leads in so many shows.

Was it any wonder Josie fell so hard? She had never even met anyone from Southern California before, much less from his celebrity circle. He'd grown up going to birthday parties with the kids of pop stars and celeb heartthrobs. He had A-list actors on his phone. For Tate, it was normal. For Josie, it was a world away from Buffalo.

It had taken her years to get her self-esteem back. Josie won't risk losing it again.

There's a knock on her door. "We don't need our room serviced. Thanks."

"Open up. It's Val!"

This is a surprise. Val had said that she'd go down to the rehearsal dinner with them, but Josie half expected her to bail–or at least, show up hours late. It's been ages since they've seen each other.

The only thing you can count on with Val is that she will be consistently unreliable. And even then, she can surprise you. Val is even unreliable at being unreliable, if that's a thing. She had come close to losing her spot on the show more than a few times for her chronic lateness, but her character Francesca was so popular that it would have been hard to replace her.

Josie opens the door, and there she is. "I can't believe you're actually here."

Val laughs. "You know I'd turn up eventually." She's the ideal bad girl, with her jet-black hair and light blue eyes. Even when she's being a bitch, she has a way of making people want to root for her.

Josie pulls Val in for a hug, and suddenly, everything is right in the world. Everyone is here, back together, to celebrate the wedding of their old friends. Whatever small resentments and snide comments they've made about each other are forgotten.

"Come in, have a drink. I have champagne." Josie pops a bottle.

"You read my mind," Val reaches for a glass and tosses it back. Her dress is a deep auburn, with spaghetti straps and a deep slit, the perfect complement to her golden skin and long, dark hair. She looks sexy and just a little bit dangerous.

Paige has on a light pink ruffled dress that's just as angelic-looking as she is. The shade picks up her pale skin and reddish-brown hair. Josie thinks Paige looks like a doll, with her wide lashes and pattern of freckles across her nose. She looks so innocent that Josie wants to tell Paige not to take candy from strangers.

They make a toast: "To us!" The nostalgia is almost too much to take in. The golden trio, back together again.

The welcome reception is being held in the hotel's main gardens. It's supposed to be more of a cocktail hour than a sit-down dinner. Josie is grateful for that. She won't be nailed down to one spot as guests wander around.

"You ready?" she asks.

Paige nods sweetly, while Val gives a wicked smile.

"As much as we'll ever be. Let's do this."

They lock arms as they head downstairs to the hotel lobby.

It's showtime.

Chapter 12

"Can't you try a little harder?
You're always so hard to get along with."
- Chase to Francesca, Season 1, Episode 2

Val, May 31

"Would you like a drink?"

"Absolutely. Keep them coming." There isn't enough alcohol in the hotel to numb Val's nerves. She grabs another drink from the waiter's tray as he passes and chugs it, then looks around for another.

Things aren't going as smoothly as she'd hoped. Josie and Paige had already split off to talk to other people, leaving her feeling like the odd person out.

At least there's an open bar. And it may be one of the most gorgeous venues on the East Coast. Before tonight, she had never heard of Goat Island. Today, she's overlooking the iconic Claiborne Pell Bridge spanning Narragansett Bay.

And all Val can do is worry about what's going to go wrong.

Val knew Sage would have an incredible wedding venue. It's literally her job to create stunning, unforgettable scenes. She used to incorporate accent lighting and special effects that became iconic moments for the show.

Nothing was too much when they were shooting *The Shallows*. Their director, Bryce Chung, believed in employing the best set designers and installers in the business. He used to poach them from the sets of other network shows by dramatically raising their salaries.

But even for Sage, this is over the top. Ten-feet-tall mirrored walls reflect the harbor and ocean back at the guests, making it seem like the entire ballroom is underwater. She's added enormous mirrored disco balls to the walls of climbing ivy. The decor picks up the light from the water, making it look like the room is floating in specks of light.

How are they paying for all of this? Val can't help but wonder.

Art assistants don't typically make millions. And wasn't Sage from some small town in Oregon? Val didn't remember Sage being a trust fund baby. And her fiancé, Simon, is a writer. Everyone knows they don't make a ton unless they're working on *Star Wars* franchises.

Well, *someone* is paying for it. Tuxedo-clad waiters weave in and out of the crowd with trays of wine and champagne, canapes and cocktails. A jazz trio is set up on the pebbled stones outside. Rows of arched doors are flung open to the elements, the sheer white curtains fluttering with the breeze from the ocean.

There must be hundreds of people here. The guest list is extremely generous. Val was invited with a plus-one, when she hadn't even talked to Sage in years. It seems like almost everyone from the show is there, along with the couple's friends and family. She bets it's costing them more than $500 a head.

Val's glad she went full glam with her long, sweeping dress. If only she had her mother's necklace. The Art Deco style would fit in perfectly with this Great Gatsby setup.

She isn't going to give the asshole blackmailing her any more headspace than they've already taken. Tonight is the time to have fun. Val reaches out for another glass, even though she isn't quite done with the one she's holding.

Josie arches an eyebrow. "Starting off strong?"

"Give me a break, Jo Jo. I haven't seen some of these people since the show ended." Josie is the last person Val is going to confide in. Explain why she's being blackmailed for what she did a decade ago. *That* will go over well. No, Val will keep that little secret, just like she always has. She and her own personal blackmailer.

When she finds out who the bastard is … Val jumps when a pair of arms close around her.

She jabs back with her elbow, striking their stomach hard.

"Ouch! What the hell, Val?" Mason says sulkily. "I was trying to give you a hug."

"Mason! You scared me."

"You sure are jumpy," he says, rubbing his stomach.

"Tell me about it," Josie rolls her eyes. "She's been like this since we got here."

Val didn't become a famous actress for nothing. She quickly laughs it off. "I just don't feel like running into Jacob," Val quips. "I'd never get out of there." The grip had a not-so-secret crush on her that had been a running joke on set for years.

Mason laughs along with her, and the tension is gone. "So, who else is here?"

"Paige came with us, but we lost her when we came in. She saw some acting friends from a commercial they worked on recently."

Sage and Simon have worked on so many productions that many of their colleagues began to overlap from working on years of projects. It's pretty common. Once a director finds the right person for a job, they will often use the same camera operators, gaffers, sound, and production departments for different gigs going forward.

Hollywood can still be a small world, with many of the same players showing up. Even when you don't want to see them.

"Where's Kit?" Josie asks.

"His ex-wife delivered a heavy dose of father guilt," Mason rolls his eyes. "He's at a family reunion. With her family, not his."

"You're still in Chester County, living it up in the burbs?"

Val still can't picture him settling down. He was one of the biggest partiers in their group.

"One big happy family. Hitting up the farmer's market on the weekends, and coaching lacrosse games from the sidelines. We even have a collie."

"Damn. Who would have thought you'd be so domestic?"

Mason nods as he looks around the crowd. "Seriously. And I'm so glad I'm out of the industry. Although I do miss the drama."

"You're in landscape design, right? That explains those muscles," Val purrs. She reaches out a hand to touch his biceps. "I miss feeling them."

"These things?" he says with a delighted smile. "Val, you always know what to say. My fave sex kitten."

They'd shared more than a few plot lines that involved heavy making out—on the beach, in cars, in bed. Val's character Francesca was the bad girl, after all. She was duty-bound to create drama wherever she went.

"You're one of the best kissers I've ever had," Val tells Mason brightly.

"That makes my heart flutter." He leans over to plant one on her cheek, careful not to scratch her with his thick mustache. "What about you, Jo Jo? Who's at the top of your list for an on-camera makeout?"

Josie doesn't rise to the bait. "I don't kiss and tell," she says as she looks over the crowd. She puts her glass to her lips and takes a sip, effectively ending her response.

Josie won't just say it out loud, but Mason and Val know the only person it could be. The flames from Jo Jo and Tate's affair were so bright that they left behind embers.

The production team didn't have to even attempt selective editing—their attraction was so fierce it leaped off the screen.

Too bad it burned them both.

Val decides to stir the pot. "Who else RSVP'd yes, Mason? Our new rock and roll recording star?" She's well aware that she's being bitchy. She still can't help herself.

"Oh, let's hope so," Mason answers. "If only to offer eye candy." An open-ended answer. Val knows Mason won't get involved. He keeps his friendships with Tate and Josie separate, not getting involved in their personal relationship.

No one can deny that what he said was true. The sex appeal of Tate Masters was off the charts. The square jaw, dimpled cheek, and golden boy sheen have always followed him. It didn't matter if he was sick or hungover; he was still devastatingly gorgeous. Combine that with a body made by the gods? It was so unfair that one person got all of that. It was simply greedy, in Val's opinion.

Val watches Josie's eyes sharpen. Of course, she would have known he was invited. But did Tate RSVP yes or no? The only people who would know that would be the bride and groom. It's going to be interesting to find out. She can't wait.

A waiter walks past. "Excuse me? Can I have another?" Val asks, trailing after him.

The party is getting into full swing, and she doesn't want to be sober for it.

Chapter 13

"Life is like a carousel. You never can predict
where you'll get on and get off."
- Chase, Season 4, Episode 3

Tate, May 31

Squeaks is taking her sweet time getting ready. They're already an hour late for the welcome reception. At this rate, they're going to completely miss the event.

He's starting to lose his patience. "What are you doing in there?" he yells to his date in exasperation at the closed hotel room door. "We need to leave soon."

"Stop rushing me!" Squeaks shouts back. "These things take time."

Okay. But what in the hell could take THAT long?

He's been sitting on the edge of the couch for what seems like forever, waiting for Squeaks to finish getting ready.

They booked two suites at the Hotel Viking, a luxury boutique in the heart of Newport. It took Tate ten minutes to get ready. Squeaks has been locked away in the bathroom for over an hour.

To be fair, Tate hadn't given her much notice. Squeaks had to rush out to the stores yesterday to get formal outfits for both the welcome reception and the wedding. They were both black tie events. He gave her his credit card and free rein to spend what she needed.

He had to. When he found out Josie would be coming, Tate bribed his partner into coming by promising her he'd take Squeaks along on his mom's next tour. He couldn't face seeing Josie alone.

He doesn't use his nepo baby status often. He only plays that card when it's badly needed.

What he didn't take into account was how *slow* Squeaks was getting ready. She tended to get distracted and lose her focus often, which actually was a gift when recording. They often went back and caught mistakes they wouldn't have otherwise.

But getting dressed for a function? It's freaking *brutal*.

Okay, so he's not used to sharing a space with another person. He's an only child. He doesn't have a roommate. And he hasn't had a serious relationship in a long time. But does everyone really take that long to walk out the door?

The fact that he's so worked up right now makes him realize it's been too long since he's been with anyone. He's becoming an introvert.

Maybe it's time he stopped shutting himself off in a recording studio and got out there. He doesn't even know what dating apps people are using these days. The last time he went on a date, people were using Match.com.

"Squeaks, do you use a dating app?" he asks at the closed door.

"I don't need to. Stop distracting me and let me get ready!"

Great. What's he supposed to do to meet someone? It's not easy dating when you're a minor celebrity. If he has a bad first date, she might go right to a celeb blog and tell them all about it. Unhappy dates have gone online and posted things about him that aren't even close to being true.

This is why he prefers to keep his circle close, spending his time with trusted people.

Like Squeaks. Who's still in the bathroom.

He's been waiting for so long that he hasn't had a chance to get something to eat. "Squeaks, we really gotta go. We're an hour and a half late."

The door finally opens, and she emerges in a bright red jumpsuit with stacked heels.

"You look amazing," he says honestly. And she does, now that he's taking the time to notice.

"Of course I do," Squeaks says. She grabs her clutch and throws her lipstick inside. "Looking this good takes time, you know."

It's all he can do not to roll his eyes. He doesn't need to risk a fight and lose even more time. They still need to get a cab.

"I'll call a car," he says.

Ten minutes later, they pull up to Belle Mer on Goat Island and walk across the sweeping gardens facing Narragansett Bay. It looks like a scene straight out of *The Great Gatsby*.

The lawns are lit with strings of lights and glowing lamps, while hundreds of people are spread out among cocktail tables and efficient waiters. The band is playing classic Sinatra as a tuxedo-clad singer belts out "My Way."

Squeak's face looks around in disbelief at the setup. "Damn, you know some rich people," she says.

Tate shrugs. "I guess so." Sage and Simon have definitely pulled out all the stops for this reception.

He's grabbed from behind and spun around. "Tate!" Thick, beefy arms squeeze his sides.

"What's up, man?" Tate smiles.

Chuck Pencha was one of the stunt coordinators for *The Shallows* crew. He also stood in as a bodyguard when needed, since they didn't have that many stunts. But they did have a lot of overzealous fans.

Chuck did a good job of keeping them away. His size alone was a deterrent.

"It's been years. What have you been up to? And who is this lady?" He turns to Squeaks.

Tate chuckles and introduces his date. "I've been producing music. This is my partner."

"Romantic or professional?" Chuck has no filter. He never has.

"We just work together," Tate says easily.

"You're a lucky man."

Squeaks has been considering this heavily tattooed, bearded man in a sports coat with some apprehension. She must have decided that he's harmless. "I'm Sasha, but my friends call me Squeaks."

He continues staring at her, obviously struck by her style. Squeaks has that effect on people. "It's a BIG pleasure to meet you. Can I get you a drink? Something to eat?"

Tate rolls his eyes. "Easy, fella. You just met her." He knows Squeaks is more than a match for Chuck. "He's harmless," he tells her quietly.

"Like I can't take care of myself." She grants Chuck a wide smile and puts her hand in his. They stroll over to the main reception area.

Great. He's already lost his date in less than ten minutes. Tate strikes out on his own to find the bride and groom. He won't let himself think about who else might be here.

Even if she's been on his mind all week.

Chapter 14

"I never got over you, Eve. It's simply not possible."
- Jack, Season 4, Episode 9 (Series Finale)

Josie, May 31

Josie begins to relax. If he isn't here by now, Tate must not be coming to the wedding after all.

With no way of knowing if he was going to make it or not, Josie has been tense for hours. She couldn't ask Sage or Simon. That would have looked pathetic. Instead, she's just been anxiously waiting to see if he was going to turn up at the event.

They've been at Belle Mer for over an hour now, and there's no sign of him. This place is something else. Goat Island's location offers ocean views from every angle. If she looks out over the water, she can see the historic Castle Hill Inn, with its rows of Adirondack chairs lining the lawn.

Josie has mixed and mingled all over the venue and hasn't run into Tate. He obviously isn't coming. Which means she's safe ... and maybe a teeny bit disappointed.

"I'm going to run to the bathroom," she tells Paige, who nods and continues talking to one of *The Shallows* sound techs.

As she makes her way to the lobby, Josie wonders if she really wants the drama that always seems to accompany Tate Masters. She honestly doesn't. The idea of seeing him again is exciting, she has to admit. She has scrolled through his social media accounts to look him up. It's a guilty and pointless habit; one that she can't seem to toss when it comes to Tate.

Josie wonders if he even remembers their time together. He's probably too busy now, with his high-profile career. Making rock stars.

Whatever. Not her problem.

The bathroom attendant is helping a few women fix their hair, touch up their makeup, and adjust any loose straps. She doesn't pay Josie any mind, just nods in greeting.

"Nice event, isn't it?" Josie says, slipping into a stall.

Josie washes her hands, gives the attendant a nice tip, and strides back out to Belle Mer's opulent lobby on her way back to the ballroom. Chaise lounges and clusters of chairs are placed around in pairs of seating. She can envision it as it was during the Golden Age in Newport, with women dressed in formal evening gowns talking to their dance partners in tuxes.

The lobby is quiet, especially when Josie considers how many people are there. The majority of guests have likely wandered into the back ballroom area or spread out across the manicured lawns overlooking the water.

Josie is double-checking her profile in an oversized mirror when she overhears someone arguing. She's not trying to eavesdrop, but the rest of the space is so quiet that they come across the corridor loud and clear. The tall ceilings make it easy to overhear a conversation happening nearby, even if she can't see them behind the mirrored wall.

"I could kill you!" a woman whispers angrily.

"Just stop," a man is saying. "I didn't do anything."

"If anyone finds out I was behind this, my career is over," the female voice replies. There's a tinge of desperation in her voice. She's speaking low, making it hard to pick up all the words.

"Then you shouldn't have fucked up so bad," he tells her coldly.

"Screw you. I was 20 years old. What did I know? I've paid my dues."

Wow. This isn't party chit chat. Josie stumbled on a serious convo. She can't help being curious. She *needs* to hear more. Wouldn't anyone?

She's inching closer, as quietly as she can, to see who these two people are. Is it possible she knows them?

They're down the hall in a shadowy alcove. She can't see their faces or even tell what they're wearing.

Damn it. She shimmies down the hallway as far as she dares without risking them hearing her. It helps to make some of their words a little clearer.

There's a deep sigh. "Well, obviously someone doesn't think so. And they want to make sure you continue to keep quiet. Or you know what will happen."

Was that a threat? She can't get any closer without giving herself away.

There's a muffled sob from the female. "This isn't the place to talk about it." She sounds like she's about to cry.

"You never could take any responsibility for your actions. But I have a way to make you some money. Take some pressure off."

The guy sounds like he's enjoying tormenting her. What a jerk. Josie wants to step in and break it up. Who could it be? His voice sounds familiar, but it's still so low she can't place it.

The woman sobs again. "I can't believe you're still pushing it in my face. It's done. I can't take it anymore."

It sounds like the woman is about to bolt. Josie takes a step back, as quietly as possible. If she's discovered, they'll know she heard everything. It will be embarrassing for all of them. And possibly make things worse for the woman.

Josie keeps walking backwards, as quickly as she can, which isn't easy to do in high heels and a long dress. If she trips, the gig is up. They'll know she heard everything. She makes it back to the main lobby area where the bathrooms are located.

Phew. That was close. Jo turns around to walk back to her friends, when her heart drops. Tate is walking across the lobby, heading straight for her.

Are you kidding me? Right now?

She really doesn't need this.

She's still reeling from the secretive conversation she overheard, and now the ex-boyfriend she hasn't seen in ten years is here.

There's no escape. His gaze is locked in. Josie knows that look.

There's nowhere to duck and hide, unless she joins the unhappy couple in the corridor. From the ballroom, a familiar song begins to play, and it's all she can do not to break down ... *The way you wear your hat, the way you sip your tea ...*

The song where they reunited for the series finale. Holy shit.

He's less than ten feet away.

Unsurprisingly, he looks devastatingly handsome in a black tux. Tate always does. It's so incredibly unfair. He's staring at her with that direct, unblinking stare he has that makes it impossible to look away.

She won't break first. Let him talk.

An awkward silence follows. He's still standing there, looking at her.

The memory of all that ... no, they can't take that away from me ...

Screw it. She'll be the mature one and go first. "I didn't expect to see you here." She keeps her tone light and friendly.

He still doesn't respond. Just looks at her intently. It's not like him.

He's not quiet or shy, so she's not sure what this is all about.

Why isn't he talking????

She isn't going to keep filling up the empty air with small talk. Two people are standing here.

"It's been a while. How have you been?"

He's still just looking at her blankly.

"Hello?" She cracks, moving closer and waving her fingers in front of his face.

Still nothing.

"Earth to Tate?" She's losing her patience. Why is he acting like such a jerk? He should at least have the decency to answer her.

Tate doesn't look well. His face is pale and sweaty. Finally, he shakes his head. "Damn it, I'm sorry. I'm not feeling great."

Now that she's so close, she can see beads of sweat have broken out across his forehead. The collar of his shirt is soaking wet. He looks like he's going to be sick. "Tate, are you okay?"

He doesn't respond, so she reaches out her hand to touch his forehead. "You're clammy." Josie grips his arm to hold him steady. "We need to call someone."

Tate groans. "I'm sorry, Jo Jo. I need to ..."

His face goes white. He passes out, falling forward and tumbling down, taking Josie down with him.

Tate has more than six inches and 50 pounds on her. She crumples to the floor under his limp body.

"Ooooff!"

Tate is so heavy that she can't move him. She tries to yell for help, but he's crushing her lungs with his weight.

This is it. She and Tate are going to die on the floor of the Belle Mer lobby. Someone will find their bodies after the cocktail hour ends.

After what feels like *forever,* she hears someone shouting.

"What the hell?" One of the rehearsal guests walking to the lobby must have spotted the two of them sprawled across the floor. He runs over.

"Are you okay? Let me help." She feels the weight of his body being lifted off hers. He's still unconscious, just completely passed out cold.

She rolls to her side and sits up. "Thank you. I couldn't move him."

"Damn," her savior says with a raised eyebrow. "How are you feeling? Did he crush any of your ribs?"

Josie shakes her head. "I'm fine."

"You're sure? Just stay there for a bit, catch your breath before you get up." The guy turns his attention back to Tate, crouching over him to check his vitals. He grabs a small light from his pocket, shining it in his eyes.

Is he a doctor? He must be looking for a concussion.

"He has diabetes," Josie tells the helpful (and she can't help noticing, extremely good-looking) guest. "His blood sugar must have dipped, causing him to pass out."

"Gotcha. I'm a firefighter. I have some EMT training."

Tate begins to come to, groaning as he sits up from his spot on the floor.

"Slow down, buddy," the guy tells Tate as he checks his pulse, then pulls out his phone. "I need help in the lobby. Can someone grab me an orange juice from the bar? ASAP."

Within moments, someone is there with a drink for Tate. Some color begins to return to his face. He thanks him.

"Give yourself a minute," the firefighter tells Tate, then turns to Josie. He grabs her hands and pulls her to her feet in one smooth move. "You're sure you're okay?" he asks.

"Everything is intact. I'm Josie." She smiles up at him as she smooths her dress. "Remington," she says as an afterthought. It doesn't look like he recognizes her name or who she is.

"Quinn Kearney. Do you come here often?" he asks dryly.

She laughs. "Not usually."
And that's how Josie meets Quinn.

Chapter 15

"She's only mad because she wants what you have."
- Shea to Eve, Season 2, Episode 8

Paige, May 31

Paige marches to the open bar to get another drink. She makes sure she doesn't make eye contact with any of the guests. She's too annoyed for small talk.

"Can I have another dry martini?" She walks right up to the bar and taps her glass. There's a line in front of her, but she's not in the mood to wait.

Someone behind her mutters under their breath. Paige whirls around. "Did you say something?" She stares the woman down, as if to say, "Just try it." Even though Paige has a sweetheart face, her eyes can still turn lethal if needed.

The woman sighs. "No. It looks like you need it more than I do."

"That's true," Paige answers. Then, feeling a little bad (and nervous someone might be recording her bitchy move), she grants the other guest a radiant smile. "It's for someone who isn't able to walk over to get it for themselves."

The woman looks appropriately ashamed, as Paige had hoped she would. She also shuts up. The rest of the people in line don't make a peep as she waits for the bartender to finish making her martini.

"Not too much vermouth," Paige cautions. "And make sure you use the good vodka."

She's so pissed off. Of course, Josie has two men falling over her. Two incredibly gorgeous, leading men material, insanely charismatic guys just dying to get her attention. Like, literally passing out and nearly getting rushed to the hospital in the middle of a million-dollar wedding weekend.

Why wouldn't she? Paige thinks angrily.

It's so typical of Josie. While Paige is slogging around during the rehearsal dinner reception, trying to get the attention of a bartender to make another espresso martini, Josie is once again grabbing all the spotlight. Hogging all of the attention.

Josie has always been the lucky one. The girl who everyone's eyes swiveled to when she entered the room. The director's pet.

Paige is so incredibly sick of it. Why can't it be her?

She remembers one time, when *Teen Crush* magazine approached her mother and then agent about Paige appearing on the cover. The title was going to be, "Shallows Star Paige DeBello: How The Girl Next Door is Taking Over Hollywood." That was, until news of Josie and Tate's real-life romance spread, and the couple was chosen for the cover story instead.

Paige never got over it. It's insulting enough that she's been working since she was a child, yet still struggles to pay the bills. Her living expenses keep creeping up while her cash flow has gone way down. There's no way she could ask her mom for money, and she never knew her father.

Paige skipped college because she couldn't afford to lose out on acting opportunities, so she only has a high school GED. Looking back, it probably wasn't the wisest decision, but what did she know then? She was a young girl, riding high with a hit TV show. She thought she was invincible.

Multiple stints of rehab haven't helped much, either. Paige has made so many mistakes that she cringes to look back on them. But she can't change it now. She can only move forward.

So many other people involved with *The Shallows* have gone on to be successful that it makes Paige feel insecure. Sage is designing blockbuster movie sets. Simon is signed on to write screenplays for superhero franchises. Mason has a successful landscaping firm. Tate just got nominated for a music award. It's ridiculous. And embarrassing.

And then there's Josie, who turned a hobby of taking photos of food into a commercially successful photography business virtually overnight. She's getting flown all over the world to photograph inanimate objects for a stable of corporate clients, her photos appearing on the covers of major magazines. Raking in tons of money.

Son of a bitch. Why not Paige? How come she still hasn't made it big?

Without realizing it, Paige starts pulling at her hair. It's a bad habit she can't stop herself from doing when she's upset, twisting and pulling at the strands.

She is so fired up that she tosses back her third drink of the night. The alcohol goes straight to her brain, as she hoped. Who cares about rehab? Paige hasn't eaten all day because her dress isn't the most forgiving, and she didn't want to look bloated, so there's nothing to soak it up.

Whatever. As if these people haven't seen her blackout drunk before. And tonight's a celebration, right?

Paige has her elbows propped on the bar, overseeing the method to make sure he's followed her exact instructions, when an arm slides around her waist.

"You're such a diva," Justin chuckles in her ear.

"You know it." Justin was Josie's agent for years, but when she retired from acting, he took on Paige instead. He knows exactly what she's been up to and how many gigs she's booked (not a lot). He's well aware of how much Paige's life sucks right now.

Come to think of it, Justin might be the only one who knows the honest truth about the pathetic state of her career.

"Want a drink?" she asks.

"Am I awake? Get me a beer?"

Paige waves her fingers at the bartender, who clearly is dying to hate on her but has to hold his tongue because he's a working stiff. "Add a light beer to that order."

The bartender sighs, but nods to let her know that he's heard her.

Once they've received their drinks (finally), she and Justin move out of the long line and back towards the reception.

"I didn't think we'd be invited," Paige says. "Did you?"

Justin doesn't take offense. "Yeah, I was surprised, too. But from the looks of it, they invited everybody." He gestures out at the crowded dance floor. "So what's got you all fired up?"

"The usual. Josie blinks, and men fall at her feet. I can't even get a guy to split the check on a Tinder date."

Justin laughs. "You know that's not true. You're gorgeous."

"Not gorgeous enough, or I'd be booking more gigs."

He nods and takes a sip of his beer. "It's probably your agent's fault."

"Most likely."

"I might have a proposition for you," Justin says. "It's unorthodox, but you might be interested."

"Really? What is it? At this point, I'd do anything." Paige is past worrying about looking desperate. Justin knows every gig she's booked (and audition she's lost out on) this year. "I mean that."

"I know what you're capable of," Justin replies somewhat mysteriously.

"You should."

"Let's talk next week." He looks around. "Where are your girls? Jo Jo said the triplets were coming together, but she and Val are nowhere to be found."

Paige rolls her eyes. "Just guess. Jo is probably surrounded by men, and Val is helping out with bridesmaid duties."

Even though Val isn't technically in the wedding party, Paige knows she'll still volunteer for the awful tasks, like corralling people for group photos or keeping an eye on the caterers. She always needs to be where the action is.

"Let's go find them." Justin tucks his arm into Paige's and leads her towards the terrace. "And stop being such a bitch."

Paige laughs. "I can't promise anything."

Chapter 16

"When you grow up as good-looking as Jack, you don't have to be skilled at anything except waking up in the morning."
- Shea, Season 2, Episode 1

Mason, May 31

"Well, that went swimmingly," Mason tells Tate as he looks down on him sprawled on the couch.

They've been taking a break in a room off the lobby to give Tate time to feel better. He's been fading in and out, but it doesn't look like he has a concussion. The very helpful firefighter has been patiently waiting with them until the sugar kicks in.

"Where are we?" Tate asks, looking around with confusion. He tugs at his tie, loosening it from his collar. Even disheveled, he still looks better than most people, Mason thinks.

"We moved you to another room so people don't start taking pictures of you passed out and make up rumors that you overdosed."

"Thanks, man." Tate struggles to sit up.

The fact that Mason is the first person Tate sees when he comes to would come as a surprise to absolutely no one who actually knows them.

They've been inseparable since the first moment they met, despite multiple false rumors of on-set tension and drama over the years. They both enjoy tacos, fishing, and surfing. What else do you need to agree on?

On their days off, they spent hours in the Atlantic Ocean, hitting the beaches in Avalon and Stone Harbor, sometimes traveling to Sea Isle and Wildwood for a change of scenery. They explored all the island towns of South Jersey.

Mason played opposite Tate as the other corner of the Josie love triangle. More like a pentagon, if you counted Val and Paige. The writers had them constantly swapping partners to keep the drama going.

It was ironic, of course, because the whole time all Mason wanted to do was date guys. But that was ten years ago. Gay characters were always the supporting roles then, never the stars of the show. The first time he ever saw a teen come out on TV was Rickie on *My So-Called Life*, followed by the first kiss between two men on network TV on *Dawson's Creek*.

Even now that they're older, they live less than 45 minutes from each other—Tate in downtown Philly, Mason in the Philly suburbs—so they get to see each other as often as they can.

They're still as different from each other as they ever were. Tate is easygoing, but quiet. He tends to be more reserved. Mason is outgoing, with a dry sense of humor that can veer towards nasty when he's not careful to rein it in. Tate works late hours mixing music, while Mason gets up at dawn for landscaping projects.

But their bond is deep. They consider each other the brother that neither of them had.

Now, Mason watches with worry as Tate struggles to rise from the couch they had laid him on. Tate blinks a few times, still disoriented.

He's well aware of the serious nature of Tate's condition. When Tate was diagnosed with Type 1 diabetes, Mason was one of the few people that he confided in.

Things kept happening that couldn't be easily explained away. His hands and feet would tingle, or his vision would blur after long days of shooting. Tate didn't like to talk about it, but Mason could tell that something was off. His friend kept losing weight and was always thirsty.

Tate hated going to the doctor. Always has. He didn't want to get checked out, but Mason had pushed him until he finally made an appointment. After the diabetes diagnosis, Tate had a change of heart and started taking his health seriously. He's been able to handle diabetes through insulin and blood sugar monitoring. Sometimes, though, he slips up.

It usually happens in stressful situations. He knows that Tate has been working long hours for that band. He's probably not paying attention to his diet. No one could ever tell Tate Masters what to do. He's one of the most stubborn people Mason has ever dealt with.

"You're okay," he tells his woozy friend. "You just passed out for a sec."

"What happened?" Tate asks. He looks around the room.

"You went lights out. Fell right on top of Josie."

"Are you kidding me? Is she okay?"

"She's fine. I told her to give you some space, but she's right outside the door."

The firefighter leans over Tate to pull off the blood pressure cuff. Tate flinches at the contact.

"Who the hell are you?"

He grins. "My name's Quinn. I'm not actually a medic. I'm a firefighter, but I have EMT training, too. Your vitals are stable, but you should rest for a bit."

Hot. Mason has always had a thing for firefighters. Who doesn't?

Quinn pats Tate on the back, like he's a little kid. Tate looks surprisingly small next to him.

The firefighter is becoming more interesting by the minute. Too bad Mason is already taken. Then again, Kit isn't here.

"Just give yourself a few more minutes before you get up," Mason tells Tate. "You have time. No one even knows you're missing."

He considers it lucky that Tate's collapse happened away from the party. It means that only a few people had seen what happened, which should limit the spread of gossip.

Mason knows all too well that could soon change. Rumors take on a mind of their own. Some are probably already beginning to spread about Tate Master passing out, people making up stories that he's using drugs, has an eating disorder, or has a medical condition.

There's never a positive spin, either. It's always nasty. Snide.

It's a damn shame, in Mason's opinion. They aren't celebrities anymore. They did their part while they were active, but now they're retired. They should be allowed to have privacy in their lives now.

The attention won't end until *The Shallows* becomes obsolete. When their fans stop watching reruns and the show is no longer aired on streaming channels.

Until then, the cast members are still easy prey for the public. To be dissected and gossiped over, photographed and studied. It made all of them a bit wary and jaded, for sure.

Some people will say it's what they signed up for. But do you really know anything when you're eighteen years old?

Color is starting to return to Tate's face. He looks at Quinn. "Thanks, man," he tells him.

"No problem. I'm going to head out, unless you think you need me?" Holding a medical kit, the guy is a six-foot-three firefighter with doctor vibes. If Mason were single, he'd be ditching Tate to spend some time with Quinn.

"Thanks again. We owe you. And I hate to ask, is there any way you can keep this between us? We don't want to ruin the wedding."

"Of course. Hippo oath and all that."

"How do you know the happy couple?" Mason wonders if Quinn's an actor, too. He has the face for it.

"I helped out with the sets when you filmed around Avalon and Stone Harbor," Quinn admits. "It was my first job in high school. I got to know the production crew."

Interesting. "Will you be there for the reunion?"

"Definitely. I live there year-round. I'll be helping with security." Quinn cocks his head. "Are all of you coming?"

"Not sure. I think about half have agreed to it. Why do you ask?"

Quinn grins. "Just wondering."

"I owe you dinner," Tate says. He's finally up and looking much better.

"Give me a call when you get to town." Quinn pulls a business card from his wallet and hands it to Tate. He waves goodbye in their general direction and heads out the door.

Mason watches him go. "How did I miss that dreamboat?"

Tate laughs. "Let's go back to the party. I need to find Squeaks. Did you say Josie is outside?"

Mason sighs. "I'll get her." When he walks out the door, though, she's no longer waiting directly outside their room, but across the lobby, talking to that foxy firefighter. They're standing close to each other, almost intimately.

Interesting. Mason decides not to say anything to Tate. He's so unpredictable when it comes to Josie.

Mason tries to walk a fine line between Tate and Josie, keeping his opinions about their relationship to himself. No one likes being told what to do or how to live, anyway.

Mason heads back to the couch Tate is lying on. "She must have just left," he announces.

Even though Tate nods, Mason can tell he's bummed.

He feels no compunction about lying. Tate and Josie are oil and water. They shouldn't mix again. It's better for both of them if they have as much space between them as possible.

He is going to make sure that happens. They all just need to get through the wedding tomorrow, and everything will be fine. Right?

Chapter 17

"You can be empathetic and poor,
or pragmatic and live a wealthy life."
- Francesca, Season 1, Episode 6

Sage, June 1

"Smile! Gorgeous. Simply gorgeous. Can we have one of the bride with her mother-in-law?" the photographer asks.

Sage beckons Simon's mom over with a wave. The sweetest lady ever, she hasn't argued with a single detail of Sage's wedding planning, even when she probably thought it was over the top.

It's finally here: her big day. The event Sage has been planning for over a year. The beginning of her new life as Mrs. Simon Hartwick.

There has been no detail too small for her to have personally taken care of. Nothing that could go wrong has been overlooked.

Sage has made sure of that.

She's used every single movie contact she knows from years of working in the industry to make this weekend an absolutely unforgettable experience. The very best caterers, decorators, musicians, stylists, and wedding planners.

Every aspect of the event has been obsessed over and pored over, from the lighting to the flowers, the favors to the food. Nothing has been left to chance.

If Sage could, she would have bought a weather machine to make sure it's sunny. But there's no need. Today is absolutely gorgeous.

The weather is in the mid-70s with sunny skies and a little bit of cloud cover. The most ideal weather possible for a June wedding. Sage has teams of videographers and photographers on standby to capture every moment. She even booked a drone to take video from overhead.

"Can we get one of you looking down at your flowers?"

Heather rushes over with the bouquets in tow. Sage didn't want any bridesmaids (too many questions about where her family was), but she has her wedding planner, Heather, to run everything that bridesmaids usually do.

"I can't wait for the reception," her soon-to-be mother-in-law confides as they smile for the camera.

Sage knows it's going to be amazing. Rosecliff Mansion sits on the cliffs of Newport. Built for silver heiress Theresa Fair Oelrichs, it was known for its opulent parties during the Gilded Age. The architect modeled it after the Grand Trianon, the retreat of French kings.

Sage thinks it might be even prettier.

The ballroom is Newport's largest. It's so huge that it was even used as a roller rink at one time. She's filled it with banks of flowers and candles, glittering branches and shimmering chandeliers.

They're getting married at Trinity Church in downtown Newport before being transported to Rosecliff for cocktail hour, where the wedding reception will be held on a sweeping lawn overlooking the Atlantic.

She's sure that everyone is wondering how they're paying for such an elaborate, expensive wedding.

Let them. They don't need to know her business. Sage told him that it would all be taken care of, and sweet Simon let her take the lead, not questioning a single choice.

Does he really need to know everything? She thinks it works better this way. It's just like not telling him where she actually grew up. He doesn't need to know the details, because it's not important. She's no longer that person anyway.

Sage will never tell him how she came up with all the money. If she did, she knows Simon would leave her at the altar.

Sage feels a momentary twinge of guilt—she's not a terrible person—but it got her where she is now. Having the best day of her life. So, does she regret it?

Not at all.

Because today is her wedding day. The one she's dreamed about her entire life. Walking down a white carpet to meet the man of her dreams, surrounded by friends and family, in the most enchanting setting anyone could come up with.

Well, Simon's family. Her family can't make it. They live too far away, in Oregon. That's her story, anyway. She couldn't risk inviting her cousins and having them show up at a black tie affair. Sage shakes her head at the thought. She can't even imagine it.

Everything she's done to become Sage Domingo would come crashing down. All the work she's put into making herself over—changing her accent, her hair color, her style, even her teeth—has all been worth it.

She wouldn't change a thing. Because here she is. The belle of the ball.

And no one will ever find out what she did to achieve all of this.

Ever.

The photographer clicks away. "Stunning! Absolutely stunning."

Sage beams.

Chapter 18

Val, June 1

Val wakes up with a raging hangover and a dry mouth full of regret. She doesn't recognize this hotel room. It definitely isn't the one she checked into yesterday.

What had she been thinking? She'd ended up at an after-hours party that saw her making terrible decisions. Like, really bad ones. The ones that have landed her in so much debt that she's barely paying her bills.

She rolls over to check the space next to her. Yep, he's still there. Another horrible decision.

The guy is still sleeping, as far as she can tell. Maybe she can make a quick getaway? She starts inching away, careful not to pull the sheet with her.

He doesn't move. Maybe she'll get lucky and manage to sneak out without him noticing.

Val has one leg on the floor and the other slowly lifting off the mattress when he stirs.

She freezes. Damn it. She really doesn't want to have the awkward morning-after conversation, when both of them want to get out of there and forget they ever saw the naked parts of the other person just hours before.

While being polite.

He doesn't move again, so she gently sits up and rolls off the bed. She looks around for her clothing. And an escape exit.

Remnants from last night are strewn all over the floor. Empty wine bottles, torn condom wrappers, and piles of wet towels from the late night dip in the hotel pool.

Why does she keep doing this to herself? It's always been her problem, acting first and actually thinking about it later. She just dives in (no pun intended) without considering whether or not it's a good idea.

Pathetic.

It's the biggest reason for her current life situation: bartending at a dive bar and taking small parts in commercials. Working conventions for people with nostalgia for a teen drama. Selling signed memorabilia on eBay. Sneaking out of hotel bedrooms. Val sighs to herself.

She spots her dress and bra over by her purse. She just might get lucky and be able to get out the door without the random booty call waking up. She nabs them off the floor.

As she's zipping up her dress, he rolls over. Shit.

The stranger raises his head. "Morning," he says sleepily.

He looks harmless. And cute. *Score, Val!*

But then again, she knows next to nothing about him. She's not even sure if she remembers his name. She opts for a pleasant, neutral return greeting.

"Good morning." Her voice is way too high-pitched, but she can't help it. She's nervous.

He reaches out a hand to pull her back. "Where are you off to? It's so early. Come back to bed."

This is odd. Why doesn't he want her to leave? He already got lucky.

"I've got this wedding today," Val offers. "I don't have that much time."

"Yeah, Simon and Sage." He smiles up at her. Now that she's got her wine goggles off, she can see he's really cute. A little scruffy. Not her usual type, but cute. And from what she can see (and remember), he has a jacked body.

"They won't miss us yet," he tells Val. He feels familiar.

It's not a surprise that he's here for the wedding. Lord knows, Sage and Simon invited everyone they've known since preschool. But she realizes she also knows him from before last night. From *The Shallows*.

It's all coming back to her, even though it's still fuzzy.

Camera crew? No. Catering? Hmm, no, not that.

Stunts! He worked with Chuck. He was Mason's stunt double. She can totally see it. They share that surfer, bohemian vibe.

Mason had never been interested in her, no matter how hard she tried, which makes sense now, but didn't back then when the cast members were all hooking up with each other. But this is perfect. This guy is like a stand-in for her teen crush.

"I can stay a few minutes more," Val says shyly.

He lifts the covers in an invitation. "Come back to bed." She drops down and slides in. He pulls her closer to spoon. It's actually really nice. And she is tired.

A little more time won't hurt.

"So, what's your name again?" Val asks brightly.

He laughs. It's hoarse and sexy, just like him. "It's Xavier."

Chapter 19

Josie, June 1

"I promise to be your biggest fan, your equal partner, and your shelter during every storm," Simon tells Sage. "I will always be there, in sickness and in health."

"You are my favorite part of every day, and the one who makes all my dreams come true. Together, I know we can achieve anything we work for," Sage pledges her wedding vows.

"You may now kiss the bride," the minister intones. An organ starts up with its deep timbre, and Simon leans in for a big smooch with his glowing new bride, Sage.

Josie can't help but melt. They're so happy.

The historic stone church is filled to capacity and overflowing with flowers. A violinist and a cellist begin to play "Ode to Joy" as the crowd gets to their feet to applaud.

Sage and Simon glide past, waving and smiling at friends and former castmates, bubbling over in their happiness.

Josie is seated towards the back with Paige, Val, Mason, and Justin. Tate and his date are in the back row; she couldn't help but notice.

Once the couple passes, they rise from their pews and file out, row by row. Groups of people are mingling as they greet old friends.

Outside, a white Rolls-Royce waits to whisk the bride and groom to Rosecliff Mansion for photos. The guests will be ferried over on classic red trolleys.

Josie spots some familiar faces, including Bryce Chung, the show's former director. He's done really well for himself, career-wise, going on to bigger and better projects. He even won an Emmy for his most recent show, *Compass Lane*. She walks over to give him a hug.

"Josie! Will I see you at the reunion?"

"Yes. Can't wait!" She's always liked Bryce. He's a bit of a control freak, but that comes with the territory, being a director. Trying to juggle multiple roles and corral everyone towards the same vision.

She spots other writers from *The Shallows*, which makes sense because Simon worked with them at their network, LJC. Once you find someone with good chemistry, you try to stick together.

There are the stunt doubles, who have always been the most entertaining characters in the crew. Willing to do anything for a dare.

Propmasters and camera masters, hair and makeup—there are people from all areas of production milling around. So many familiar faces. She loves seeing them all back together.

It's an absolutely gorgeous, fairy tale wedding. Every detail is perfect, from the flowers to the music. Sage has always had impeccable taste. Josie doesn't know how she does it.

A pair of doves flies over her head, making Josie duck for cover. She almost falls over in her heels.

"Watch out for those birds," Justin says with a dry chuckle. He makes a half-hearted attempt to steady her, but he's holding cups of edible glitter meant for throwing at the couple. He hands her one.

"They could have given us a warning," she tells him.

"I don't think they felt they needed to. Doves aren't known for their high threat level."

"Honestly, they should be. You never know."

Val hooks her arm through Josie's. "Take it easy on her, Justin," she says cheerily. "I personally hate all birds."

"Kit just took up bird watching," Mason offers. "I feel like we're becoming an old couple."

"Speak for yourself." Justin is the oldest of the group. "I'm older than you, and I'm not old."

Josie wonders how old Justin actually is. Her agent has been representing actors since he was in his late 20s, putting him anywhere between 40 and 50 years old. It's hard to tell. He does a great job maintaining himself, and in this industry, you never know someone's true age.

As Justin said, Botox isn't cheap. Neither are facelifts.

"Let's get going. I need a drink," Paige says brusquely. She's been in a bad mood all morning. Now that Josie notices, Paige has been grumpy this entire weekend.

"Everything okay?" Josie asks.

"It's fine," Paige snaps. "Not everyone's life is a cakewalk."

Well, there it is again. That fierce snap at her.

Something is definitely not right. "Do you want to talk about it?" Josie asks again, this time more gently.

"No, I don't, Jo Jo. Stop trying to solve everything."

Josie remembers that when Paige was like this when they were filming, it was always better to leave her alone. She walks away and heads towards the bright red trolley parked nearby.

Mason is already on board. She plops down on the seat next to him. "Bird watching, huh? Tell me about it." She nudges his shoulder.

"God, I miss Kit," he moans. "After I kill him for abandoning me, I'm not letting him leave me again."

"Sounds like a solid plan."

Mason slides his arm around her shoulders, then pulls a flask from his pocket. "Keep me company tonight? I need it."

"Of course." Josie reaches over and takes the flask from his hand. "It's me and you against the world."

Chapter 20

"A man does not choose his outfit.
His outfit chooses him."
- Chase, Season 4, Episode 8

Tate, June 1

The wedding band is rocking out to "It's Fun to Stay at the YMCA," and Squeaks is right there with them, enthusiastically making the letters in swooping arm movements. She nails every beat.

Tate can't take his eyes off her. He's not sure whether to applaud her or join in on the dance floor. With her sequin jumpsuit flashing off the strobe lights, she looks like she could pass for a member of the Village People.

"You can get yourself clean, you can have a good meal … " She's singing along with the band, her arms flying in all directions.

Squeaks has been on the dance floor since the ten-piece band started up, horns blaring and guitar players wailing. Two solid hours, and no one has been able to keep up with her. She's outlasted a few dance partners, including Chuck, who she pulled onto the dance floor when the band started up.

Chuck eventually waved the white flag and went to the bar.

Tate has a feeling Squeaks is going to end up joining the lead singer on stage before a few more songs go by. He'd put serious money on it.

"That's a sucker's bet," Mason says next to him, and Tate realizes he's said it out loud. "You know Squeaks will own that mic."

They've finished the obligatory wedding toasts, the four-course sit-down dinner, and the cutting of the cake. Now, it's time to party. Most of the guests have passed the threshold for making good decisions. The dance floor is starting to look like an underground rave.

After last night's scare, Tate is trying to maintain his blood sugar levels by making sure he's eating enough and staying hydrated. From the looks of it, he's the only one.

Their table is riddled with empty wine and cocktail glasses. The champagne is long gone. Tuxedo jackets are off, bow ties are loosened, and shoes have been discarded.

From their seats, Tate and Mason have the perfect view of the shenanigans on the dance floor. Competitive dance circles, couples grinding, other couples fighting … it's endless entertainment.

Paige is at the bar with Justin DeRose. Tate has never trusted the guy. He's such a scam artist. Always up to some kind of con.

It's supposed to be a wedding, but Tate has watched him working to get some of the smaller cast members to commit to the upcoming *Shallows* reunion.

"You'll make so much money!" he keeps saying, handing out his card. "Just give me a call, and I'll set you up."

The guy is such a sleazeball. There's a time and place for everything, and this isn't a work function.

Everyone is trying to cash in on their reunion. They've never done one before, and it's the tenth anniversary of their final season.

There's no doubt it will be huge. All of them, back in town where it all began. Having to face everyone they worked with after nearly a decade. So much time has passed, and things have changed. People moved on or are still trying to make it in the industry.

It wouldn't be a new idea. Tate has seen a lot of sci-fi and teen shows do the same: *Star Wars, Vampire Diaries, The Walking Dead,* and of course, all the guys from the Marvel comic universe. The fans all dressed up in cosplay, paying to see their favorite TV show and teen drama stars in real life. Willing to fork over cash to get up and close. Have a memento to take home.

The company that plans the event makes a killing on tickets, meet-and-greets, and autograph sessions. In Tate's opinion, it's a ripoff, but some fans are willing to pay anything to get up close and personal with their favorite stars.

Surprisingly, Paige and Val have both committed to doing the convention in July. Mason told Tate that he had, too.

It will be fun to have the whole gang back together, Mason had said.

The actors who played Josie's mom and dad on the show, Elise DeLonghi and Marty Lawson, also agreed to attend. Scotty, who played Tate's little brother Liam on *The Shallows*, and some of the more prominent extras, originally agreed to do the show but have since backed out for another gig. Rebecca Radcliffe, the actress who played Josie's sister Hazel, hasn't been heard from since the show ended, so he doubts she'll be there.

Why did they say yes? Did they really want to revisit all the drama? Apparently, they do.

Other than saying a few sentences and then fainting at her feet, Tate hasn't had a chance to talk to Josie. They hadn't seen each other in person for years, and then he fell on her. Literally.

"How many years has it been since you last saw Josie?" Tate asks Mason. His friend has stayed in touch with the crew and cast members much better than Tate has.

"At least five," Mason confirms. So he's not exactly up to date on what she's been up to, either.

"You should go talk to her," Mason says, his arm draped across the chair.

"It's not going to be easy," Tate responds. "Nothing ever is with Josie." To be honest, he still doesn't even think he really knows what happened between them.

It had all been on her end. He thought they were doing great. Happy. In love.

Until one day, out of the blue, she dumped him, with no explanation. Even now, years later, it stings. When he'd tried talking to her about it, she always found a way to avoid him and end the conversation. He'd stood there, heartbroken, wondering what he had done wrong.

He tried writing to Josie. Long emails, even a letter he mailed to her house. A few times, when he wasn't exactly sober, he'd left pretty embarrassing voicemails on her cell. He hoped she erased them. He *really* hopes she did. It's so damn humiliating.

The song ends, and Squeaks heads back their way. She must have worn out all of her past dance partners.

"When are you two going to dance?" she asks, her hands on her hips.

"You know I have no rhythm," Mason shrugs.

"Doesn't mean you can't try." She grabs his hand and hauls Mason to the floor.

Tate stands up to go find something to eat. He needs to keep his insulin levels steady.

Josie is making her way off the dance floor. There's no polite way to avoid running into each other, even if Tate wanted to.

Might as well go for it. He takes Mason's advice. "Josie, can I talk to you?"

She hesitates, then nods in agreement. "Sure, Tate."

"Thanks again for what you did for me last night. I'm so sorry that I collapsed right in front of you."

"I'm just glad you're okay." Jo shakes her head. "That was scary. I wish I had reacted quicker."

Before he passed out on the floor. He wants to ask her if he should do the reunion—if she even wants to see him—but he can't make out the right words.

Why didn't he practice what he was going to say when he finally got her attention? Tate should have thought of something. Try to get some key points down instead of winging it. He's good at memorizing lines, terrible at improv.

"You're feeling okay, right?" Josie asks. Great. She must think he's going to pass out again.

"Oh, yeah." He tries to think of the next thing to say, but everything he wants to ask seems too personal. There's too much left unsaid. The silence is growing longer and risking getting awkward. Josie is standing there, her arms crossed, waiting to hear him out.

"Look, I know we haven't seen each other in years. I feel like there's unfinished business here."

Jo looks at him cautiously, giving him a chance to add to his impromptu speech.

"Maybe we can sit down and talk about it." Not here, while the band is playing "The Funky Chicken."

"That sounds good," Josie agrees. She looks less concerned now that he's making coherent sentences.

"Can we get coffee? Catch up? It's been years. "

"I'd like that."

Her friendly agreement causes something in his chest to ease. "Are you around tomorrow? I was going to go to brunch, but we can skip it. Grab something in town."

"I can't tomorrow, but I'm around for the next few days. I'm staying in Rhode Island for a project. Can we meet on Tuesday?"

He sighs in relief. "Sure. Let me check with my business partner about when we're heading back, and I'll let you know. Can I get your number?" he asks.

Jo tilts her head. "It hasn't changed. It's still the same."

"So, you did get my voicemails?"

She looks at him. "Yes, every single *one*. There were so many."

Is she being sarcastic? He can't tell.

Fuck it. "Then I'll see you soon. Looking forward to it."

Josie doesn't answer him. She looks like she's about to say something, then stops, before turning and walking away from him.

At least she agreed to sit down and talk. They just need to get some kind of closure to that terrible ending for their relationship, and then he can move on.

Tate just hopes he'll be able to deal with whatever she has to say. Explain why she broke his heart and ripped him to shreds without ever looking back.

Chapter 21

*"Sure, he is cute if you like guys who go shirtless
on rollerblades down Third Ave."*
- Francesca to Shea, Season 1, Episode 4

Mason, June 1

"You're sure you're single?" Mason asks Quinn.

They're standing at one of the cocktail tables near the dance floor, watching some of the guests getting down to the wedding band.

"Didn't I already answer that question?" Quinn takes another sip of his vodka tonic, eyes raised.

"And you were on Seven Mile Island the whole time we filmed there?"

"I was," Quinn laughs. He rattles the ice in his glass. "I remember all of you running around town, but you probably didn't notice me."

"How is that possible?"

"It was so long ago. I was in college, so I wasn't there often. You guys came in during the off-season, so I would only see you around when I was home on break."

"Interesting. Did you ever come to any of our parties?" Mason can't believe he never noticed Quinn in such a small beach town.

"I don't think so. Your crew stuck to themselves a lot."

"Yeah," Mason agrees. "We probably did. Shame, though. You would have been a fun addition to our pack."

"I don't know if I would have fit in with this country club scene." Quinn looks around at the guests in black tie. "I'm pretty casual."

Mason snorts. "I own a landscaping business in Pennsylvania. I'm usually in cargo pants, not a tuxedo."

"Fair enough," Quinn agrees. "That's more up my alley, too."

"Really? What do you do during the offseason?"

"Everything," Quinn says. "It's the best part. Avalon goes from over 40,000 visitors to less than 1,500 full-time locals. You can eat at all your favorite places, take your dogs to the beach, grab some friends, and drive your Jeep on the sand."

"It's not too quiet?"

"Not at all. But I guess I'm used to it. And I have friends who live there year-round, too. My buddies Tyson and Eddie, and Tyson's wife Margo. Tyson works at the Stone Harbor Yacht Club, which stays open all year. And Margo runs *The Plank,* a fitness center."

"I always felt like the whole island was built on the summer months. But you make the off-season sound better."

"It's my favorite time of the year," Quinn says simply.

"We were always working long hours, so I feel like I didn't get the chance to really know the town." Mason regrets it, now. Oh, well. Add that to the list.

"When you're back, I'll show you around. The good spots."

"I'll be there at the end of July for the reunion. I'm going to hold you to it." Quinn is definitely off limits, but Mason likes the idea of knowing more about the local scene. Seeing a part of the Jersey Beaches he overlooked.

Quinn pauses, then looks up from the drink he's holding. "Josie Remington. What's the deal with her and Tate Masters? Is there anything still there?"

Mason isn't surprised by his question. *Everyone* knew they were the teen couple while the show was being filmed. And Mason is friends with both of them.

"I'm sure one of them hopes so, and I'm not going to say which one," he tells Quinn. "But it's over. They haven't been together since the show ended."

"So, there's a chance?"

"Not with me," Mason sighs. "I'm taken. But yes, Tate is single."

Quinn grins. "Good to know, since I am too."

Chapter 22

"People say that high school is the best time of your life.
I'm still waiting."
- Hazel, Season 2, Series Finale

Paige, June 12

Paige flips through the audition sides she is reading for a major role in a new crime drama. The director is one of the hottest names in the business.

She can't afford to be distracted. This is her first big shot in more years than she'd like to admit. Much better than the zombie penguins or the zookeeper.

A few months ago, Paige never would have even gotten this call. It has to be all the buzz about their reunion.

"Paige DeBello? Are you ready?" The AP is waiting with a clipboard, ready to bring her into the audition room.

"Absolutely." Paige stands up.

Twenty minutes later, she's finished. She can't tell if the director was impressed or not. This is such a huge opportunity. She can't afford to fuck it up. Anxiety begins to creep in.

She needs to talk to Justin. He's her agent now, after all. He'll make her feel better. That's what he does. He's a fixer. Even when he's an asshole.

It's amazing how he got exactly what he wanted, in the end. Just like he always does. He managed to convince every single one of the original stars of *The Shallows* into doing a reunion in Avalon for the first week of August. Even Tate Masters, who had been holding out for months.

For the first time, they'll all be together—in person—at the same place. What a coup! It's a once-in-a-lifetime event: *Eve, Jack, Shea, Chase, and Francesca back together. All in one place! All at the same time!*

Seeing old friends has also recharged their connection to each other. A group chat has been resurrected. Even some of the lesser-known characters, like summer crushes and a random cousin who made a few short-lived appearances, are planning on coming to the reunion, or at least sending signed memorabilia.

It's like the band is getting back together again. Nostalgia is at an all-time high.

The news has been a much-needed boost to her career. She's had a huge bump in popularity since *The Shallows* reunion was announced. Thousands of new followers and multiple offers of endorsements. And good ones too, not just scam companies. Are things finally looking up? Or did she blow her chance already?

She grabs her phone out of her bag and clicks on Justin's name in her contact list.

The call goes right to voicemail. Either he has his phone set to private, or he's avoiding her.

Both scenarios piss her off. Justin knows she has this big opportunity today. It's his job to be available.

Years of therapy have helped her to recognize her addictive tendencies. She still isn't comfortable sitting in uncertainty. She usually needs instant gratification. Despite knowing that, Paige can't help from panicking. She needs to feel better. Be reassured.

She grabs a piece of her hair and twirls it so hard that a few strands pull right out. It doesn't help her feel any better, but she can't stop herself from doing it.

Paige calls again. Right to voicemail. "Justin, I need to talk to you. Like, right now. If you don't call me back, I'm going to find another agent pronto."

She disconnects the call. Maybe he doesn't think she's worth picking up a call for. She shouldn't have called him twice. It looks desperate.

Dread starts to kick in, coupled with anxiety. Paige starts sweating, her breath getting shorter as she tries to get more air, but can't take any in. She knows she needs to talk to someone, or she's going to spiral. This is when she would try to score some drugs to keep the panic at bay.

Maybe it wouldn't be such a bad idea. Just one more time. And then she'll be clean again.

No. She can't fall apart right now. There's too much to lose. She needs to get hold of someone badly. Who would even be available?

For obvious reasons, she can't call her mother Jean, the epitome of a Stage Mom. Not Josie, who is still annoyed with her, for reasons Paige doesn't want to think about.

Mason will just make light of her anxiety, telling her not to worry about it. Sometimes his casual sarcasm is too much to take.

Val? From what Paige understood at the wedding, Val has hung up her hat with acting. She doesn't feel competitive with Val. The passive-aggressive, back-and-forth bullshit wouldn't be there anymore.

She doesn't have many options. Val, it is.

Paige dials her number.

Thankfully, Val answers on the second ring. "Paige? What's up?"

"I'm so sorry to bother you, Val, but I'm having a panic attack. I just had a major audition and now I'm freaking out."

"Oh, honey. Take a deep breath."

"I can't breathe."

"Yes, you can," Val answers firmly. "You're talking to me. You're already breathing. Now just take a deep one."

"Okay, okay. Give me a sec." Paige allows herself to pause, leaning against a nearby building.

On the other end, Val waits patiently, not saying anything. It gives Paige time to get a hold of herself.

"Oh, Val, I'm sorry. I'm making such a mess of myself. I just had to talk to someone."

Val has never sounded more confident and in charge. "Oh, honey. I've been there. Why don't you tell me about it?"

For the next half hour, Paige spills it all out to Val. Her dismal audition record. How she was dropped by her agent. The lack of money coming in is causing her to sell off her most valuable items to pay rent. How even her own mother dropped her when Paige wasn't something to brag about.

Val listens to everything without interrupting, besides making comforting noises.

Paige doesn't tell her *everything*, but enough to get the big things off her chest. There's no use confessing what happened ten years ago.

"Honestly, Paige, I don't blame you for panicking. You've been through enough. But good things are coming your way."

"I hope so," Paige gulps. "I just really need this, Val."

"I know you do. I love you. And I'm always here for you."

Paige feels a bit better. Disconnecting the call, she sees a text from Justin: *Sorry I missed your call, but I was on the other line. You got the gig! Way to go, girl!*

Maybe things are actually lining up. First the reunion, and now this role.

She wipes her tears off her face. Things are going to be okay.

Get it together, Paige. Stop blowing everything up. Again.

She can't help it. She reaches for her hair and pulls some more.

115

Chapter 23

*"He is one of those psychos who go skiing on
President's Day Weekend."*
- Francesca, Season 1, Episode 5

Mason, June 26

The phone rings yet again. "Can somebody get that?" Mason shouts down the hallway from his office. He's wrapped up with putting together a client proposal for an elaborate outdoor living space, and he can't afford to be distracted.

"I've got it," Ida yells back.

It's probably another media outlet. The phones at Stauffer Designs haven't stopped ringing since the *People* magazine cover spread hit. The popularity of *The Shallows* cast members has spiked. Suddenly, the crew from Duffy Beach is all over social media. It's all anyone seems to be talking or posting about.

He can't believe how much nostalgia there is over the show. It's like everyone wants to know what they've been up to. How well they've aged.

Mason loves hearing that he still looks good. But he's out of the showbiz industry. Out of their original crew, only a few are still working in the industry.

Josie's on-screen dad Marty Lawson had gone on to star in a family sitcom about starting over in a blended family called *Step Ladders*. It's one of those shows everyone knows and is ranked high in Nielsen ratings. It was set in the Midwest and basically a takeoff of *The Brady Bunch* and *Cheaper by the Dozen*.

Mason has never watched it. He doesn't do laugh tracks.

The actress who played Josie's show mom, Elise, is one of the more popular actors in Hallmark Christmas movies, appearing to drop succinct words of wisdom at the ideal time to convince the heroine to leave her soul-sucking job in the big city to become a baker in a small town. Or save a Christmas tree farm. Same thing.

Ida walks into his office. "Mason! We booked the job at the Branton estate."

"Really?"

"Yep," his assistant says. "We're starting in six weeks. They want everything you proposed to them."

"The pool house, stone patio, and pool deck surround?"

"All of it."

Mason rubs his hands together excitedly. He quoted them a few months ago and never heard back. He figured he'd been outbid by the other competitors.

"This is huge, Ida. Major bonuses all around." The house and grounds are among the largest in the Brandywine Valley. It's going to take a good four months to complete.

"We're going to need to order everything and wrap up the CAD designs before that beach reunion thing you're doing," she reminds him. "When do you leave?"

"July 31. About a month."

Ida frowns. "That doesn't give us a lot of time."

"I'll make it happen."

"Are all of you kids going?" Ida has worked with him since he left *The Shallows* and started Stauffer Designs. She knows everyone's personalities, for better or for worse.

"The main six, and the actors who played Eve's parents. Her sister isn't going to make it, and neither is the kid who played Chad's little brother."

Rebecca (Becky) Radcliffe played Josie's character Eve's little sister. She was a supporting character in small TV dramas and documentaries before she hit the big time with their teen drama. When they were filming *The Shallows*, she used to follow Mason around like a love-struck teen. Then all of a sudden, she stopped talking to everyone.

It's too bad she's not coming to the reunion. She was a good kid. He doesn't think anyone has heard from Becky in years.

She was always hanging out with their crew, until she started ghosting them to hang out with some guy she met. He must have been controlling, or she was obsessed, because she completely dropped all of them and then mostly disappeared from acting. Someone said she was now living in Ohio, he thinks?

Mason heard Tate's on-screen brother won't be able to make it, either. Tate said he's living in Portugal. Scotty Redcross was one of their crew to pal around with, but he could get into trouble quickly. He always found the best weed on the island, though.

"Where are you staying?"

"This is the cool part. We have a huge mansion right on the beach." The event planners had sent him details about the multi-level beach block property they were all sharing. They had been given full use of his twelve-bedroom mansion. It was owned by Roger Elliot, a big Stone Harbor and Avalon real estate tycoon.

Mason remembers Roger's daughter hanging around their set, trying to get in on their crew. Sabrina was a pretty thing, but obviously spoiled rotten.

"I wish I could come," Ida grumbles. "You get to have all the fun."

"Next time, you'll be my date."

"I don't need a date," she tells him. "Just a pool boy."

Mason chuckles. "I'll find you one. I already met a hot firefighter."

This cheers Ida up. "I'll take one of them, too."

"Done. Thanks for covering for me when I'm gone."

"Just don't get into any trouble," Ida warns. "We need you back in one piece."

"Promise."

Satisfied, Ida heads out of his office. He doesn't know what he'd do without her. She's the glue that keeps their company together, even when she's scolding them.

He has to admit that the timing isn't ideal for his firm. This is their busy season, when everyone wants their properties looking great for outdoor parties and events. It will be tight with all the other projects they're juggling, but Mason will make it work.

Like anything, life is just a matter of luck and timing. And his luck looks like it's changing for the better.

When Kit calls to tell Mason that he's definitely going to join Mason on the trip to the Jersey Shore, Mason is sure his luck is at an all-time high.

Life is great. Perfect right now.

It's all coming together—everything he's ever wanted. Financial success, a thriving business, a beach vacation with the love of his life.

Things have never been better.

Chapter 24

Val, July 5

Val reaches for her mailbox knob, then hesitates.

The letters have been arriving with greater frequency between the demands. They used to come in every few months or so, without any detectable pattern, but now they're even less predictable. And much more threatening.

The increased pace and sense of urgency have ratcheted up ... and it's scaring the shit out of Valerie.

She still has no idea who could possibly know her secret.

It was just a stupid mistake, but once she made it, there was no way to fix it. Make things go back to the way they were.

Val has never told anyone. Why would she? It would be a catastrophe. This kind of bomb would destroy her relationships if it ever got out. She'd lose all her friends, the fans who looked up to her, and probably even the respect of her family.

Val swallows, gathers her courage, and opens the mailbox. There's another letter.

Well, she isn't going to open the letter today. She does what she always does and ignores it. She'll deal with it later.

There's always later.

She unlocks her door and dumps the mail on top of the rest of the pile in her hallway. Her shift at the bar is in less than an hour, and Val still needs to get ready.

After a quick shower, Val pulls on her bartender outfit: a black crop top and low-slung pants that show off her toned abs. She slicks her thick black hair in a high ponytail so it doesn't fall all over her face.

Winged eyeliner to accent her almond eyes, some cream blush and highlighter. Undereye concealer to cover up less than eight hours of sleep. A swipe of red lip gloss, and she's ready to go in less than 20 minutes.

She could get ready anywhere under any tight deadline. It's one of her best talents.

Val snags her car keys and heads out to her dark blue Subaru Outback. Over a hundred thousand miles and counting, but it's still running.

O'Donoghues is packed when she walks in. The dive bar isn't much to look at, but it's a solid place to work, with a lot of the same crowd, week after week.

Tall wooden stools line the bar, which has seen better days. It could use a fresh coat of stain to rub out the drink stains and dings from years of heavy use. The bar menu is heavy on fried food and red meat. No one cares.

It's the 4th of July weekend, a Friday night, and the Nationals are playing on the TV's above the bar. The perfect trifecta to earn some serious tip money.

And she needs it. Val got a small upfront bonus when she committed to the reunion, but it wasn't much. Definitely not enough to take a break from work or pay off any loans.

Still, it's nothing to laugh at. She needs all the money she can get.

"Vince, you bad boy. How long have you been at my bar?" Val purrs to one of her regular customers. He'll sit there for hours just watching her pull beers from the tap.

"Keeping it warm for you, Valerie," Vince returns.

They might flirt all night, but he's harmless. He's never tried to make a move. If he did, he'd be on his ass in a second.

"Val, I need a pitcher of Miller Lite and two Tito's and sodas. Doubles." MJ, one of her favorite cocktail waitresses, sets down her tray on the bar.

"On it." Val quickly pulls the taps and assembles the order.

Val, MJ, and the other bartender, Pat, are so busy that they don't come up for air for a good two hours.

Val needs a break. "Pat, can you cover for me?" she asks, and he nods.

She heads outside to take a hit of her nicotine pen. She might have given up cigarettes, but she can't quit everything, can she? Sometimes, she dabbles with weed pens too. Depends on her mood. Anything to help take the edge off.

Tonight's too busy for that, though. She needs to keep her wits about her. She can't be stoned while she's mixing drinks at the bar. That didn't go so well the last time, when she screwed up all the checks.

Val is heading back to her spot behind the bar when she spots Justin sitting at a stool. He's sitting belly up at the bar, resting his elbows on the counter. Her stomach drops.

She had no idea that he even knew where she lived, much less where she worked. This can't be a coincidence.

Val plasters a smile on her face, which probably comes off like a smirk. Even when she's trying to look sincere, people say she comes off as slightly catty. A little dirty.

It was the role she was usually slotted, that of the unreformed bad girl. The one that men always wanted to take home at the end of the night, but never thought to take home to meet their parents.

"Of all the gin joints in the world … fancy seeing you here."

"Long time no see, Valerie," he says jokingly. He looks completely out of place at O'Donoghues, with his black, gelled hair and suit. Everyone else is in shorts and T-shirts, maybe a pair of jeans.

"Sure, less than a few weeks since the wedding. What are you doing at my bar?" There's no reason not to be blunt. Justin expects it of her.

"Can't a friend stop by and say hi?" he asks.

"We were never friends, Justin."

He shrugs agreeably. "True. I just wanted to come by to run some things by you for the reunion."

"What kind of things? I already committed to the damn thing. Just like everyone else."

"You aren't doing as well as you'd like to be doing." He flicks his eyes around the weathered bar. "Thought I could help."

"Saint Justin DeRose of Hollywood. Try some other sucker."

"No, really. I can help out. Make things go a little smoother for you. Like we discussed before we were …" he pauses, choosing his next words carefully … "interrupted."

She doesn't ask how he knew that she is being blackmailed. It's his business to know. The dick.

"So, what would you need me to do?" She props her elbows on the bar and leans over to stare at him. Anyone watching would think they were lightheartedly flirting. Anyone who didn't know their history. Val has always despised Justin. It's hardened into hate.

He hesitates, then plunges in. "Let me leak a piece that you and Tate are dating. It's still new, but you're excited—yada, yada—and can't wait to see where it's going."

She raises her eyebrows. "Seriously? You want to add another plot line to an old teen drama?"

"The fans will go crazy over it."

"Everyone knows Tate is still in love with Josie. And vice versa."

Justin smiles. "That's what makes it so good."

"I wouldn't do that to Josie."

"Why not?"

"Because she's my friend. No one would believe it, anyway." Val can't see anyone falling for it. "Tate and I weren't even close. We haven't seen each other for years."

"Don't you remember?" Justin pauses meaningfully. "At the reunion, when Tate passed out, you helped him recover and realized you had feelings for him."

Val scoffs. "What do I get out of it?"

He looks at her steadily. "It will be huge. For your wallet and your career." He looks pointedly around the bar again. "I can guarantee you ten grand."

"You're such an asshole," Val responds good-naturedly. "I don't need your help. I'm doing just fine on my own."

"Yeah, I can see that." He rises out of his stool and places a business card on the bar. "Call me when you're ready to play in the big leagues."

Justin walks out of the bar in his shiny suit. Val looks down at his card. It's glossy, just like him. A shithead agent who's too slick to trust.

She wonders if Justin ran the idea by Tate. She can't see him going for it.

"Who was that guy?" Vince pipes from his spot at the bar. He's watched their exchange the entire time he was sitting there.

"No one important," Val returns.

She taps the card as she considers Justin's offer. It might not be the worst idea. Make some money and get this asshole blackmailer off her back. Put a little aside so each month isn't a crunch to figure out how to pay all her bills at once.

It's just a little bit of acting. Something she's done well for years.

What's the big deal?

125

Chapter 25

Josie, July 11

Josie is waiting in the checkout line at the supermarket when she spots a familiar face on the cover of *US Weekly*. Two faces, in fact.

Shallows Stars Tate Masters and Valerie Worth: How They Found Their Happy Ever After!

She blinks. Did she just read that right?

Oh yes, she did. Because the next issue she scans is *Life & Style's* weekly edition. This one says: *Reunited at Last! Tate Masters and Valerie Worth Share Their Love Story.*

What in the living hell?

They're not the top story for *In Touch Weekly* (a soap star's reported relapse is), but Tate and Val share a prominent photo in a large box on the right-hand side.

Oh, and there's a subtitle underneath: *Josie Remington Devastated: Shares Her Top Regrets*, accompanied by an unflattering photo of Josie with her mouth gaping open that must have been taken years ago.

This has to be a joke. There is no way Tate and Valerie are together. They can barely stand each other.

Plus, she literally just saw Val. Wouldn't that have come up? Val would have told her if she were dating her best friend's ex. Especially the one who *took her virginity.*

The Tate she once knew wouldn't do it either. At least, not without notifying her first. He would call to let her know that this was about to hit the press, dragging her into the drama along with them.

Were they actually dating? She doesn't believe it.

Josie isn't sure what to do. She would have laughed if she didn't know that the photo of Valerie and Tate is, in fact, a newer one, with Val's fringe bangs and Tate's scruffier beard that he was sporting at the wedding. It's not an old pic that the magazines found in their files. This one was taken recently.

If the photo wasn't taken at Sage and Simon's wedding, did they actually have a photo shoot? Joined together to make their couple announcement public right before the *Shallows* reunion?

The timing is ironic, to say the least.

"Wow. Jack and Francesca? They look SO cute together!" A high-pitched voice screams behind Josie in the grocery checkout line.

"I can't believe I never thought of it," her friend responds. "I love this so much."

Josie freezes. They're looking at the same magazines. She sneaks a peek discreetly, trying not to show her face.

Two 30-something women, the show's biggest fan base, are standing behind her with their carts. They probably grew up watching the show, relating to the characters. And have absolutely no idea how much they're making it worse for her.

She ducks her head back towards the cashier so they don't realize it's her. That would be humiliating.

Were there signs she missed at the wedding? Sure, she didn't talk to Tate for long. They never managed to meet up for that cup of coffee afterwards. By the time he reached out to her, she had already wrapped up her work and was on her way back home.

Regardless, she was with Val for most of the wedding. And they've talked frequently enough since then that this should have come up. At some point!

Shit.

She can't call Val to verify if the articles were true. She'd look so petty. Or naive. They all know these stories weren't usually based on facts, just mindless rumors that were always attributed to "close sources."

Maybe she should ask Paige? Josie isn't sure if Paige would even know. She doesn't see Valerie making a big confession to Paige. Val has always said she never fully trusted Paige, because she's been brought up her entire life to act like someone else. No, Val wouldn't have told Paige about it.

There was another option: don't say anything. But then, how would Josie find out if it is true?

Her stomach is in knots. She feels her hands getting clammy.

"I always thought they were adorbs," her friend coos. "They're going to have the hottest babies!" She grabs a couple of the magazines. "My cousin and I have binged every season at least three or four times."

Josie knows they are just two young women squealing at each other about two people they've never met, but it feels like they're personally rubbing it in. Making it worse. If only they knew that Eve was standing right in front of them.

No point in taking any chances. Josie pulls her baseball cap further down on her head and doesn't dare look behind her again. From the way they are carrying on, she doubts they even notice her.

It's hard not to grab one of the magazines herself, to examine at home. Although she wants to, she can't risk anyone snapping a photo of her reading this tabloid crap about her ex-boyfriend. That would be humiliating.

Josie thinks about all the time she and Tate spent together. They were each other's firsts in almost everything—first time saying I love you, first time making love, first time confessing their major hangups and insecurities. He knew every detail about her.

And then one day, he threw it all away. Dumped her and everything they had built together. Made her cry for weeks to her friends. Never responded to her texts.

In all the years since, Tate has never explained why. And Josie has always had too much pride to ask him. She tried to act like she never dated him and shut that part of her life down. Never to be repeated.

The grocery clerk smiles at her politely and scans Josie's items along the conveyor belt.

"Do you want any bags?" she asks.

"No, thanks."

"And you found everything you were looking for?"

"Absolutely." Josie is starting to sweat. The first woman is right behind her, loading her items onto the belt.

"Cash back?"

"I'm good." *Can this take any longer?*

"Will you round up for charity?"

Josie shoves the cap down even further over her eyes. "Sure."

She needs to get out of here now. Josie grabs her two bags full of snacks (her main food source) and sets off for the parking lot. She can't get away from the women in line fast enough.

Forget taking the high road. She's still angry.

As soon as she's inside her car, her first call is to Justin. "Are you kidding me?" Josie asks as soon as Justin picks up.

To Justin's credit, he doesn't ask what she's talking about. He just sighs. "I told them they should tell you. But they didn't want to upset you."

"I honestly don't believe it. They have zero chemistry. They don't even like each other."

"Isn't that what happens, though? Opposites attract? Enemies to lovers?"

"Do *not* say lovers to me, Justin," Josie scolds. "This is out of left field. I saw them both a month ago. They didn't even talk to each other at the wedding."

He gives another deep sigh, as if he's feeling her pain but can't do anything about it. "I'm sorry, Jo Jo. You can't help what the heart wants."

Josie rolls her eyes. "I think you've been in La-La Land too long. This is so obviously a gimmick to get attention before the reunion."

"We'll see," he says easily, and Josie feels like a bitter ex.

"Let's drop it," Josie replies.

"Sounds good, kid. I'll see you in a few weeks at the reunion."

It's always about the next gig. "Nice talking to you, Justin." She hangs up.

They want publicity? She'll give it to them. Val and Tate will *definitely* be seeing her at the reunion. She wouldn't miss it for the world.

Jo decides not to call Val. It's better to let her sweat, knowing Josie has heard the news and hasn't reacted. Especially considering that they'll all be living in the same house for three days and nights.

Josie is done running away from all of them, done being the more mature person. Enough is enough.

Chapter 26

"I got tickets to Bruno Mars! Want to come?"
- Chase to Eve, Season 3, Episode 2

Tate, July 12

The phone rings, waking Tate out of a deep sleep.

Why is Squeaks calling him at 6 am? It's not like her to call so early. Or to call him at all. Squeaks is mostly on a text-only basis.

"Why is your pretty face being plastered all over magazine covers?" Squeaks asks by way of greeting. "And when did you start dating? You never date."

Tate rubs his eyes. "What are you talking about, Squeaks? It's six in the morning."

"Your new *girlfriend,* Tate. That's why I'm calling. Valerie Worth."

"Um. Now I know even less about what you're talking about."

"You, Tate Masters. And your co-star. It's all over the papers."

"What is?" Tate is still not coherent. He needs coffee. He tucks his phone to his shoulder and pulls on a pair of pants as he makes his way to the kitchen to make some coffee. "I honestly don't know what you're telling me."

"Shit, Tate. You're front page news. It says that you and Valerie have made it official. You're in love. Babies are coming."

"Oh, please. You know how that stuff works by now, Squeaks. It's all smoke and mirrors. I didn't think you'd fall for it."

"Normally, I'd agree with you, but this is uncanny. It looks like the real thing. There's a picture of you and Val from the wedding, and you two look like a couple. Your hand is around her waist. You're *smiling.*"

He dismisses it. "It was a special day for two of our old friends. I took lots of pics that day."

Squeaks pauses before asking, "Maybe you should call Val and see what she's doing about it?"

"I'm sure she's ignoring it just like me. We've never had so much as a spark." Tate isn't going to call anyone. He doesn't like confrontation. That's one of the reasons things are still so unresolved with Jo. When she wouldn't respond to his calls and texts, he gave up. Moved on. Tried to, anyway.

Squeaks laughs. "It's just so funny. I never heard of these people, and now you have a wedding and a reunion, and all of a sudden, you're all over my Insta feed. Girls were so in love with you. They're still so in love with you!"

He's been dealing with it for years. "It will go away and die down when they discover something new. It always does."

Squeaks still doesn't seem convinced. "Might be worth calling Val anyway, just to see how this came about."

"Yeah, I might. Now, can I get back to sleep?"

"Sure thing. And hey, Tate?" She pauses. "If you want, I can come to the reunion, too."

Tate knows this is her way of showing support. "I'd like that," he responds. "You've already met most of the crew."

"I wonder if that hot stunt double will be around?" Squeaks muses. "He was a dish."

"I'll make sure you see Chuck," Tate promises.

"Deal."

They hang up, but Tate knows he won't be able to go back to sleep now. He hauls himself out of bed and pads over to a bookcase filled with books and picture frames. On the top shelf is a box that he's kept private, hidden away from prying eyes.

He heads back to his bed and sits down before opening it. Inside, there are pictures of the cast. Candid shots of Tate and Josie at the beach, happy and in love. When they were together. Before it all broke apart.

He knows too much now. It was a happier time, before he became sick. Before his parents split up. When he and Jo were still together.

Tate would do anything to go back.

Chapter 27

"Ugh. Is Fran really going out with that surfer dude?"
- Eve to Shea, Season 4, Episode 1

Paige, July 12

Paige is getting her nails done at one of her favorite spots in Hoboken. They've been booked solid with appointments, but she managed to nab a mani and pedi by dropping her name. And by repeatedly calling. She's not sure which method worked, but she's glad they squeezed her in.

"Can I get this chrome color?" she asks.

The nail tech nods agreeably. "That's a popular look."

"In that case, let's go with a reverse French manicure using the chrome and light pink." Paige can't afford to look basic.

There are only two more weeks until *The Shallows* reunion. She can't believe it's right around the corner. Her anxiety is through the roof. She even had to put in extensions to fill the bald spots on her scalp from twisting and pulling her hair. The appointment took hours.

She still has so many med spa appointments to make, so she looks her best—lashes, peels, fresh extensions, maybe a little lip filler touchup.

Things have never been better. The ten-year reunion has been a huge boost to her career. She's booking auditions left and right, with some pretty promising callbacks, too.

It seems like early 2010 nostalgia is making grown women feel like they're in their teens again, going through all the angst they experienced with their first crushes. Gay men, too. They *love* the show.

July 31st to August 4th. Five days of chaos. Giddy fans, self-absorbed influencers, and aspiring actors all looking to get a piece.

An admissions pass starts at $150, with each of the sessions going for another $100 to $500 a pop. The bigger stars generate more money, naturally. The actors who played Josie's character Eve's mom and dad aren't generating the same crowds as Tate.

Regardless, the fans will all show up. She's seen how many guest stars are at *Vampire Diaries* or *Supernatural* comic cons. Even the lesser characters from *Star Wars* are still making money off a movie that was filmed nearly 50 years ago.

It's quite a living, but it doesn't mean she doesn't find the entire process tedious. She's so tired of answering the same questions: "Yes, Josie and I are friends in real life." "No, she didn't lose her virginity to Mason." "Of course, they all got along on set." Enough already.

She won't tell them the truth. No one deserves that except the people who were there. As the tech soaks Paige's gels off with remover, she leans over to grab a magazine off the rack, risking getting a disapproving look for moving in the middle of a manicure.

Paige can't help it. She just noticed the headlines of the magazines:

Spotted: Valerie Worth and Tate Masters in Love.

Is Valerie Worth Pregnant?

The Shallows Cast Tells All!

And then there's the last one—*Josie Remington Devastated: Shares Her Top Regrets*—with a terrible photo of Josie with her mouth gaping open.

Holy shit. Tate and Val?

This doesn't make any sense. Paige just saw them. They weren't even together for much of the wedding. Tate spent most of it staring hopelessly at Josie.

Paige grabs her phone, which earns her a glare from the nail tech. But this is life and death. It can't wait.

To her surprise, Valerie picks up.

"Hey, Paige," Val says breezily. "What's going on?"

"You tell me," Paige answers. "I'm sitting here in a nail salon, and I see a magazine declaring you and Tate are a hot item."

Val laughs nervously. "I know, I've been getting calls too. I don't know where they got that from. Must have been someone from the wedding who thought something was going on."

Paige knows Val well enough to tell that she's lying. Val isn't that good an actress.

"From what I remember, you were draped over some cowboy at the reception," Paige responds. "I'm pretty sure you left with him, too."

There's a brief pause. "Oh. Well, yeah, I guess I did."

"Then how is there an official statement from you in Life & Style? They quoted you."

"Must have been a mistake."

"Hmmm. Okay. Well, congratulations. I'm glad to see you've never been so happy and in love."

"You know how people run with things."

But Paige isn't about to. This is unusual, even for the press. "Have you talked to Josie yet?"

Valerie sighs with frustration. Paige must have hit a nerve. "Can you let up? I've been meaning to. I figured she'd think it was a joke. Besides, she and Tate are ancient history."

"Darling, in two weeks, this is about to become very present history. I hope you know what you're doing."

"It's not a big deal," Val insists. "Don't make this into more than it is. Please, Paige."

Paige can't figure out why Valerie decided to create unnecessary drama. Especially right before they would all be together again. It was so typical of Val, screwing things up.

"Well, it's going to be an exciting reunion for sure. Are you and Tate sharing a room?"

Val laughs. "You're such a bitch, Paige. If that's all you have to say, I gotta run."

"See you in two."

"See you." Val disconnects the call.

Paige can tell Val was nervous. This isn't something Valerie would normally think to do on her own. One of their publicists? Maybe the company is running the event? Or was it really just a silly piece of gossip someone ran away with?

Paige decides to call Justin. He'll know what's going on.

Straight to voicemail. Disappointed, Paige turns her attention back to her nails. She's got too much to do.

She should probably check in with Josie, too. Make sure she's okay and not taking this seriously.

Right now, though, she's got too much going on. She'll let this drop right now and see what she can find out later.

"Excuse me?" Paige asks the technician. "Do you think you could squeeze in an eyebrow wax after this?"

Chapter 28

"If I had known how much fun being rich was,
I would have made sure I was born into it."
- Francesca, Season 3, Episode 5.

Sage, July 19

"Isn't this the life?" Sage asks Simon as they lie on striped lounge chairs overlooking the water. The sun makes the water of Lake Como sparkle as they soak up the last day of their honeymoon in Italy.

Set against the backdrop of the nearby Southern Alps, the lake stretches across the Lombardy region, with three distinct branches forming a Y. Majestic villas line the waterways, their terraced gardens blooming with flowers.

They can make out the terracotta roof of Villa del Balbianello, the lavish home that served as a backdrop for major movies, including the *007* and *Star Wars* franchises.

"You called it," Simon responds, leaning over to pick up his Aperol Spritz from the table nestled between them. He downs the rest of his drink and signals a hovering waiter for another. "I didn't think I'd like it this much. Or that we could afford all this."

They'd flown into Rome and made their way up the coast before ending up in Lake Como. Everything was first class, from their luxurious villa to their airfare. Simon has no idea how much it was actually costing them.

"God bless Aunt Frances," Sage responds. She'd told him about an aunt on her dad's side who had left her money because she felt so bad that Sage grew up without her father. The wealthy aunt wanted to leave her funds to fall back on if tragedy ever happened to her again. She'd made up Aunt Frances years ago to cover her tracks.

The story about her dad was another lie she crafted, telling Simon that her dad died in a boating accident when she was six years old. It gave her an excuse for why it was so hard for her to go back to the West Coast and see her family. She just couldn't handle the memories.

Simon doesn't need to know that her father is alive and well. At least, as far as she's aware. She hasn't been in contact with him for decades. He left her and her mom when she was a baby. So while it's true that she had grown up without a father in her life, the details surrounding it were a little murky.

"You're sure you still want to go to the reunion in Avalon?" Simon asks. "We're going to have a lot of work to catch up on when we get back." They were starting a new TV show that had been adapted from a popular Nantucket book series.

There's nowhere she'd rather be. "It's a great opportunity, though. They asked me to be one of the moderators for one of the panels about love triangles." She takes another sip of her drink. "I get to do it with Tate, Josie, Val, and Mason."

"That's fantastic, honey."

"Yeah, I'm excited."

"You're going to do an incredible job." Simon has always been supportive of her career. It's one of the things she loves most about him.

Sage grew up fending for herself and learned how to take care of things on her own. Her husband doesn't have the same background.

Simon came from a nuclear family that actually enjoys spending time with each other. The first time she met them, she couldn't believe it. She thought families like his only existed in Nancy Meyers movies.

Sage came from a poor neighborhood filled with families always working to pay the bills. She never knew her father, and her mother was an absentee parent at best, until she became sober and started working again. Mostly raised by her grandparents, she never had the nice things that people on the other side of her town had. Her grandparents didn't set much stock in labels, and even if they did, they wouldn't have been able to afford them.

She was always trying to catch up, to make the money and have the name-brand clothes that seemed to come to the other kids so effortlessly. It got better once her mother straightened herself out, but she still struggled to fit in.

Sage always felt like she had to do more, work harder, make a bigger sacrifice to get ahead. But it wasn't like that with Simon. He made her feel special. Sage was no longer the welfare kid whose parents never came to school events. She belonged.

"It's going to be a blast. All of us, back together at the Jersey Shore, ten years later."

Sage loves being part of the Hartwick family. And sharing the spotlight with the rest of the Shallows cast, who were part of her early adult years.

If you had asked her ten years ago where she'd imagine herself to be, it definitely wouldn't be soaking up the sun in Lake Como with her husband. A successful career in set design. Thinking about starting a family.

Sage has to admit, she couldn't have planned it better herself.

The waiter returns with two orange cocktails, holding striped straws. "Godere!" he tells them, which means "enjoy."

"Grazie," Sage answers. She fully plans to. Especially since each cocktail is costing her $75.

Chapter 29

"You want to go all the way to Calabasas for a party?
Why don't we just go to Santa Monica, then? What's the difference?"
- Francesca to Eve, Season 3, Episode 4

Mason, July 31

Mason drives along the long, winding roads of South Jersey, through arching avenues of trees and past scattered reserves of saltwater. He passes farm stands advertising fresh Jersey tomatoes and corn, freshly baked apple pie, and cider donuts.

The bucolic scenery might distract someone else, someone more flexible with their plans, but not Mason. He doesn't stop. He doesn't have time.

There's a rumor that the Jersey Devil lives here, in these woods—a gargoyle-type creature with horns who prowls the marshes of the Pinelands looking for victims. The devil was spotted in this area by generations and generations of people until he finally became a local legend. He's even the mascot for New Jersey's professional hockey team, appropriately named The Jersey Devils.

Mason finds himself identifying with the Jersey Devil a lot today. Give him a little sympathy. The poor guy isn't a dick. Everyone else is the problem, and he's just doing his best, trying to make a life, and eventually he loses his temper. And then they call *him* a devil! Have a little sympathy for the guy. The Rolling Stones had that right.

He thinks back to the long night he had with Kit. It was their first time getting away in months. His husband was supposed to come with him to the beach after they dropped the girls off at Alex's in the morning, but at the last minute, one of them came down with a fever.

The youngest, Maeve, had padded downstairs as they were sitting on the couch watching the most recent season of *The Last of Us.*

"Daddy-O?" she said, her face flushed and her eyes watery. "I don't feel right."

Mason could tell right away what was about to happen. Rushing over, he picked her up to make a run for the bathroom.

He was still too late. Maeve got sick over both of them, throwing up down his back.

All night, he and Kit took turns cleaning her up, giving her cold cloths, and trying to make her comfortable as she battled a stomach bug and high temperature.

By 5 am, the worst of it was past, and Maeve was sleeping it off. Both he and Kit were exhausted.

It's not that he doesn't understand that these things happen. They're eight and ten years old. It just seems like it crops up *every single time* there is a big event that's important to Mason.

"Do you think Alex can watch Maeve after she's feeling better?" Mason had asked last night, but his partner wouldn't budge. "You could maybe come down a day later?"

"How could I leave when she's sick?" Kit barked. There was no compromise when it came to the girls.

Mason understands and empathizes. He's not an *asshole.* But he can't understand why Kit has to always be the one who stays behind to take care of their daughters if anything comes up. Why can't his ex-wife ever do it?

It's so damn unfair. And yes, Mason knows he can be selfish and shallow at times. Petty as hell, if necessary. But this event is important to him.

So, Mason took another shower, hugged the girls goodbye, and put his bags in the car before he left the house this morning, filled with resentment for the sacrifices he had to make. It's the first time in his life he's ever had to put others before himself. It's *exhausting*. And all because he fell in love with someone who was a dad. And his girls.

Compromise is important. Isn't that how relationships work? That's what Brené Brown says, anyway. And she's usually right.

His SUV glides through the town of Cape May Courthouse, passing a lot of the locations they used for filming: the Cape May Zoo, the Wetlands Institute, and one of Rutgers University's branch locations. Mason is always nostalgic whenever he passes a former filming location.

His favorite episode of the show was the third season, when they closed the Ocean City boardwalk down for three days to film. It had been right after their school won the state basketball tournament, similar to *High School Musical*. They were riding high until Josie's character, Eve, found Jack (Tate) kissing Francesca (Val) on a bench along the boardwalk.

Of course, it was all a big misunderstanding, but Eve then went on to date his character, Chase, until the fourth season, when Jack and Eve got back together.

It's probably why the press is eating up the same love triangle of Tate/Val/Josie taking place in real life. Mason doesn't buy it. Tate has only ever had eyes for Josie Remington.

Damn, they had a good time. Youth is wasted on the young. Who said that again? Mason knows he'll forget to look it up.

He's drenched with memories as he crosses the 96th Street Bridge, the gateway to the town of Stone Harbor. The drawbridge rocks under his wheels. Mason passes a guard stand where the gatekeeper raises and lowers the bridge for larger boats.

The bright blue water tower looms above the town. At more than 100 feet tall, it can be seen from almost every spot on the island. It's one of the most recognizable landmarks of 7 Mile Island. Further down the island, there's an Avalon one, declaring their town "Cooler by a Mile." It's a friendly dig at their neighboring town.

It's a hell of a view. Multi-million dollar beach houses spread out over the bay on both sides, their wooden docks safeguarding boats and expensive water toys.

Avalon and Stone Harbor were ideal locations for a television show. Together, they make up Seven Mile Island, a narrow strip of land perched off the Atlantic Ocean with some of the most beautiful stretches of coastline on the East Coast. Only three or four avenues wide, the island has enviable views of the bay and the beach.

There were a lot of benefits to filming on the island. It was convenient to New York City and Philadelphia, major hubs that the cast and crew could fly in and out of when they weren't filming. They had plenty of space because they filmed in the off-season, and a lot of the homes were available to rent.

The smaller numbers gave the crew plenty of freedom to film on less-populated streets. They had easy access to the town's restaurants and storefronts along 96th Street that usually hibernated in the winter. Business owners loved the additional use.

The lively downtown of 96th Street between First and Third Avenue is lined with boutiques, restaurants, and bars. Mason passes the Harbor Square Theatre, a classic movie venue with a marquee banner announcing new movie releases and wedding celebrations.

When they filmed there off-season, the theater marquee would be lit up with Duffy Beach events, while some of the boutique and bar signs were traded out for ones that were part of the set.

He takes a right at the intersection by The Reeds hotel and spa. He doesn't even need his GPS. It all comes back to him.

The house they're staying at is on 115th Street, which is towards the southernmost part of the island. The area is a little more private, closer to the Point, where the public beach meets the end of Stone Harbor's coast.

Mason pulls up to the main entrance, flanked by white-washed stone pillars with lights. The place is huge. Three stories of white brick and shingle siding take up nearly the entire beach block.

The street is already filling up with cars. He wonders if their host, Roger Elliot, will be there. He remembers that his young daughter, Sabrina, was a bit of a brat, always trying to get in as an extra on set by bragging that her dad owned so many businesses in town. She used to hang outside their trailers when they were filming, hoping to catch one of the actors' attention.

Even if his daughter was spoiled, they're lucky they have Roger in their corner. He stepped in and offered them the use of the Seven Mile Hotel's ballroom and conference rooms for seminars, photo opportunities, and autograph sessions. Anyone from the crew who didn't fit into the mansion on 115th was able to secure a room at his hotel at a substantial discount. It's extremely generous of him.

A guy with a clipboard approaches Mason's SUV. "Can I help you?" he asks. There's an earbud in his ear. He must be some kind of security guard.

"I'm one of the actors. Mason Stauffer, here for the Shallows reunion." The guy looks familiar. "Do I know you? From Newport?"

"You do. Quinn Kearney."

"How could I forget? Did you work security when we used to film here?" Mason's day is looking up.

He laughs. "No, I wasn't around then. I'm freelancing this week. I did a couple of 24-hour shifts to free me up for a few days."

"That's right. You're a firefighter now." Mason had been thinking how good-looking the guy was when he swooped in and rescued Tate, helping with his diabetes. "You know, you saved my friend."

"How's he doing?" Quinn asks. He's dressed more casually now, in board shorts and a button-down, short-sleeved shirt.

"Oh, he's fine, now. He's staying at another place, but you'll see him around." Mason leans over to get a peek at the clipboard. He can't help being nosy. "Who else is staying here?"

The bodyguard shakes his head. "Sorry, I wish I could help you, but that's on a need-to-know basis."

"Fine," Mason sulks. "Have it your way. Are you really a firefighter?" Mason wonders what this guy looks like in his uniform.

Quinn grins, and it's all Mason can do to keep from sweating. "Avalon Fire Department. They asked me to help with the reunion for the next few days."

That meant he'd be seeing a lot of Quinn. "What do you do around here for fun?" Mason asks. "It's been a while since I've been back." Quite a while.

"The Princeton is still the spot to go," Quinn answers. "A lot of us go there."

"I'd love to join you," Mason tells him. "Just let me know when."

"Most weekends we're there, if I'm not working a double shift. I'll let you know." He hands back his license.

They exchange numbers, Mason trying hard to look casual. A night out with a battalion of beach firefighters? Who wouldn't say yes? It would make a great reality show.

Mason's not going to feel guilty, either. He needs a little man crush right now. Even though he's not going to do anything, it doesn't hurt to flirt a little to boost his ego. Send Kit some pics to make him feel left out.

They're standing out front when a baby blue vintage convertible pulls up behind him. Their host has arrived.

Roger doesn't look pleased. "I thought I was paying you to keep this place organized," he barks at Quinn as he strides up the driveway.

Quinn swivels around. "I'm sorry, sir. We had a lot of guests show up at once. We're working on it." He doesn't seem concerned.

"You do know who I am, right?" Roger asks.

The guy is giving off major douche chills. Mason's impressed with Quinn's calm demeanor.

"Sure," Quinn answers easily. "Roger Elliott. You own this place."

"That's right. So make sure these bags are off the street and the cars are parked before I leave. Or find yourself another job."

"Yes, sir," he responds with a grin. "Nice car." He doesn't seem like he's taking Roger's concerns seriously.

Roger walks across the lawn and heads into the mudroom entrance.

"Swell guy," Mason says as he watches him go. "I'd better get in there. I'll be in touch." He shakes Quinn's hand and strides in the same direction that Roger was heading.

There must be twenty people in the downstairs kitchen, milling around and talking while they grab food from the island. It's a good thing there are two kitchens in the place, as well as multiple living rooms, two guest houses, and several levels of porches.

Roger walks in and claps his hands. Everyone pauses. "Hello, I'm Roger, your host," he introduces himself. "Welcome to Stone Harbor."

Everyone listens as Roger gives them the rundown of the house, explaining the rules and how things work. Once he's finished, Roger heads back outside.

Mason recognizes a few actors from the show and the network, LJC. Two of the main characters are there, too. The guy who played Chase and the girl who played Eve. The director, Bryce, is a decent guy. A little bit of a micromanager, but that makes him good. There are some people from the film crew milling around.

It's great to catch up with his colleagues. He's in the mix, giving hugs and high fives, getting updates on their lives and careers.

He wishes Kit were with him. This is going to be a hell of a reunion.

Chapter 30

"Do you really think I can trust him?"
- Eve to Hazel, Season 1, Episode 6

Val, July 31

Photographers line up outside the hotel, snapping photos of the guests as they arrive. When it's Val's turn, she gets assaulted with questions.

"Valerie! Look here! Can we get a picture of you with Tate Masters?"

"Where is Tate? You look so good! One more shot!"

Val does her best to ignore any of the questions they shout. She just smiles and swivels back and forth, signing autographs as she goes. She hasn't even *seen* Tate yet.

When the Jack and Francesca love story line took off with views, reposts, and likes, they were inundated with influencers taking sides on the love triangle. Coupled with the nostalgia over the past decade, they're getting lots of extra publicity.

Why did she let Justin create this stupid storyline for attention? She knew it was a ridiculous idea when he proposed it, but she needed the ten grand. And now it's time to pay the piper.

They're swarming like vultures, the entertainment reporters and photographers covering every day of the reunion. It's more press than anyone expected–their event blew up on social media.

The opening night reception is a cocktail party being held at the Seven Mile Hotel. All of the stars are required to be there for a meet and greet with the VIP guests attending the reunion. Tate, Val, Josie, Paige, and Mason all arrived at the designated time for maximum exposure.

This is just the beginning of the four-day extravaganza. Tomorrow, there will be a red carpet to walk on as they enter the historic Harbor Square Theater for the official start of the reunion.

Fans are lined up on the sidewalk outside the hotel, hoping to catch a photo with one of their favorite characters or even snag an autograph. The sidewalk is crowded, making it hard to maneuver.

As soon as she arrived, she tried getting Josie's attention when she spotted her, waving and shouting her name, "Jo Jo! Hey, it's me!"

Josie turned at the sound of Val's voice, flicked a stare, and turned right back around. An ice-cold shoulder.

Obviously, Josie is going to do everything she can to avoid her. Every time Val gets close, Josie slides away.

Paige keeps looking back and forth at them, not sure what to do. Mason is positively basking in the attention, while some of the other cast members, like Tate, wave and keep going inside.

Val pretends like everything is fine. "Great to see everyone! Thanks for coming!" She turns and makes her way into the hotel lobby.

"Do you want to mingle for a bit?" Paige asks her.

"No, I don't. I need to talk to Josie." Val hates this passive-aggressive shit. If you have a problem, just say it. Val walks over to where Josie is standing at the wraparound bar, waiting for a drink.

"Josie, could I have a word?" Val reaches out to touch Josie's shoulder.

Josie flinches, pulling away. She gives Val a cold stare. It's unnerving. Josie's usually so open and friendly, so in all of her golden glory, that it can be hard to stand next to her. It's easy to envy her for her glossy perfection.

"I don't think so," Josie answers coldly before turning and walking away.

Val watches her go. "Maybe later?" She asks Josie's departing back. No response.

Val gives Josie an hour to settle down. The girl has never been one to hold a grudge. She's too damn nice. Everyone knows this.

She watches Josie carefully for a while as she mingles with guests, making small talk and taking selfies. She seems less agitated.

Finally, Val sees her opening. Josie has peeled off from a pack of groupies and is heading to the bathroom.

It's her cue.

Val plops down her drink and follows close behind. Josie's already walking into the stall when Val steps in after her.

"Jo Jo, I need to talk to you."

Josie is turning around to shut the door. But Val is already there, her body blocking the door and pinning them in together. "Please let me explain."

"Are you *stalking* me?" Josie asks in disbelief. "I told you I'm not interested in hearing from you. Get out."

Val doesn't budge. "It's all a big misunderstanding," Val insists. "I'm sorry."

Josie's eyebrows raise. She's quivering with anger. "I don't give a damn. Now, leave me alone."

"Please, Jo Jo. Give me five minutes."

Josie pushes Val out and slams the stall door. Val hears the lock click.

Fine. Valerie can work with this. She leans against the gold-veined marble of the double vanity. The lights shine bright on both their faces, illuminating their expressions.

"It was stupid. They thought it would generate publicity for all this," Val casually waves her hand. It might have worked if Josie wasn't so spitting mad. "It didn't mean anything."

"Go away, Val. I have nothing to say to you."

"I didn't think you'd be this upset. You know I'd never hurt you." At least, not deliberately.

"Upset? That you make up a story and drag me into it? And don't have the decency to tell me that it was coming out so I could prepare for it?" Josie's voice comes from the stall. "C'mon, Val. We're not kids anymore. You knew what you were doing."

At least Josie is finally talking to her. "We're such idiots, Jo. I told them it wasn't going to work."

"Who's them?" Josie opens the stall door and walks up to the mirror. She washes her hands, then pulls open her bag to rummage inside. She still hasn't made eye contact.

"The press. Social media. PR agents. You know, the usual. They thought it would make a splash right before we all got together. Create another love triangle."

Josie pulls out her lip liner and applies it over the sink. "It was dumb."

"Yes, it was. I already told you that. It was a stupid thing to do."

"It doesn't matter what they did. It's what *you* did. My friend. Stabbing me in the back." Her eyes glitter with rage or tears. Val can't tell which. She tries again.

"I know. I'm sorry. More sorry than I can say. I got caught up in it." Val smiles, hesitantly. "You know, I haven't been on the radar in years. It felt good."

Josie drops her lip liner into her clutch, snapping it shut. Val can't let her leave. She grabs Josie's arm.

"Josie, I tried to fix it. I made a statement yesterday. It's going to hit today: magazines, Instagram, TikTok, you name it. I told them it was a big mistake."

"What kind of mistake?"

Val hesitates before answering. "The truth. That Tate and I have never been an item. You two were always each other's first choice."

Josie swipes at her eyes, the tawny gold flecks that made her famous now brimming with emotion.

Valerie doesn't think she could feel any worse. "I honestly didn't think you had any feelings for Tate anymore." Josie never talks about him, not in all the years since the show ended. Val just figured it was a one-time fling they both outgrew. Childhood sweethearts who moved on with their feelings.

Josie sighs, but she looks less angry.

"Jo, I didn't know. Really. You still love him?" Val asks, hesitantly moving closer. She's not sure if Josie will let her give a hug.

Josie smiles as she dabs at her tears. "No, not like that. We've been over for a long time. I just didn't like being hit with this story out of nowhere." She tilts her head. "You know what you did was low. You could have given me a heads up."

Damn. Val thinks she might feel even worse. "I know. I'm so sorry. It was Justin. He paid me to do it."

"Justin?" Josie's eyes widen. "But Val, why? Did you need the money that badly?"

"I did," she says sheepishly. Val's pride is really taking a beating here. "I'm flat broke."

"I could have helped you," Josie offers. "You didn't need to go with Justin. He's always been an asshole, but I didn't expect him to pay you for press."

"Yeah," Val nods. "He's getting worse." She hesitates, then adds, "It's not the first time he's planted stories."

Should she tell Josie everything now that she's being honest? Finally fess up to the other things she did years ago? Does she have the guts?

Josie sighs. "I've heard that. I guess I didn't expect Tate to go along with it, too."

Shit. "Jo, Tate had nothing to do with it."

"He didn't? I figured he knew."

Val shakes her head. "Absolutely not. He would never do that to you." The truth is hanging in the air between them. That Valerie would. And did.

She wonders if she has the guts to tell Josie. It feels like the right time to rip off the band-aid.

Val takes a deep breath, opening her mouth to finally spill the truth.

The bathroom door opens, and two young girls walk into the bathroom.

Spotting Valerie and Josie leaning against the sinks, their eyes widen. "Oh, my God. Eve and Frankie?"

Val and Josie automatically straighten up and paste their happy faces on.

"It's us," Val says with a bright smile. "Are you here for the reunion?" And just like that, they're back on *The Shallows*.

The show must go on.

Chapter 31

Tate, July 31

Tate sips a glass of whiskey at the bar while he listens to Mason complain about Kit and gush about his crush on Quinn, Avalon's finest firefighter. The very one who rescued Tate from a diabetic episode. In front of Jo Jo.

It's going to be a long night.

This welcome reception is already giving him a headache. This doesn't help. Tate had been reluctant to come back. He never should have said yes.

He's not sure exactly why he did. He has a fulfilling career with Squeaks, producing albums with talented bands. Mixing music is what he's always dreamed of doing, not trying to come back and make pocket money off of nostalgic fans.

The Shallows was so far in his past that it seems silly to try to bring it back. It's done and dusted. He's gotten over it. Why hasn't everyone else?

"I can't believe you talked me into coming to this," Tate moans. When their former director, Bryce, had first asked, he'd said no without a second thought. But Mason wore him down.

"Of course I did. I wasn't going to face the gauntlet without you. Give me some credit."

"At least you have Kit for support. I'm here solo."

Mason's eyes darken. "I'm still pissed. He'll be lucky if I let him get away with it."

Mason wasn't the only reason Tate agreed. He has to admit to himself that he also hopes to finally get the chance to talk with Josie. To clear up the things that have been unresolved and weighing on him for years.

He's been scanning the room for the past hour to catch a glimpse of her. He saw her walking around earlier, but then he lost track. He really needs to talk to her. The number of times they've been interrupted is getting ridiculous.

He's sure Josie isn't annoyed about that silly story about him and Val. Who would have expected that to go viral? One of the wedding guests must have seen him hanging out with Val at the wedding and interpreted it as something more, and it spiraled from there.

Growing up with famous parents, Tate has seen so many gossip items in the press that were completely wrong. There had been rumors he was a love child, that he had been adopted from missionaries, that he had a tail … you name it, there's been a story involving Crew Masters and Kate Noble, Hollywood royalty. Just having their faces on the covers sold magazines and generated website traction.

You'd think with that kind of upbringing that he'd be over show business, but here Tate is again, standing around a room full of former castmates and crew members in the heart of a coastal beach town. Anxiously looking around for his ex-girlfriend. Munching on a granola bar to keep his insulin levels steady. Nursing a glass of whiskey.

It's pretty crowded. Besides the cast members and production crew, there are also Shallows influencers who are being paid to build up the event. They're circling the main actors, trying to get photos and inside gossip about their lives.

It's obnoxious, in his opinion. And it's exactly why Tate does his best to avoid most HBs: Human Beings. That's why he got his own place.

He hates drama. And small talk. This is Tate's personal version of hell.

Which makes it so ironic that Mason is his best friend. Mason, who brings both drama and small talk in equal spades wherever he goes.

"I swear, there was a zing with Quinn as soon as we laid eyes on each other," Mason says, sloshing the ice in his drink. "Right over your prone body. It was an instant attraction. He's just hiding it."

"I'm sure," Tate says agreeably. "But do you really want to mess things up with Kit for a weekend fling? You've been together a long time. There's a lot there. Not to mention, you're married. And I'm pretty sure Quinn is straight."

Mason sighs. "I figured he was, too. The spark might have been with Josie. Isn't it always?"

"Pretty much." Tate is barely paying attention to Mason's bitching. He's too busy watching Josie heading towards the restrooms. Val is trailing right behind her.

"I will say that it has been hard lately. Really hard. We don't have fun anymore."

"Doesn't that happen sometimes? You go through stages?" Not that Tate would know. His longest relationship was when he was 20 years old. Which is freaking sad.

"Not like this. I don't see how we can get out of it. The same fight, over his kids." Mason looks down at his drink sadly. "I love those little devils, but his ex-wife won't stop using them against him."

"I'm sorry," Tate responds. "But that's not worth giving up on him. And you love the girls too much."

"I do. So let's just get drunk and then head to Fred's Tavern later. Maybe I can convince everyone to meet us." Mason wiggles his eyebrows.

"Sounds like a solid plan." It seems like Josie and Valerie have been in there for ages. They should be out any minute. Tate had better think of the right thing to say when they do.

The last time he saw Josie, he *literally* passed out at her feet. Tate is hoping he can talk to her without fainting this time.

He wouldn't be surprised if Josie and Val were discussing the recent stories about their little love triangle. Basic bullshit, but still something that could aggravate them both. Josie knows enough about the industry not to get upset, though.

Tate thinks back to when he first met her, when they were teens. They were both at a follow-up audition to read lines together, and you could tell the casting director was thrilled. They had instant chemistry. They could barely keep their eyes off each other.

"I'm Tate Masters," he said.

"Josie Remington," she answered, tucking her long blonde hair behind her ear self-consciously.

Josie was every fantasy: the golden girl, the girl next door, and the unattainable crush. Tate didn't stand a chance.

And now they're all here, ten years later, in a ballroom in Stone Harbor. Getting paid ridiculous money to sign autographs and pose for pictures with avid fans.

You can't make this stuff up.

After what seems like forever, Tate finally spots Josie and Val leaving the women's room. He'd been about to give up hope.

"I gotta go," Tate says, and starts to walk away.

"Where are you going?" Mason asks, but Tate doesn't pause.

He's not letting Josie run away from him again. He manages to cut Josie and Val off on their way to the bar. Mason has caught up with him and stands right behind him.

"Josie, can I have a moment?" Tate reaches out to touch her arm.

Josie whips around, but she doesn't pull back from him. That's a good sign. Her mouth opens in surprise. "Tate. Hey. Sure. Just give me a second."

She looks at Val. "I'll go get a drink," Val says and heads to the bar. She doesn't even greet him or kiss his cheek, which confirms his suspicions that she's never been interested in him.

It's better, anyway. Tate doesn't need another picture of them in proximity to keep that storyline going.

Mason cocks his head. "I'll go with her," he says, hurrying to catch up.

Tate leads Josie to an open cocktail table tucked away from the crowds. He sets his whiskey glass on the high top table and clears his throat. How should he start?

He has one chance to make it right. One last shot before she leaves his sight yet again. "I didn't get much of a chance to talk to you at Sage and Simon's wedding," he begins tentatively.

"I'm sorry, I should have asked," Josie says with a shake of her curls. "How are you feeling now? How's your head?"

"It's fine. I'm fine. My diabetes has been in check. It hasn't been an issue in a while, except for the last time I saw you." He clears his throat. "That's not what I hoped to talk to you about."

Jo smiles, and for a second, he's lost. He hasn't been this close to her for years. It takes him back to the beaches of Avalon, where they spent all their time, all while he wondered if she wanted him half as bad as he wanted her.

"What, then?" Josie asks. What did you want to talk about?" She's turned her full attention to Tate, and it flusters him. He forgot what it was like to have the full focus of her attention. Those speckled eyes.

He hesitates. "I'm sorry. I know I'm going about this all wrong."

"It's fine, Tate. Whatever you have to say, you can say to me."

"This whole reunion thing has thrown me, as I'm sure it's done for you. I saw you and Val talking, so I'm sure you realize there was nothing behind that stupid rumor."

"Not on *your* part," Josie mutters under her breath.

"What do you mean?" Tate's not sure how to respond. He only has so much time before they get interrupted, and he still hasn't had a chance to say what he wants to say.

"I thought you might have been involved, but it was all Val. Typical of her."

"I'm sorry." What can he say?

Josie crosses her arms. "It is what it is."

Not exactly the opening he was looking for, but he plunges ahead anyway. He can't miss this opportunity. "I know this isn't the place or the time, but you've never responded to my emails or voice messages. So I wanted to see if we could find somewhere to talk."

There. Finally. Phew.

Josie looks confused. She tucks a strand of hair behind her ear. "Sure. Did you mean after the wedding?"

"No, ten years ago." What is she even talking about?

"Ten years ago?" She pauses. "Okay, I'm not exactly sure what you're talking about, but I'm happy to talk anytime you want to."

Tate is about to respond when he feels an arm clutching his neck, preventing him from responding. He's been ambushed by a superfan wearing a shirt with *"I'm having Jack Tucker's baby!!!"* emblazoned across it.

"Oh my GAWDDDD I can't believe it!" the woman screams in his ear as she clutches his neck. "It's you!" She has him in a death grip.

Josie chuckles. "Good seeing you, Tate." She walks away to meet Val, leaving Tate to untangle himself from an unfamiliar set of arms and legs.

Damn it. He forgot how crazy the fanbase is. *The Shallows Suckers.* They still live for the show, living out their fantasies in Duffy Beach. They send him fan mail with slightly threatening plans of the lives they'd have together.

Tate curses his luck. He can never just get some alone time with Josie. He always screws it up.

It doesn't mean he won't stop trying. He promised himself he'd finally clear the air with Josie.

"Can I just grab a drink, and I'll be right back?" he asks.

His newest enthusiastic fan hugs him tight. "Of course! I'll be right here waiting," she says as she releases him.

Tate runs to the exit as soon as he's free. He's making a mess of this.

It's time to call in reinforcements. He needs Squeaks.

Chapter 32

"Duffy Beach is the perfect beach town.
Trust me, you're going to love it."
- Mrs. Mattson to Eve and Hazel, Season 1, Episode 1

Josie, July 31

It's past time to go home. She's been hit with more drama this evening than she can cover with hours of therapy. It's time to make a swift exit.

"I've had enough." Josie bends over and gives Paige a peck on the cheek. "I'm out."

"You're sure?" Paige looks worried. "Want me to come with you?"

"I'm beat. We've been here for less than one day, and I'm already ready to pack up and head home. I need a break."

"Text me when you get home."

"Promise. Love you."

It's not a hard decision to make. Josie is sure the party will keep going late into the night without her. She whips out her phone for an Uber that arrives in minutes. Getting into the car, she leans her head against the seat.

The evening had been brutal. She was ambushed twice, once by Val and once by Tate. It's way too much—it felt like they were trying to get her forgiveness automatically, just by asking her. It just doesn't feel right. Why isn't she allowed some time to be angry? Why does she always have to be the nice one who forgives everyone right away?

It's been so long since she and Tate broke up that it didn't affect her like it once did, when it was fresh. But damn, Val had just blindsided her last week. She needs some time to process it.

Tate and Val both have larger-than-life personalities. Val isn't afraid to say what she wants. Tate was born knowing he was special, with his movie and rock star royalty lineage. Having Mumford and Sons playing at your birthday parties isn't typical for most kids.

Josie likes the life she's made. She found her calling. But right now, she needs some peace and quiet.

Back at the house on 115th Street, Josie checks her phone for the entry code the organizers gave her to enter the property and shoots Paige a text that she's home safe.

Now that she's successfully inside, she heads to the kitchen to find something to eat. The house is big and silent. It's incredible. She has some space to breathe.

She opens the refrigerator door and grabs a plate of food from the fridge. She considers for a second, then grabs a can of hard seltzer off the side door as well.

She's about to close it when she hears a soft noise behind her. A squeak on the floor.

She whips around.

Someone is standing under the arch of the hallway. He looks familiar. He has a head of dark hair with a thick set of eyebrows on top of heavily lashed eyes. There's a hint of stubble across a strong jawline.

"Sorry." He clears his throat. "Don't worry, I'm harmless. I didn't mean to scare you. I'm helping with security."

It clicks. "You helped Tate," Josie remembers. He was the one who rescued her when Tate passed out.

"That was me. Quinn."

"Thanks again." She smiles. "You saved the day."

"That's my job." He raises one of those thick eyebrows. "Do you want company? If you need some space, I totally get it. No pressure."

"As long as you're not recording this conversation, we're good."

"I have a non-disclosure. You're safe with me."

Josie cocks her head, considering. "You were in Newport and now here. How come?"

"I became friends with Simon when you filmed here. I'm a townie," Quinn says comfortably. "He used to come into the restaurant my parents owned in Avalon."

"I never met you."

"Most of you didn't socialize outside of your group." He says it easily, without judgment.

Josie looks around at the dark kitchen. It's just the two of them, but she isn't nervous. "Want to sit down?" Now that she has friendly company, she doesn't feel quite so much like being alone. "Can I get you something to drink?"

Quinn looks at the can of hard seltzer in her hands. "I'll have one of what you're having, thanks. I didn't expect anyone to be home this early." There's a question there. She likes how he dropped it, without outright asking why she left the party.

Josie sighs. "It was just too much. I needed some space."

Quinn flicks a glance around them. "Well, this house has plenty of that." He takes a seat at the island.

She laughs. "That's true."

Josie hands him a glass and sits down next to him. There are ten other stools she could have chosen from, if she wanted. The island is massive.

She wants to sit next to him, though. For the first time in a while, she feels a spark of interest in someone. There's something about Quinn that's compelling. Inviting, without being overbearing. She's so *curious* to hear what he's thinking about this weekend and learn more about him.

"How did you end up working this security gig?" Josie asks.

"I usually work a set of 24-hour days in a row. So then I'm off for a few days," Quinn answers.

"That's an interesting schedule. What's your day job?"

"I'm a firefighter for the town of Avalon."

"That's right. Did you tell Mason that at the wedding?" She pictures Quinn in a firefighter's uniform, holding a hose, and she rolls her eyes. "He'll lose his mind."

Quinn laughs. "I met him after you left the lobby. He's very friendly."

"Oh, I'm sure. He's always dreamed of dating a firefighter. It's one of his top three fantasies."

"I'm not going to ask what the other two are."

Josie hasn't felt this comfortable with someone for a long time. Quinn is so easy to talk to. She's very glad she decided to duck out of the party early.

She thought she'd be alone at the house. Some of the actors are staying at other places, like Tate, who rented a condo for the week. There's a group of production team members who pitched in for a house.

Still, Josie and Paige decided to share a spot at Roger Elliot's place. Their room has a balcony overlooking the water and its own en-suite bathroom, which is a nice perk. And it's free, which was an even nicer one.

Mason and Justin are also staying at the mansion. Sage and Simon will be, too. They're arriving later for the panel discussions. Bryce is arriving tomorrow afternoon.

The actors playing Josie's mom and dad in the show, Marty and Elise, are arriving tomorrow as well. They're only going to be there for a couple of days. Marty showed up at the party with a very young female assistant in tow. Josie has only seen him with twenty-somethings, even though he must be nearly 50. It's such a cliche.

"Can I ask you something?"

"Sure."

"You didn't want to continue acting, but you're here for this. How come?" His question seems genuine.

Josie takes some time to finish the rest of her seltzer. No one has actually asked her that specific question. Everyone kept telling her that she *should* attend the reunion, but no one has thought to ask *why* she'd want to.

"I guess I felt an obligation to the cast and crew. Everyone was such a piece of my life for so long, nearly five years if you count film and production. They needed me, so I came."

"That's truly nice of you. But it doesn't seem like you're thrilled to be here."

Josie silently gives Quinn bonus points for noticing. "I guess I'm not. It's been too long since we did the show. I'm over it."

"What do you do now?"

"I'm a commercial photographer. Mostly advertising shoots, product placement, things like that."

"Do you travel all over for it?"

"No, most of the time I can do it from home. I also live in New Jersey, but on the west side along the Delaware River. I only fly out a few days a month. Or I drive, if it's New York or DC. They're both a couple of hours away."

"So you can live anywhere you want. That's nice."

"I guess so. I never really thought of it that way."

"I've always lived here. I grew up fishing in the bay and sailing on the Atlantic. I left for a while to attend school in Georgia, but I decided

I missed the barrier island and came back."

"It's a great town."

"It's my place," he answers simply. "There's nowhere else in the world like it. Did you know it has the best sunsets in the entire world?" A dimple appears in his cheek. Is he putting her on?

"The best sunsets? In the entire world?" Josie asks skeptically. "That's a pretty big claim. Have you ever been overseas?"

"I grew up on Seven Mile Island," Quinn answers. "They're not even close. I'd bet my life on it."

"What do you do when it's off-season?"

"Everything. We have the run of the island. My best friends live here year-round. They just got engaged."

"That's sweet."

"Well, it wasn't the most romantic beginning, but they worked it out. They both lived in other places before they came back home. And a lot of people are coming back, realizing how great this spot is."

Quinn stops to take a sip of his drink. "You just have to know the good spots. And the right people to hang with."

The way Quinn describes Stone Harbor makes her appreciate it more. The show was filmed on location here in the winter, when the weather was colder, and fewer people were around. They also frequently shot in the studio, so Josie didn't have the same experience he's describing.

"I wish I had met you when we were filming. I feel like you would have shown me all the best spots," Josie says.

"I still can. Do you want me to?"

Is Quinn asking her out or just being friendly? Either way, she wants to go.

"I'd love that. When do you have a break?"

"I'm working security for the reunion tomorrow, but I'm off by 5:30. Would that work?"

"I'd love that."

They exchange numbers. "The first thing to do is go for a twilight cruise out of the marina at the Stone Harbor Yacht Club," Quinn says.

It sounds perfect. For the first time in a while, Josie has flutters of excitement over a date. Or is it a date?

Whatever. She's going to see what happens. "I'm in."

They're interrupted by the sound of the front door opening and slamming shut.

"'Honey, I'm home!" Mason shouts as he walks in. He casts an eye on the pair of them. "Did I miss anything?"

"I was just going to bed." She gives Mason a peck on the cheek. "Good night." He looks like he's about to say something, but stops himself.

Quinn gets up and excuses himself. "I've got to go, too. See you in the morning."

They didn't make an actual plan or a day to hang out, but Josie isn't worried. She's pretty sure that she's going to be seeing a lot of Quinn around Avalon.

She's counting on it.

Chapter 33

"Shots! Shots! Shots!"
- The crowd to Shea, Season 2, Episode 9

Paige, August 1

As the alarm on her phone rings, Paige is seriously regretting many of those decisions. Ugh. Her head is pounding, and her mouth is a dried-out wasteland.

"Water," Paige whimpers. "Please, for the love of God. I need water." Is anyone around to save her from near death?

There's a knock on her door, and Saint Jo Jo walks in. She has come to her rescue with aspirin, toast, and a huge ice-cold glass of water on a tray.

"Whatever you want, whenever you want it. It's yours," Paige tells Josie as she lowers the life-saving tray to the bed. She picks up the water glass, careful not to spill. "First child, first dog, or the password to my TikTok account." It feels like heaven as she takes a large drink.

Josie comes and sits down at the foot of the mattress. "What time did you get in?"

"Who knows? I remember closing the place down. After multiple rounds of shots."

Paige didn't get back to the Elliot mansion until past three in the morning. After the opening night reception, a motley crew from the party had gone to *The Princeton* in Avalon, an iconic nightlife spot with three bars and clubs under one roof. The group, including Val and Xavier, had stayed out dancing to live music, slinging shots of tequila, and scream-singing along to cover songs.

Val was cozied up with Xavier, the same gorgeous stunt double she had hooked up with at Simon and Sage's wedding. They were all over each other on the dance floor.

"I guess this will take care of the rumors about us!" Val shouted in Paige's ear.

"We'll make sure we send the pics to Justin, the dick."

Val laughs. "He really is. But tonight we're having fun. Xavier is so cute, isn't he?"

"Adorable." Paige saw them go home together, hand in hand. She has to admit, they look good together.

You just can't have a bad time at *The Princeton*.

The rest of the gang finished up the night with multiple orders of pizza to soak up all the booze, but now Paige feels like it wasn't enough to make much of a dent with how much she drank over the course of the night.

It probably wasn't the wisest move for the first day of the reunion. She's supposed to be up by eight for hair and makeup, with the first set of meet and greets starting at ten this morning.

It's a long schedule. Tomorrow, they'll break up into panels with titles such as "Love Triangles" and "Creative License." She's scheduled for a panel with Elise and Marty about what it's like to have a long career in film—how things have changed over the years. The three of them have all had the longest careers in Hollywood out of the rest of the cast.

Josie rubs a spot on Paige's face. "I hate to say it, but it looks like you went somewhere to eat, too."

Paige sighs. "Probably. It's all hazy." She's not even going to try to remember everything that happened last night until the aspirin kicks in. It gives her too much of a headache.

She takes a piece of toast from the plate Josie made for her. "You really are an angel. What time are we due in the chair?"

"I'll go first, so you can get a little more sleep. They should be here soon, though."

Paige groans. She doesn't know how she's going to get through the next seven hours. "I'm going to look terrible all day."

"Never. Not my Paige."

The sheer love and acceptance radiating from Josie makes Paige feel like shit. Here is Josie, taking care of Paige when she isn't even sick—she just had a few too many drinks. She brought it all on herself.

She always does this. Creates her own problems.

Before she can think better of it or consider the outcome, Paige blurts out the secret she's been hiding for so long. The one she's never dared to say.

"Jo, it was me. I ruined your relationship with Tate." Paige squeezes her eyes shut. She can't look at her friend, she's so upset. She grabs a lock of her hair and begins pulling on it.

There's no response. Total silence.

Paige peeks an eye open.

Josie is still sitting there, her legs crossed. She looks bemused, not upset, her golden curls highlighted by the sun behind her.

"You had nothing to do with it," Josie tells Paige.

"No, I did. I really did."

Josie still looks like she doesn't believe her. There's a smile on her face. *Is she actually humoring her?*

This wasn't the reaction Paige expected.

Maybe she should recant what she said—pass it off as a joke. She's already kept this secret for so long. More than a decade. Never spilling what she'd done to anyone who wasn't involved.

It feels like it's time, though. She's carried it too long.

"It was me," she insists.

"And how did you break us up? Tate did that all on his own."

"Because I was an idiot. I was so scared the show was ending, and I'd be alone again. It became my life. My family. I didn't want to lose it."

Jo finally seems to take her seriously. She dips her chin, sending gentle waves through her curls. "What did you do, Paige?"

"I made up a lie."

"What lie?"

"I told Bryce and Simon you were leaving. That you'd been scooped up by another studio and you were going to break your contract."

"How could I even do that? I would have been in breach." She gets off the bed.

"I said it was the opportunity of a lifetime. And then I told Tate the same thing. He didn't believe me at first."

A hot rush of shame goes through her. Saying it out loud makes it seem so much worse. "I didn't want him to try and talk to you, so I might have done a few other things too."

"Go on." Paige has Josie's full attention now. Even though she kind of wishes she didn't. Josie is standing there, completely still, listening.

"It was bad. I changed his name in your contacts so you didn't realize it was him calling, and I deleted some of his texts and calls, too. It seemed like you were ignoring him. He didn't understand why."

"And I thought he was pulling away."

"Yeah, I know." Paige looks down at the strands of hair in her hand. She pulled them out without even realizing she was doing it. It doesn't make her feel any better. "And since the filming had wrapped, you weren't forced to see each other. Made it easier."

"But why would you do that? Didn't you realize the show would be canceled? Without me in it?"

"Yeah, um. I thought Simon would just write a scene where you died. I mean, it's happened before. I didn't think it would make the show *end*. Just switch it up."

"Of course. And you could just slide into my spot, saving the day."

"I didn't think it through, Jo Jo. I was scared. I did a shitty thing." Paige looks down again, unable to keep eye contact. "I was just so jealous of you. Everyone loved you."

"They loved you too," Josie responds. "We all did."

Josie walks over to the closet. Paige watches her warily.

"What are you doing?" she asks as Josie picks up her things from the side table, sweeps her bathroom products into a case, and tosses the smaller bags into her luggage.

"I'm leaving. What did you think I would do?"

"You can't leave! The conference is just starting."

"I can do whatever I want to. And I'm not staying." Tugging the strap over her shoulder, she strides out of the room angrily.

Paige's hangover is instantly gone, replaced by a sick feeling in her stomach. She ruined everything. Josie will never forgive her. She races down the stairs after her.

"I'm sorry, Jo Jo. I was an idiot. A kid. That's why I'm telling you now."

Josie is moving so fast that Paige can hardly keep up.

"Fuck you, Paige. You told me because you were tired of feeling guilty. And you thought it was long enough ago that I'd be okay with it."

Paige follows Josie outside, where they end up on the expansive driveway in front of the house. "I can't tell you how sorry I am."

"No, you're not. You messed with so many lives. Our careers and our friendships. Because it was always all about you."

"I was an idiot," Paige cries, her stomach churning. She's never seen Josie so angry.

"I'm out of here." She won't look at Paige. "Don't ever talk to me again." She flies down the sidewalk.

"Please?" she whispers. "I'm sorry, Josie."

What had she done? Why had she told Josie the truth? Paige knows Jo won't answer if she calls now. She'd blown her shot at explaining why she had done what she did, simply because she was feeling so crummy.

Damn. She's never seen Josie so angry.

She needs to reach out to the only person who will be able to help her out. Who might be able to fix this horrible situation she created and get her out of the hole she's dug herself. He might not always be a good guy, but he can get people to listen to him.

She grabs her phone and makes a call to Justin.

Chapter 34

"Becky isn't responding to any of my calls and texts.
I think she ran away."
- Eve, Season 3, Episode 10 (Season Finale)

Mason, August 1

Mason hasn't heard from Kit in two days. It might be one of the longest they've gone without talking since they started dating years ago.

And it's all Kit's fault.

Really. This time, it is.

For once, Mason is not the one being the drama queen. When normally his husband is the laid-back, "go along with it" guy in their relationship, Kit is now the one being a complete asshole.

Kit knows just how important the reunion is to Mason. After he didn't make it to the wedding, Mason was sure that Kit would feel guilty and ask Alex to help with the girls, now that Maeve is feeling better. But instead, Kit kept telling him that he was being selfish.

Screw him. Mason is going to have fun and not worry about what his partner is doing back home in Pennsylvania.

After a quick shower, he throws on a set of tailored slacks and a short-sleeve, button-down shirt. Mason doesn't have to be told that it suits him. He knows it does.

He trots down the stairs to the main kitchen, where there's a huge breakfast spread. Bless them.

He doesn't know who's doing all the cooking, but there's always food around: pastries, breakfast sandwiches, and quiches in the morning; pasta salads, fruit, and French bread sandwiches in the afternoon; bowls of nuts and spreads throughout the day. Stacked cans of sparkling water and Italian sodas with cut limes and lemons nearby.

He could get used to this kind of life. And the people in it.

Quinn is leaning against one of the counters, sipping a cup of coffee. He's wearing a light blue polo that shows off tanned and toned arms. When he shifts positions, Mason can see a glimpse of his stomach. He doesn't have to check to know the man has a solid six-pack under there. You can just tell.

"Morning," Mason says brightly, heading over to the coffeemaker. "Are you the only one up?"

"Josie left ten minutes ago."

"Oh, she's going to be early for today. We're not due for a couple of hours."

Quinn pauses but doesn't say anything. Mason immediately knows something is off. "What happened? Is everything okay?" he asks.

"She's pretty upset," Quinn says. "I don't think she's coming back to the house. She had all of her things with her."

"That doesn't make any sense. Did she say where she was going?"

"I'm not sure," he hedges. "I didn't want to ask too many questions, but she and Paige were arguing."

"Interesting." His interest is piqued. What could they have been fighting over?

"Yeah. I got her an Uber. I couldn't drive her, since I'm on security detail," he explains.

It's the first day of their reunion, and there's already drama. Mason isn't surprised. There's always drama.

"I'm going to run upstairs to their room and see if Paige knows anything," Mason looks at Quinn. "Will you be around later?"

Although he doesn't want to miss out on this unexpected one-on-one time, he also NEEDS to find out what happened. He *loves* gossip, and hates to be left out.

"I'm working this shift, but I'm off duty from the fire station tonight," Quinn says. "I'm going to hit the beach and surf for a while, then head out for some drinks."

Dear God. Mason had pictured Quinn in his firefighter gear, but to find out he's also a surfer? Can this man become any more of a fantasy? Wiping the drool from his mouth, Mason heads back upstairs to find Paige and Josie's room.

He's not familiar with where everyone is staying. There are so many hallways and side rooms. He finally gets lucky and finds Paige sitting up in bed, staring at her phone.

She looks like hell. Her dark red hair is up in a messy bun, while the white cotton tank top she's wearing has a strap falling off her shoulder. Streaks of eyeshadow and mascara are smudged under Paige's brown eyes, making them look darker than usual.

"Good morning, darling. Don't you look shitty?" Mason greets Paige. He hands over his cup of coffee as a mercy offer.

"Leave me alone, Mason. I don't need your commentary," she grumbles, not looking up.

"What did you do now?" he asks as he plops down. Mason knows the long laundry list of problems Paige has had over the years. She seemed like she had been doing pretty well lately. Getting back on her feet.

"Are we back to doing lines in the bathroom? Hope not." Mason shudders. "That's so 2010."

"Funny. No, Josie and I had a fight."

"When does Saint Josie ever get that mad? She'll be over it in no time," Mason consoles Paige. "Five minutes tops."

"Not this time," Paige groans, pulling her knees up and resting her head on them. She starts crying. "I really fucked up."

"It can't be that bad."

"It is. I told her that I'm the reason she and Tate broke up. And I ruined the show. She *hates* me," Paige wails.

"What did you do, Paige?"

She sniffles, wiping her nose with the back of her hand. "We were so young. I was freaking out, Mason. I was tired of it always being Josie, Josie, Josie. So I told a few lies."

"What *kind* of lies, Paige?" Mason has gone still.

"I told Bryce that Josie was planning on leaving the Shallows. And then I told Tate she was leaving too."

"I'm sure he didn't believe you, though. Bryce is the director. It's his job to hold her to her contract."

She looks away guiltily. "I sent an email to Bryce saying that it was from a law firm. They threatened to cut short her contract based on emotional distress. Caused by him."

"Wow. That was harsh."

"I know. And I also sent some texts from Josie to Tate and then deleted his responses. You know Josie. She always left her phone lying around. It was easy to break into it and send them out, then just erase the history of what I sent."

"Damn, Paige. You're a psychopath. With anyone else, I'd be impressed."

"Everyone just took it and ran with it. It just kept getting bigger, and I couldn't stop it." She sniffs. "I thought Simon would rewrite the show and bring in some other people. But instead, they all believed me. The show was canceled."

"Why is that a surprise? They were going to lose one of their stars!" He can't believe what he's hearing. "Paige, what were you thinking?"

"I was so young, Mason. Cut me a break. I didn't mean it to get out of hand."

"You put hundreds of people out of work and broke up a couple in love so you could have top billing. I'm not giving you any break, Paige." A sudden thought occurs to Mason.

"You were the one who told me that Jo was leaving. And I confirmed it to Bryce. You made me complicit!"

"I didn't mean to, Mason. I keep telling you guys this!"

"You can't even take responsibility for what you did." Mason grabs the cup of coffee from her hands. "I'm taking this with me. I hope you have a hell of a hangover."

Paige starts crying again, even harder this time.

'I said I'm sorry!"

"I'm going to try and fix this. Don't say anything to Tate until I talk to him first."

Mason stalks out of the room. He needs to find Josie.

What a mess. He doesn't even get the chance to say goodbye to Quinn, who's still standing watch downstairs in the kitchen. Mason is so concerned about finding Tate to tell him what happened that he doesn't even have time for the firefighter/surfer god.

Mason has to say, he's a hell of a friend.

Chapter 35

*"Should we be worried about how much
time you're spending with that boy?"
- Francesca's parents, Season 4, Episode 3*

Val, August 1

Waking up next to Xavier after another hook-up sesh feels more comfortable the second time around. Maybe Val's just getting used to it—going home halfway drunk with him and waking up in his arms, slightly hungover and very thirsty. Craving carbs.

It still feels exciting, but also familiar. There's something about him that makes her feel safe when she's with him.

"Xavier? Hey Xavier," she says as gently as possible. It's literally like waking a sleeping giant. Made of stone.

He doesn't budge. She tries again, swiping her hand through his thick head of hair. "Hey, buddy. We need to get up. It's late."

He's so damn cute she can't help it. Even now, sleeping next to him, she gets a little flutter in her belly thinking about how much fun they had last night.

"Give me your best knock-knock joke," Xavier asked her. Val couldn't think of a single one.

"Knock knock."

"Who's there?"

"Snow."

"Snow who?"

"It's snow use. I can't stop thinking about you."

Okay, so it took her off guard. Made her belly laugh out loud in front of everyone at the bar. Which is *so* unlike her.

Xavier has no issues with self-confidence. He has no problem looking silly, even in public, which is a refreshing change from some of the assholes she's hooked up with.

She guesses it's hard to get embarrassed when you're six feet four and 250 pounds of sheer muscle. No one's going to call you out unless they're looking for a fight.

He's also a cuddler, which she didn't expect. Val finds she doesn't mind being swamped by the weight of his massive arms. It's kind of endearing, even though she probably wouldn't admit it to her friends.

He has her locked in a hug right now, his upper half wrapped around her waist with one of his legs stacked on top of her. Xavier won't let go. It's as if he doesn't want her to get away, even for a second.

The scruff of his facial hair scratches the side of her cheek, but surprisingly, she doesn't mind. She might even like it.

Val tries sliding out of his tight grip, which is as difficult as it sounds. She's going to have to wake him up.

She can't tell how late it is yet, but they have an early roll call for hair and makeup, and the sun is already shining.

There's no response. "Xavier, you gotta wake up," Val says.

Nothing. Val puts all her strength into her right arm to push him. "Xavier!" she yells. He grunts, but doesn't stir. Absently, she wonders how much he can bench press.

It's time for drastic measures. She pinches the soft area of his tricep. He yelps. "Hey!"

Finally. "Morning," Val says brightly. His eyes are starting to open.

"Mmmm," Xavier says sleepily. "It's not morning yet. A few more minutes." He nudges her cheek again.

"No, it really is morning. And I think we're seriously late."

"Five more minutes," he counters.

"Come on, big guy. We gotta get up. We're going to miss the conference."

Xavier finally rolls over, taking his gigantic arm off her. Instantly, she misses the warmth of his body. Until he picks her up and brings her on top of his chest.

"Screw the conference," Xavier says. "I can think of better things to do." He pulls her down for a kiss. Normally, she hates morning breath. But he is so damn sexy that she doesn't mind it one bit.

Honestly, no one would be surprised if Val were late. She has a long history of blowing off important events. Why should she turn over a new leaf now?

He looks so good, too. Her gentle giant. They've exchanged messages a few times since the wedding, but haven't been able to see each other in person.

When will they get this kind of chance again? She'll probably never see him. As a stuntman for different productions, Xavier zigzags all over the country, depending on where and when the studio needs him.

Still, Val is under contract. And she has bills to pay. Not to mention, a persistent blackmailer who won't leave her alone.

It's enough to make a girl want to stay in bed all day. Even with all of their obligations. She makes one last, valiant effort to get up and do the right thing.

"Xavier, we have to go. Do you think we'll get in trouble for being late?' Val asks. She's not sure if there's much concern in her voice.

He makes her feel so good about herself. What would he do if she told him her secrets? Showed him the side of herself she kept hidden? Would he still look at her the same?

"Who cares," Xavier responds, nuzzling her neck. "I want to spend more time with you. In this big bed." His hand moves down to her underwear, which is all she's wearing at the moment. He's warm and snuggly. Her resolve fades.

"I mean, you're not wrong," Val smiles sleepily. "One hour." She shifts to give him better access.

Xavier smiles back. "Deal."

They miss the entire day.

Chapter 36

"I will never forgive you, ever. Don't try to get me to ever talk to you again. The door is closed from now on."
- Eve to Francesca, Season 3, Episode 9

Josie, August 1

Josie stares out at the water from the balcony of her hotel room. The million-dollar view should feel peaceful, but she can't relax.

It was a stroke of luck that there had been a last-minute cancellation at The Reeds and she had been able to book a luxury suite. Otherwise, nothing would have been available during the peak of summer.

There was no way Josie could stand to stay and look Paige in the face every morning, much less share a room with her. She was never going back to the Elliot house. Between Val lying to the press and Paige's confession, Josie is done with both of them.

If she hadn't signed an extensive contract to do this reunion, she would have already left Avalon and Stone Harbor behind. But legally, she's stuck for a couple more days, forced to keep seeing them in public.

Every time she tries to think of something else, Josie's mind goes right back to the betrayal. She feels like she's spiraling. She doesn't know how to come to terms with the idea that her both her "friends" would do this to her.

She's too angry to cry, she tells herself, as the tears fall down her face.

Paige DeBello. Josie has known her for nearly 15 years. Had been unbelievably proud of her friend for cleaning herself up, getting help with her addiction issues, and facing years of control issues with her mom.

She was practically the only one from their cast who was still acting and auditioning for roles, which Josie had felt was admirable. Paige just kept chipping away, giving it her best while waiting for her next big break.

To think that she'd been so gullible! She trusted Paige with all her secrets, when this whole time, she was working to sabotage both Josie's career *and* her personal life. Not because she had ever done anything to Paige, but because she had simply been in the way of what her friend wanted.

She doesn't see how she can ever forgive Paige. Their friendship is over, especially considering Paige never fessed up, keeping her nasty secret for all these years.

The news makes Josie reconsider the ending of her relationship with Tate. Looking back, it *had* seemed so out of character for him. She thought they were head over heels in love—completely smitten with each other.

Josie was so young then. She was full of insecurities from having her face and her body judged by the public, people she never even met. They all had an opinion on the level of her talent, making her think her fame was too soon, too much. Unearned by someone who didn't really deserved it.

Even with all the smoke and mirrors, it's good to realize that what Josie had experienced with Tate was real, until it all blew up.

When she tried reaching out to him, Tate had brushed her off. All she remembers was him saying that he was too busy to talk. His responses were so cold that she eventually turned away, too, and left him on read.

To think, that all along, Tate had been feeling the same way. They'd both been too proud (or young) to show up in person and talk it out. So they let the gulf between them deepen until it became too wide to bridge.

Josie remembers one of the final days of filming, when Tate had caught up to her and tried to talk. After days of brooding, she told him to go away. It was another decade before she saw him again.

There's a knock on her door.

Josie goes back inside the room to check and see who's there. It better not be Paige.

She peeks through the eye hole. There's no way she's opening the door.

"Open up, doll."

It's Mason. How had he found her? He must have called all the hotels in the area until he discovered where she was staying.

Why doesn't he leave her alone? He must know she doesn't want to talk to anyone right now.

"Josie!" He knocks louder. "I know you're in there!"

She knows how Mason is. He's not going to stop until she answers. The guy won't be ignored. Giving in she, turns the lock and opens the door. He walks right past her into the hotel room.

Josie sighs, turning to him with her arms crossed. "What are you doing here, Mason?"

"I came here for you." He takes in her tear-stained face and gives her a peck on the check. "You need a shoulder to cry on, Jo. Let's talk about it."

"I'm completely done with them. I'm never talking to Val and Paige again," she sniffs.

"I get that. But give it some time," Mason tells her. "You just found out. Let it settle for a bit."

"Is that what you're asking me to do?" Josie asks. "Just let it go?"

"Not at all. I'm just asking you to give it some time before you say or do anything you'll regret."

"Did you tell Tate?"

"Not yet. I wanted to talk to you first."

That makes her feel a little better, that he came to her. But she's still angry. "As long as you don't try to calm me down. I'm freaking pissed."

"I don't blame you. Honey, I'd be just as mad at Paige."

"Really?"

"Of course. So, can I stay? Keep you company?" Mason wanders over to the mini-bar and grabs two glasses. "We can get drunk on airplane bottles of booze."

Josie relents. He's too adorable to say no to, especially with his big mustache. "Only if you promise not to talk about them."

"Deal."

They order room service—margaritas, guac, and chips—and when those are finished, order another round of drinks.

Josie turned off her phone hours ago. When she finally turns it back on, she deletes multiple voicemails from Justin, Val, and Paige. The only message she's interested in hearing is the one from Quinn.

She immediately calls him back, despite Mason's warning her about the dangers of drunk dialing (as if she didn't know). He hands her a bottle of water instead of a drink.

"I wanted to see if you were still up for meeting me tonight," Quinn says.

How could she not? Josie tries to keep it casual. "If you're free."

"Absofuckinglutely. Do you like sailing?"

"Who doesn't?"

"Meet me at the Stone Harbor Yacht Club. Near the docks. I'll be there before six."

Mason hovers near her phone as he tries to listen in. Josie pushes his head away and turns her attention back to Quinn. "I'll be there."

Mason gives Josie a knowing smile. "Are you seeing my potential trophy husband?" He sighs, but she can tell it's not serious.

"I'm calling dibs."

"Fine," Mason says as he refills Josie's glass with another pour of whiskey from the bar. "Leave me here, bored. But when you get back from your date, you have to tell me *everything*."

Chapter 37

Tate, August 2

Someone is banging on his front door. Reluctantly, Tate gets out of bed to answer it. Mason is standing on his doorstep. Without asking permission, he steps inside.

"Come with me, we're getting coffee," Mason tells him.

Groaning, Tate looks at his watch. "It's 6 am."

"Doesn't matter." Mason collapses on the couch. "It's important."

It looks like he doesn't have much choice. "Give me five minutes."

He throws some clothes on, and they walk over to Mason's car, which is parked out front. Tate is too tired to even ask where they're going. He leans his head back as they drive down Dune Street.

They're about to begin the second full day of the reunion. After yesterday's meet and greets, guests have registered for individual panels about various topics featuring their favorite actors and crew members as special guest speakers.

The cast and crew seemed happy getting together with each other after all these years. Sure, there were side conversations and eye rolls from a few people, but they managed to grin and bear it for the most part.

Funny enough, the guy who owned the hotel and the house they were renting stuck around for most of the time. Roger Elliot seemed besotted by Elise DeLonghi, who played Josie's mom on the show.

Josie's "dad," Marty, was there, too. It was cool catching up with the "TV parents" and seeing what they were doing.

"Did you get that shot?" Marty kept asking the photographers. He made sure he was in as many of the photos as possible. Tate remembers that he always loved the spotlight.

Marty also spent a little too much time with the younger female fans, something Tate remembered him doing a decade ago as well. It was a little gross, to be honest. Marty's date looked young enough to be his daughter.

There were a few actors who couldn't make the reunion. Scotty, the actor who played his brother, was out of the country working on a documentary. Tate hadn't seen him for years. And Josie's "sister" Becky was missing as well.

A few guest actors had shown up to fill the gaps. They had played smaller roles, such as a potential love interest or rival, in some of the show's episodes. Tate got to reconnect with the guy who played Zad, one of the short-term boyfriends. It was great to catch up, but it wore him out.

"Where we're going–will there at least be coffee?" Tate asks.

"There will be," Mason confirms.

He pulls up to Isabel's, a small bakery and cafe on 22nd Street. Dark green awnings frame the windows, and a white wrought-iron fence surrounds tables on the brick patio. It's still early enough in the morning that there isn't much foot traffic yet. They park the car and walk inside.

"What can I get you to eat?" Mason asks.

Tate stares at the shelves lined with baked goods. The cinnamon crumb buns look incredible, but he'd better keep his sugar levels steady. "I'll have a breakfast sandwich with egg whites," he orders instead.

He grabs his glucometer from his pants pocket and checks his blood sugar. Yeah, he's in a higher range than he should be. Tate grabs a bottle of orange juice from the fridge and chugs it. Instantly, he's feeling better.

"Let's get a seat." Mason gestures to a table. They sit down as they wait for their food to arrive.

"So what's going on? Why did you get me out of bed so early?"

Mason stretches out his legs and takes a huge yawn. "I know, it's so damn early. I needed to get you alone."

"For what?" Tate has a feeling he's not going to like what Mason is about to say.

"Did you hear anything about what went down at the beach house last night?"

"No," Tate answers. "I've been trying to avoid any of the drama that usually follows this crowd."

"I hate having to tell you this." Mason pauses before continuing, "Paige made a big confession to Josie. She told Josie how much she's always resented her. So much, apparently, that Paige got Josie kicked off the show."

Tate scoffs. "There's no way. They wouldn't have had the show without Josie."

"I agree," Mason answers. "But Paige was savvy. She told Bryce and Simon that Josie was offered a big movie role and was leaving after the season. It's why they decided to wrap everything up so quickly, before the news broke."

"How would a teenager have done that much damage? They never would have fallen for that."

"I guess she used fake emails, and they thought they were talking to her agent. She was clever. And it was a decade ago. I feel like it was easier to impersonate people then. Log in to an email or open a phone."

Tate sits back. "Holy shit. I knew Paige had her issues, but that's another level."

They're interrupted by the arrival of their food.

"Eat up," Mason tells him. He takes a bite of his bagel and keeps talking. "Remember how Simon wrote such abrupt endings for our characters?"

Their lead writer had drafted a finale for the show that had the characters going in all different directions. They got a lot of bad reviews for their series finale. Some of the story lines seemed rushed or pretty unbelievable.

In the last episode, Jack and Eve started college still together, but ended up breaking up. Chase and Shea had the happy ending: they went off to separate schools, but rekindled and moved to Duffy Beach after graduation. Francesca had moved to New York to pursue her dreams. It all wrapped up quickly.

"I guess so. I just went along with what Bryce told us to say. We didn't have much contact with the network executives." They were so young that the adults handled everything.

"Yeah, our agents did all of that," Mason says. "I don't think I ever talked to a single person at LJC."

Tate pauses to consider. "My parents were going through their own stuff, so they just went along with what I told them I wanted. So, Paige was the reason the show ended?"

"I'm actually impressed," Mason responds. "I didn't know the girl had it in her." He shoots Tate a look. "Are you ready for the kicker?"

"I'm not sure."

"She's also the reason you and Josie broke up. She pretended to be

Josie, sent you texts, then deleted your calls and responses on Josie's phone so you never got them. She was always on set with Josie. It wasn't hard to get access to her phone when she was filming."

"No way." This was insane. Tate honestly can't believe what he's hearing. "There's no chance. Why would she do that?"

"Because she wanted Josie gone. She needed her out of there. And she would have stayed for you."

"That can't be right. Josie ignored me. She was the one who ended things."

"And Josie thought you were acting odd. I guess it snowballed from there."

Tate doesn't know what to think. But so many things fall into place— Josie blowing him off, telling him she needed space. Not answering his calls, giving him so many mixed signals. When he'd see her in person, she'd act affectionate, but then she was a completely different person over the phone. And then she just left the show and never responded to his emails.

It had been Paige. Tate didn't know how she managed it, but she had.

There are no words for how he's feeling right now. Looking down, Tate stares at his hands, which are shaking, from anger or being upset, he doesn't know.

All these years. All this wasted time. It wasn't about him and Josie, and what went wrong. It was about Paige wanting to be a bigger star.

Mason has been watching him cautiously. Finally, he reaches over and puts his hand on Tate's leg.

"You okay, buddy? I know this is a lot to take in."

"I can't believe it … I really can't."

"I know you're upset, but it's been so long. You and Josie haven't talked in years."

"But we could have. All this time, I thought she wanted nothing to do with me. That I did something wrong." Tate pauses. "I thought she was leaving the show so she wouldn't have to see me again."

Even now, after all this time, Tate still can't get over how betrayed he'd felt. The lack of closure has haunted him in every relationship he's ever been in, with every person he's gotten close to.

There's always the doubt in the back of his mind that they'll walk away from him as Josie did.

"What did Josie do when Paige told her?" Tate can't imagine it went over well. One of her good friends trashed her career and her first relationship, and then kept it a secret from her for so many years.

"She's not staying at the Elliot spread, if that's what you're asking." Mason answers. He shifts in his seat and sits up. " She got a room somewhere else for the rest of the reunion."

Tate can't blame Josie for wanting to leave the mansion. "Do you have her number? I know it's not the same one I used to use." Stalkers make changing numbers a frequent hazard in the celebrity biz.

"I'll give it to you. I just have to clear it with her first." Mason looks right in Tate's eyes. "You okay?"

"Define okay. But yeah, I'm fine. Just want to get this day over with." They have the breakout panel sessions today, and then the final day tomorrow, followed by the farewell party.

"Only a couple more days, and you never have to see these assholes again," says Mason.

"You'll stick with me? I don't feel like dealing with Paige."

"Don't worry. She's in another panel with Marty and Elise," Mason answers. "I'll run interference for you, too."

Tate knows how lucky he is to have Mason as a friend. Especially knowing how many people live to bring you down. Mason has always been there.

He chugs the rest of his drink. "Let's get this day over with."

Chapter 38

"Why does everyone always listen to the mean girls?"
- Hazel, Season 1, Episode 3

Val, August 2

Val strides into the conference room. "Did I miss anything?" she asks. Tate and Mason are looking way too serious for an audience participation session.

"You have no idea," Mason answers dryly. He pats the seat next to him. "Come and spill what you've been up to."

"I'm not gonna lie, spending time with the stuntman was worth it. Although I missed my boys." She plops down on the chair.

"Bragger." But Mason says it with a smile.

Val scans Tate briefly. He doesn't look well. It doesn't seem like he's shaved this morning. His face is drawn, and his jaw is clenched. His leg bounces up and down, up and down, without him seeming to realize he's moving his body.

"Are you feeling okay?" Val asks. "Is it your blood sugar?" Tate's diabetes isn't something he advertises, but she knows it's something he navigates daily. Stress, long days, and late nights are probably not helping things.

Tate smiles tightly. "I feel fine."

"You don't *look* fine."

"We should all hope to look as fine as Tate does on his off days." Mason jumps in to ease the awkwardness.

"So true." Val drops it. They obviously don't want to talk about it, whatever it is. "What's the title of this panel again? I can't remember what we're supposed to talk about."

Val has participated in a few of these panels in the past. Some have been absolutely hilarious. The moderator usually starts on topic, gets inundated with questions about the actors' personal lives, and loses complete control of the session. Honestly, Val thinks the panels can be absolutely hilarious sometimes. The things people say. The stories the cast hears.

"Love triangles. Even though there are four parts: you and me, Tate and Josie," Mason responds. He quirks his head at Val. "Too soon?"

The reference to their media blitz isn't lost on Val. Of course, Mason would be the one to bring that up. "Screw you, Mason. We resolved it."

"I'm sure our little Jo Jo feels great about that," Mason says with a smirk.

"If we're doing love triangles, why isn't Paige here?"

"She's doing the 'Career in Film' panel with Marty and Elise. We don't have the same tenure as she does. They've all been acting for decades."

"Don't tell Elise that. She still thinks she's 30."

"That second face-lift really helped."

"Meow." Val does love it when Mason is catty ... as long as it's about someone else. It's one of his most endearing traits.

Mason shrugs. "I call it how I see it. I can't wait for Simon to start giving a Venn diagram of how he charted our relationship story arcs."

Val snorts. "No one takes the show as seriously as Simon." It had defined his career.

"Where's Josie? It's about to start." She hasn't seen Josie—or anyone else—since before her date with Xavier. You're bound to miss some things when you're in bed all day—not that she regrets one second with Xavier.

They had spent hours talking, spilling secrets, and being honest with each other. She told him about her experiences on the show.

"I did a lot of dumb things," Val shared. It was her biggest shame. "I had an affair with an older actor."

He was completely supportive. "Everyone does dumb things," Xavier answered. "Don't beat yourself up over it."

"We used to meet at the Avalon Fishing Pier. We'd have sex in the dunes under the pier late at night." She didn't disclose who it had been (she wasn't *that* naive), but she did give Xavier details about how their relationship started. How he had complimented her so often that she believed him, until she finally began to fall for him."

"He took advantage of you," Xavier says bluntly.

"I was old enough to know better."

"He groomed you," Xavier told her. He made her look at the situation differently. And he listened intently to everything Val had to say, without being put off by anything she told him. It was a heady experience. He made her feel good about herself.

"Knock, knock."

"Who's there?"

"Wendy."

"Wendy who?"

"Wendy-ya think we can go on a date?"

Val laughed, but Xavier had been serious. He really wanted to go out on an official date with her, even after they had slept together. How could she say no?

In fact, they have plans for a romantic dinner tonight. Thinking about it makes her shiver. He told her she'd be the dessert …

Val notices Mason shoot Tate a look and is brought back to reality. She pounces on it. "Honestly, what is going on? You guys are acting so weird."

"Just tell her," Tate says to Mason.

"Remember how Jo and I just broke up out of nowhere? It was Paige."

Val shakes her head in complete disbelief. "I don't believe it."

"Well, she did. She said she was tired of feeling like second best."

"The final straw was when she was replaced on the cover of some teen magazine by Josie," Mason adds. "She was apparently really good at faking email addresses and using phones that were lying around."

Her stomach drops. "I can't believe Paige is capable of inflicting that much damage."

"Well, she did. She finally confessed. That's why Josie's not staying at the house anymore."

"That is so messed up. And also impressive, quite frankly," she blurts out loud without thinking. Privately, it does make her feel a little bit better about her own secrets. Maybe she's not the worst person there.

"I know, right?" Mason responds with a wry laugh. "I didn't think she was smart enough. Nasty enough, sure. But to keep it going all these years?"

"Gee, thanks, guys. I'm glad you're entertained by it," Tate mutters.

"Sorry." Val puts her hands up. " Everyone has done something terrible at some point. Although even I have to say this is bad."

Val should know. If she ever stops paying her blackmailer and anyone finds out what she's done, her career will be over, too. "The question is, will Josie show up?"

"I think so. She's a pro." The door opens, and they all turn to see who's there.

It's not Josie. It's Sage, who's moderating the event. "Good morning, guys!" She flashes them a bright smile as she makes her way to the podium and makes adjustments to lower the microphone to her height.

They wait.

By the time guests start filing in, there's still no sign of Josie. It isn't like her to be a no-show. They still have a few minutes before the panel is supposed to start.

There's an empty seat with Josie's name on it, right between Mason and Tate.

Sage looks towards them with her eyebrows raised, as if to ask what she should do. As the moderator, she needs to get the event started on time.

She starts talking. "Welcome, everyone. We're so glad you're here." She keeps talking, but Val is too stressed to listen.

A few minutes in, Josie casually strolls in and takes her seat. Val sees a thrill go through the crowd, as if Josie's late arrival had been part of the plan all along. Audience members murmur to each other.

Val tries getting Josie's attention from one seat over, but she folds her arms and won't make eye contact. In a sleeveless navy maxi dress and stacked heels, with her mane of blonde hair in a chic bun, she looks formidable.

Josie doesn't look at Mason or Tate either; she just stares straight ahead into the crowd. A fake smile is plastered across her glossy lips.

Val can tell Josie is pissed, but keeping it professional. What a pro. Val suddenly starts to feel sorry for Paige. She messed with the wrong person.

"Can I get everyone's attention?" Sage taps the mic. The audience begins to calm down. "Thanks for coming out. We have a lot of topics to cover, so we need to get started."

"Are Francesca and Jake really together?" a fan shouts from the back of the crowd.

Sage looks annoyed. "Please, no questions until the end."

"That rumor was never true!" Val responds, shaking her head. Why did people always want to hear the bad news?

"Are Eve and Jake together then?"

"Absolutely not," Josie answers.

Sage shoots them both a look. "Let's stay on track. We're going to go over a set of questions and answers, and then open it up to the floor. Please respect the process." That finally shuts the crowd up, and Sage begins with her first question.

This is going to be fun, Val thinks to herself.

She can't wait for it to be over with.

Chapter 39

"You really know how to show a girl a bad time."
- Francesca to Jack, Season 2, Episode 1

Paige, August 2

The first fist doesn't land, but the second one does.

SMACK. Right into Marty's face. His neck snaps back, a stream of blood running down his mouth from being struck.

Marty tries to defend himself by putting up his arms, but he has no shot against his huge opponent. He gets punched again.

There are high-pitched screams from teenagers in the audience.

"Ahhh! It's a fight!" a young girl shouts.

"What the hell!" a dad yells.

"Run!"

Frantic guests rush out of the conference room, damaging furniture and dropping their belongings on the way. Some guests bolt, running outside to get away from the mayhem. Others stay, out of a desire to help or morbid curiosity, Paige doesn't know.

It came out of nowhere. The title of their panel was "A Career in Film." It was being led by the director, Bryce, and the main screenwriter, Simon. They were supposed to talk about what it was like to have a long career in Hollywood and how things have changed over the years.

Perched on chairs with mics in their hands, Paige, Elise, and Marty had been answering questions from Simon and the audience.

The panel started completely normally. Boring, actually. A few superfans who wanted to wax nostalgic about classic TV shows, and others who loved seeing Marty or Elise on older 70s sitcoms.

Elise, as cool as a Hitchcock heroine, is talking about how she's managed to keep booking shows ten years after the series ended. She's been extremely savvy in navigating her career. She's aloof, not giving much away, but Paige is sure that she's seen a lot. She doesn't have time for bullshit.

Marty is a lot more outgoing. Throughout the reunion, he's been constantly putting his arm around fans and posing for photos and autographs. There were a few fans from Marty's big movie break, where he played a kid from the other side of the tracks in love with Miley McCallister, the screen siren. It earned him an Oscar nod.

Paige answers questions about her early days of acting, when she copied Shirley Temple's playbook as a precocious young girl. She also describes what it was like filming *The Shallows*. "It was an experience unlike any other," she tells them. "I don't know if I'll ever be a part of something as big again."

Most questions had been what you would expect to be asked: "What was Hollywood life like?" "How many times did you audition before you got a part?" "What's the craziest thing you've experienced?"

Your basic, everyday questions for a Q&A discussion.

Until today, Paige would have said having a dog cast as her romantic co-star was memorable. But now, it would be seeing Marty Lawson have his face punched in by Xavier the stuntman.

Paige saw Xavier in the audience. He's sitting off to the side, his large frame dwarfing the folding chair. It doesn't even seem like he was listening to their conversation very closely.

Marty cracked a joke, saying something about spending nights underneath the Avalon Fishing Pier. "I had lots of fond memories with a special someone," he smirked.

That's all it took before Xavier leaped out from the audience and flew up the aisle, knocking over chairs to get on stage. He pulled Marty up from his seat by his jacket. The rest was chaos as fans screamed and ran out, except for the few who came closer to take photos.

Marty is probably five feet ten, maybe five feet eleven, but he's not built. He's got your classic dad bod. Xavier is six feet two and ripped.

It's no contest.

The older actor tries anyway, slapping Xavier's face with as much force as he can muster. "Get off me!" Marty shouts, struggling to pull free.

"It was you! You asshole!" Xavier yells. "Pedophile *prick*."

Marty slaps Xavier away again, which sets Xavier off. He cuffs him again, right across the face.

Quinn comes to the rescue, leaping on stage and grabbing Xavier. He puts him in a choke-hold to keep him off Marty, giving the actor a chance to break free.

"Easy," Quinn struggles to keep a grip on Xavier. "Take it easy."

"You have no idea what he's done," Xavier pants.

"Doesn't mean you should have hauled your ass up here like that."

Snap! Snap! Paige is sure the photos are going to be all over social media. It will undoubtedly make the event promoters happy.

More security guards rush in to control the situation. Former stunt double Chuck Pencha is in the mix, too.

"Get him out of here!" the guards yell. Paige watches as Stone Harbor Police officers arrive and take Xavier out in handcuffs.

The only weapon the stunt double had was his fists, but the guy sure could use them.

Marty is panting heavily, his shirt covered in blood. Someone hands him a towel, which he takes gratefully as he wipes his face.

The man is the epitome of the suburban father. A nice, middle-aged actor who's been playing a caring dad for decades. What could he have possibly done to make Xavier go after him?

Paige is shocked. She turns on her heel and heads backstage to an area that's been sectioned off as a dressing room.

She needs to decompress. Paige wishes she could talk to Josie about it, but Josie still won't even look at her. It's all Paige's fault.

She feels like she's going to be sick. As she rummages in her bag for a mint or granola bar, Paige wishes she had a dime bag of blow to help ease the edges. Make things less stressful, even if just for a little bit.

Who could she call for a hit? She doesn't know anyone in this area. She starts to sweat, the nausea and anxiety threatening to overwhelm her. She needs to get out of here. She doesn't even care what happened at the panel. She just needs to get away.

Tonight's dinner won't help. Most of the cast is meeting up at *The Crew Room* tonight. It's the second-floor space above *The Stone Harbor Pizza Pub.* They have the whole upstairs rented out.

She doesn't think she has it in her to see everyone after the long day today. And she doesn't need the snide comments. Paige isn't sure who else knows the truth of what she did.

She has wished for years that she could take it all back, although it's obviously too late. They're all going to hate her for ruining the world they created, simply because she was being a petty, shallow brat.

There's a knock on the door. "Miss DeBello? Is everything okay?"

"I'm fine, thank you." At least someone is worried about her. She has no idea who it is, and she's not about to come out. "I just need a few minutes." She pops a mint in her mouth, wishing it were something else.

Paige needs some time to decide what she's going to do next. Is the reunion still on? Things are unraveling rapidly.

Chapter 40

"Just shut up and kiss me."
- Eve to Jack, Season 4, Episode 9 (Season Finale)

Josie, August 2

Josie's Uber pulls up to the address Quinn gave her. His apartment is above a boutique clothing store on one of the main business streets in Avalon. At seven, the sun is starting to make its way below the horizon, sending streaks of pink across the water.

She had texted him as soon as the conference wrapped up: *What are you up to tonight?*

Whatever you're doing, he had replied.

With all the drama going on, Josie feels she should really be talking to her cast mates and getting to the bottom of why everything was burning down. Why did Val lie about her and Tate being a couple? What made Xavier attack Marty on stage? And seriously, what the hell was wrong with Paige?

She knows she probably should be with all of them, but she doesn't have it in her. They can all duke it out at the cast dinner at the pizza pub tonight. Argue, explain, make up. Do whatever they need to get through the next few days. Josie can't make herself go.

She only wants to see Quinn. Hear his sharp bark of a laugh, see the dimples in his cheeks when he smiles. The dimples only show up in the big grins, not the ones he granted others when he was working or being polite.

Jo loves it when she can make them come out. When he gives her the full shine of his smile. It's only been one day, and she already misses it.

The night before, Quinn had shown her his version of Stone Harbor. They'd taken his boat out on the water a couple of hours before sunset, where they navigated the marshes, thoroughfares, and water channels.

Waves from the wakes of other boats rocked them as they flew past orange buoys and bird nests on top of piers. Josie wore a striped, oversized sweater and jean shorts. Perched on a cushioned seat next to Quinn, the wind blowing her hair, the grin on her face said it all.

He showed her areas that only locals would know about. He took her past a long row of houses that had been abandoned and were slowly deteriorating into the water. On the way back, they docked at The Lazy Bass for cocktails.

Josie asked a million questions: "How do you use the radar?" "What does that sign mean?" "Why is that marker red?"

Quinn answered them all. What he didn't know, he promised to find out. "You'll have to meet Tyson," he said. In his best friend's role at the Stone Harbor Yacht Club, Tyson was an expert on everything water-related.

"I'd love that," Josie had said. It was a promise she meant to keep. Because she can't wait to do it again.

If she were honest, she was developing a major crush. She couldn't wait to spend time with him again.

He was the perfect company. It seemed like he just wanted to be there, with her. The real Josie, not her character Eve. He didn't ask her for anything but her time.

Quinn opens the door before she even makes her way to the top of the stairs and pulls her in for a hug. "Hey, pretty girl," he says over her head.

Josie squeezes him back tightly. This. Yes, *this* is what she needed. A landing point. Understanding. Acceptance. It doesn't even feel strange that they are so comfortable with each other after only meeting a couple of times.

He lets go, and Josie follows him inside. His place isn't big, but it's neat and welcoming. An L-shaped couch lines the wall with a big screen TV over a fireplace. The navy kitchen has a long white counter with wicker cast mates. There's a hallway most likely leading to a bedroom and bathroom.

"Glass of wine?" Quinn asks.

"I'd love one."

"Coming right up."

Josie sinks into the couch. Quinn hands her a glass, then sits, leaving space between them.

Josie sidles over to him without asking for permission. She doesn't want that extra space.

She doesn't know why, but she doesn't feel any reserve with Quinn. She knows he likes her. He knows she likes him. There's no need for any pretenses.

He picks up his arm and drapes it around her. He's drinking something dark. She leans in to sniff it.

Whiskey. It smells sharp, with notes of cinnamon.

Quinn looks down at her and grins. "Want some?" The dimples appear.

Josie couldn't stop herself if she wanted to. She leans in for a kiss. His mouth tastes like whiskey, smoky with a bite of pepper. It's intoxicating.

She needs to get closer. Putting down her glass, she shifts to straddle him without breaking their kiss.

Quinn's hands cradle both sides of her face, pulling her closer before sliding back into her hair. His mouth tilts, doing incredible things with his tongue. She aches for more.

Josie is drawn into his spell, the hold he has over her. She feels him growing hard under her. All she has on is a pair of jean shorts and a camisole. There's a lot of skin available for him to explore. He does so, carefully and confidently, guiding his hands up her sides.

Where did he put his drink? Josie thinks hazily. He must have put it down without her noticing. Those clever hands. They move faster than you'd expect.

"Josie," Quinn says gruffly. It's a warning or an invitation. She's not sure which. "God, you're amazing."

"Same goes," she pants. Quinn's fingers slip under her shirt, touching the lace of her bra. He looks to her again for permission. Josie nods. "Yes. Please, yes."

Then his hands, those remarkable hands, pull off her shirt, and his mouth is on her breast, taking and tasting, giving and getting.

It's not fair. Quinn still has too much clothing on. She grabs his shirt and pulls it over his head.

Dear God, his abs. He must spend all of his free time doing sit-ups. Like a full-time job working out. She thanks her lucky stars.

He picks her up effortlessly, and her legs wrap around his waist. Then he carries her down the long hallway to a bedroom.

Josie can't see anything but Quinn. He's taken all of her senses: touch and smell, taste and hearing. Any semblance of thought is gone.

"I want you," Josie tells Quinn. "All of you."

"Are you sure?"

"Absolutely."

They shed the last of their clothes. She falls to the bed, and he covers her body. She feels small in comparison.

She gasps when he enters her. "Are you okay? Did I hurt you?" He looks worried.

"Don't stop."

Quinn groans. "As if I could." He nuzzles her neck, granting her silent request to speed up, matching her rhythm. Giving her what she wants, what's she begging for. He's been patient so far, but she can feel he's losing his self-control.

"Take me over the edge."

Quinn does, all through the night. Again and again, until they're both spent and exhausted. It simply sweeps her away.

Nothing else has come close. And in the morning, she wakes up to him making banana pancakes. Something she had mentioned on their date, in passing, as her favorite breakfast.

Between the whiskey last night and the pancakes this morning, Josie realizes the smell of cinnamon will remind her of Quinn. She rolls over, holding the blanket to her chest, listening to him move around his kitchen.

One more day of the conference. And then what?

Josie is not going to think of that yet. She's just going to enjoy the pancakes.

Chapter 41

"If it doesn't affect me, I don't care."
- Chase, Season 4, Episode 5

Mason, August 3

"Hold on a second," Mason says calmly from the kitchen of the beach house. "You said your part. Now, let him speak."

"I'm not going to give that prick the time of day!" Val shouts. "He ruined *everything*!"

"I get it," Mason answers. He's trying desperately to control the situation. "But we haven't heard his side of it."

"I don't give a damn what he has to say! Why would you believe anything that came out of his mouth?"

"Which has been nothing so far, because of you," Mason answers good-naturedly. Come on, Val. Let him talk."

"Do you want him to tell you how he paid me to act like I was with Tate? Because that's exactly what he did. Ten grand." Her eyes flash in anger. Something else is there, too. Fear? Hurt?

Mason wonders what else Val has to hide. She's always been wily. "See, that's what I mean. Let's get it all out."

"Fine, be an asshole. But I won't be here to listen to it. I'm going to visit Xavier." She stalks out of the kitchen. He hears the door slam.

"What's going on?" Paige asks as she comes down the stairs. "I heard yelling."

Bryce is right behind her. "Was that Val?"

"Briefly," Justin picks up his cup of coffee. "Luckily, she just left."

Mason rubs his eyes. It's only seven in the morning, and he's already exhausted. He grabbed Justin and brought him to the kitchen for an explanation. Or confrontation, whatever you want to call it.

They were talking when Val joined them downstairs. She was on her way out the door to visit her new boyfriend in jail.

"I'm glad you guys are here," Mason tells them. "It's time we all had a talk."

If anyone knows any secrets about this crew, it's Justin. The agent has a knack for either knowing or finding out.

Val might be gone, but at least Justin, Bryce, and Paige are still here. Sleepy, but present.

No one can get hold of Josie.

It's past time for an explanation of all the stuff that was going on. Why Xavier attacked Marty, how much Justin knows about Paige sabotaging the show, and why Justin paid Val to pretend to be in a relationship with Tate.

They need to stop keeping all the secrets. It's confession time. If they just get it all out, then they can figure out where to go from here.

Mason had tried to see what Val knew, but that obviously hadn't panned out. It's time to see what he can get from Justin.

He forges ahead. "It's time for you to come clean, Justin. We know you have a hand in what's been going on. Let's hear it."

"I don't know what you're talking about." The agent sits on a stool at the expansive kitchen counter with his arms crossed and a smirk on his face.

"As Val so graciously told us, you paid her ten grand to say she was with Tate."

"That's business. It gave this event free press."

He's such an asshole. "Noted. Can we talk about what happened last night? I was interviewed by the police, too. I saw you leaving the station at the same time. You were in there a lot longer than I was."

"They just wanted to know how to be an extra."

He's such a prick. This isn't going to be straightforward. And they don't have much time—less than an hour and a half before they need to be back at the hotel for photos and autographs.

"What do you know about the fight yesterday?"

"Nothing." Justin shrugs.

"Why would this guy try to attack Marty? I don't think he ever met him before."

Mason hasn't expected any response, but for some reason, Justin looks surprised. Caught off-guard, as if that wasn't the question he thought Mason was going to ask. "Because he took advantage of Val when she was a teen. You didn't know?"

Bryce drops the mug of coffee he's drinking. "WHAT? During my show?

"Yep." Justin casually takes a sip of his coffee, as if he didn't drop a bomb.

"There's no way. We would never have let that happen," Bryce exclaims. "We had guardians on set to watch over all of the kids."

"Apparently, they weren't very good," Justin replies flippantly. "Marty took Val's virginity. Right there under the Avalon fishing pier."

So that's why Xavier attacked Marty. Val must have told him about what happened. It was crazy that she never confided in anyone else, especially Paige or Josie.

"Paige, did you know anything about this?"

Paige shakes her head. "No way. I mean, I know they used to hang out sometimes. But I thought it was a father/daughter thing. They were more than 20 years apart. Yuck."

Mason couldn't agree more. Marty Lawson is America's dad. An icon. He's been on sitcoms for decades, giving fatherly advice alongside laugh tracks.

To think he had been taking advantage of young actresses is sickening.

"Have there ever been any whispers about him doing this?"

"Not that I'm aware of," says Justin. "There was a flare-up a long time ago—we're talking 20 years—about him and a young co-star, but it's just a rumor. I don't think it was ever verified." He pauses, considering. "That was on his old show, *Hutch Offline.*"

"Well, it's all coming out now," Mason replies.

"I remember Val was sneaking out to the pier with a guy, but I thought it was you," Paige says. "Didn't realize you were gay."

Mason laughs. "It wasn't me."

Bryce is frantically texting on his phone. He's probably contacting his PR crisis team right now. "How old was she?" he asks, typing quickly.

"Pretty sure she was legal, but barely," Justin answers. "I don't think he'd go to jail over it. But it will destroy his reputation."

"Oh, if that's all that is," Paige says sarcastically. "At least it wasn't breaking the law. You know, stealing the virginity of a teenager."

"I get how serious it was," Mason says calmly. "Do you remember anything from back then?"

"I can't say I do, but to be honest, I wasn't paying that much attention to anyone else," Paige admits. "I was too caught up in my own bullshit."

They all were. Poor Val. While they were wrapped up in their own drama, an older man was taking advantage of her.

At least someone did something. It can't help but make him respect Xavier. The guy might have chosen a less *violent and public* route, but he was standing up for his girl. Val could use someone in her corner.

Everyone goes silent, lost in their own thoughts.

Paige holds up her hand. "I have something to confess." She looks over at Mason guiltily.

Mason turns to her. "About breaking Tate and Josie up?"

She nods sheepishly. "So, you already heard. And getting the show canceled. More or less."

"Wait, what?" Bryce looks like he's about to faint. "Can someone fill me in?"

And they do, while Justin sits there smugly. Mason just knows he has more in his arsenal. He's a slimy, sketchy weasel who's been wreaking havoc throughout the industry for years without any repercussions.

It's past time he kept getting away with it. Before this weekend is over, Mason is going to make sure Justin's career is over, and his reputation is trashed.

Things are getting heated between Bryce and Paige. The director is not happy to learn he was tricked into ending one of his most successful shows ... especially by a kid.

Mason lets the conversation flow without interrupting. He knows he'll forgive Paige—it was so long ago—but that doesn't mean she's off the hook with everyone. She still needs to accept blame for blowing up people's lives for her selfish purposes.

It's one of the main reasons Paige has struggled her whole life. She kept getting second chances without realizing the grace she was given. She's going to need to earn it now.

The doorbell chimes, and Mason hurries to answer the front door.

Is Val back? This is going to get dicey.

But it's not Val. Not even close.

Kit is standing in the doorway. The familiar sight of those brown eyes and warm caramel skin that Mason has been missing like crazy. He's dressed all preppy, like he's going sailing, with a button-down, khakis, loafers, and a cable sweater tied across his broad shoulders.

Even better, the kids are with him. Maeve and Ivy, in the cutest little sundresses that Mason bought them over spring break.

Mason's face breaks into a wide, happy smile. "You guys!" He crosses over to squeeze his family in a solid embrace.

He grabs Maeve and plants a kiss on her cheek. "Daddy-O! Your mustache tickles!" She giggles.

"You love it." He looks at his family. "I can't believe you're here."

"We wouldn't be anywhere else," Kit smiles.

And suddenly, all is right in the world.

Chapter 42

"Can you believe she repeated that outfit?
Give me a break."
- Francesca, Season 3, Episode 9

Tate, August 3

Tate surveys the "selfie stations" set up around the ballroom. There are cordoned-off areas for attendees who pay extra to take photos with actors. The show's *Shallows* logo is splashed all over the room, from photo backdrops and huge signs to tables of overpriced hoodies and pieces of merch.

Tate bets they're making millions off this event. It makes him wonder just how much money the show's creators and producers have made on the show—and the actors—over the years. It must have been substantial.

Once the photo and autograph sessions end and the reunion wraps up, he hopes he never sees some of these people again. He had nearly been late, the chaotic conversation with Val taking longer than anyone had anticipated. They'd had to rush over to the hotel, dashing up the stairs through the back entrance to evade the hordes of fans outside, waiting to come in.

Josie is already there, calmly sipping on a cup of coffee with that security guard who's always hanging around. Quinn, who saved Tate when he fainted.

It made him look really good in front of Josie.

Josie looks up as he approaches. "Hey, Tate," she greets him with a friendly smile.

She's glowing. Absolutely radiant. He'd place bets it was because Quinn was standing next to her. The firefighter is eyeing her up like she's a Popsicle he can't wait to melt.

Tate doesn't like the guy on principle. He's one of those types that everyone wants around. Easygoing, friendly, athletic, charming. Life of the party.

He's a freaking firefighter. A hero who jumps into burning buildings to save kids. How could Tate compete with that?

Even though his face has been on posters tacked around the bedrooms of teen girls across the country, Tate has a hard time talking to most people and connecting with them about their interests. His life was so different than most, traveling on tour buses and doing homework with tutors while his parents performed. It was privileged for sure, but also isolating.

That's why he prefers recording music. Working alongside Squeaks. She never tries to pull anything from him—get him to open up with what it was like growing up with famous parents, or seeing them split up. Most people can't relate, but Squeaks just accepts him for who he is.

Tate sucks in a breath as he realizes how much he misses Squeaks right now. He could really use someone in his corner.

"Morning, Josie." He dips his head in greeting. "Quinn."

He knows Josie well enough to tell that she's happy with Quinn. He accepts the fact that, even though they learned who broke them apart, it's been too long since they were together.

It's never going to be the same. They've outgrown the overwhelming feelings they had as young people. Whatever closure Tate was hoping for with Jo will never happen.

It's over. They've both moved on. And he's going to have to deal with it.

Tate sighs and plops himself down next to her. "Missed you at the house." At least he's finally comfortable around Josie, now that they're on more friendly terms.

Quinn looks over towards the doors. "I'll start letting guests in about ten minutes." He stands up and walks away, giving them privacy.

"Tate mentioned a meeting. Sorry to miss it." She hesitates. "I was … busy."

"I get that."

All their history, and Tate only has ten minutes to wrap it up. "Josie," he starts hesitantly. Big statements aren't his thing. "I loved you. Really loved you. When you turned away, wouldn't let me in, it was really hard."

Josie's famous pale green eyes soften. "It was hard for me, too. You were so important to me." She looks at him fondly.

"You were my first everything—my first girlfriend, my first time, my first love," he says. "What we had was special. I know it's over, but I want you to know how much of an impact it had on me. I'll never forget us."

Josie smiles sadly. "I wish I had done things differently. I mixed it all up … the end of the show, with our relationship, when they should have been separate. I'm sorry."

"It wasn't your fault. We had no idea what Paige was doing. As for us, I should have fought for you." Tate takes her hand. "If you ever need me, I just want you to know that I'll be there."

They hug tightly, and Tate feels a piece of his heart crack. Nostalgia for what could have been if they had tried harder. Suppose they hadn't listened to the rumors or the background noise of fame. But now they're back. Their reunion might be too late, but he has finally found some peace.

Tate hugs Josie once more, then stands up. "I need to eat something before the guests arrive," he tells her. "I can't risk passing out in front of that freaking firefighter again."

Mason, Val, and Paige are standing against the wall. Tate hadn't even noticed they were there.

"Oh, you guys," Paige says. "I love you all."

She rushes forward, and suddenly they're all embracing. One big group huddle. A huge smush of their pack of five.

Val starts crying. "I'm being blackmailed, guys. For something terrible I did."

"What?" Tate asks.

They all start talking at once.

"What did you do?"

"For how much?"

"Do you have any idea who's doing it?"

"Really? How much are they asking?"

"Wait, wait, hold up," Tate breaks in as he checks his watch. It's hard to hear who is saying what. We have less than a minute before the doors open. Can we shelve this and meet up right after this session?"

"Absolutely." Val swipes her eyes. "You're right. This isn't the time. Can we meet back at the house at three?"

"Rendezvous at the Elliot mansion at three," Mason confirms.

"Got it," says Paige.

It will give them a few hours to find out what's going on.

"This event is over at one, and we have the reception at six," Tate tells them.

"That's perfect. I'll be there," Josie says.

"We all will," Mason tells Val. "We're going to help figure this out."

Val comes in for another group hug. "I love you guys."

The doors creak open, and Bryce strides in. He's followed by a team of assistants hurrying behind him.

"Let's get into position." Bryce starts pointing. "Tate, you're over here. Mason, there. Go!"

Tate heads over to his backdrop for meet-and-greets. One of Bryce's admins hands Tate a stack of photos to personalize for each fan.

Lines begin to form, mostly young women who can't wait to put their arms around him. Tate can't tell one from the other. They all want something from their teen crush. It's almost too much right now. He needs some space from all the news that's being thrown at him.

"Do you think you could sign it to Mom?" a woman asks, and at the sound of his mother's voice, Tate's face breaks out into a real grin.

Kate Noble is standing there, in the flesh. His dad, Crew, is right next to her. His parents are here, on Seven Mile Island.

Tate can't believe it.

Seeing them, when he needed them the most, is more than he could have expected. Could it get any better?

"How did … ?" Tate starts to ask, but then he spots another familiar face. Squeaks' breaks into a huge smile, her brown eyes dancing.

She's here. Tate suddenly sees things a lot more clearly.

Today is turning out to be a really great day.

Chapter 43

"I'm worried about Francesca. Something doesn't seem right."
- Eve to her parents, Season 4, Episode 3

Val, August 3

Val takes a sip of her Diet Coke and looks around the room nervously. Josie, Paige, Tate, and Mason are all squeezed into the room to hear her confession. "We're really doing this?"

"No time like the present," Mason confirms.

It's finally time for Val to come clean and spill her awful secret. To tell them what she did in Los Angeles.

All this time, she's kept it to herself. Never opening up to anyone for fear they might confess what she had done. Using her dwindling savings and royalties to keep it from reaching the public.

It was never going to end, was it? Whoever is behind this will keep sending her letters. Why wouldn't they? She keeps paying up.

She's finally done hiding. Her cast mates are all there, waiting to hear what she has to say.

Xavier hasn't been released from jail, but it looks like Marty isn't going to press any charges, so he should be able to post bail soon.

It doesn't hurt that Justin had done Val a favor and called Marty to let him know he was considering leaking a story confirming the rumors of statutory rape.

"There are a lot of questions about how legal the girls were that you took advantage of," he told Marty. "Either way, you're no longer America's dad. You're a filthy predator who took advantage of young women."

It was one of the first decent things Justin has done in years.

Detective Shroud is still interviewing witnesses about what happened a decade ago. Since no one has come forward with any solid facts, they have a long process ahead. Val fears the scandal will likely be swept under the rug.

Even if he doesn't get charged, it's unlikely Marty will book another acting job after this. The rumors will dog him for the rest of his career.

Val can't say she's bothered by that. The man is a creep. She plans to talk to the police detective when this is all over. Give a statement.

After she finally comes clean herself.

She perches on the desk chair, facing the group. Her former costars are all sprawled across her bed and the couch in the room, waiting for her to speak.

Val takes a deep, shuddering breath, then looks at Tate. "I owe you a huge apology. Years ago, when we were on a break from shooting, we all went to your house in LA. You flew all of us privately in your family jet. Do you remember?"

"How could I forget? We had a long weekend without filming, so we took off on a group trip," Tate recalls. "Spent it doing what dumb 20-year-olds do, getting drunk and high for five days straight."

"Yeah. A little too high." Can Val go through with this? She has no choice. "One night, when everyone else passed out, I wandered into your parents' den. There was this huge wall of awards."

"I remember that room," Paige says. "It was so cool."

Val starts to cry. "It made me sad. That you had this amazing house, with all these fabulous trophies, and I had nothing. Then I got angry, thinking how your life was so perfect."

Tate looks uncomfortable. "That wasn't my intention, to bring you there to brag."

"I know that now." Tears keep coming. "And I'm so sorry. But I was drunk, and stoned, and I did a terrible thing. I saw your mother's Grammy and your father's Oscar. Some lifetime recognition thing, too. And I ... swiped them."

There's silence.

"Wow. The press was all over it," Paige recalls. "I remember the headlines–no one could believe that Kate Crew and Tate Master had been robbed. Didn't some of your parents' rivals issue statements that they hadn't taken the awards?"

"They did," Tate confirms. He looks shell-shocked. "What did you do with them, Val? We never found out where they went."

Val swallows hard against the tears. She's never felt worse, having to confess her most horrible secret in a room full of people she cares so much about.

"I put them in my bag. I don't know what I was thinking. I just wanted to have them. I'd never seen anything so fancy."

"And then?"

"The news broke, and the police came and interviewed all of us. I was so scared. They had their names all over them. How was I going to keep hiding them without being found out?"

"So you hid them?" Tate's voice is cold. He grips his hands tightly. She can't imagine how mad he is right now.

"Not exactly. I freaked out and took them to a pawn shop in LA. I couldn't risk someone finding them on me."

"You *sold* my parents' trophies?" Val now knows there are rules in place, that you can't just sell an Oscar or a Grammy. They're actually "on loan" from the Academies that presented them, although they can stay with the winner forever. They're supposed to be given back to the Academy that awarded them first.

But just like the art world, there are sketchy gray areas where collectors are willing to pay a substantial sum for a piece by their favorite artist. Or in this case, actors and musicians.

"How much did you get?" Tate asks.

Val swallows. "Five hundred."

"Damn. Only five hundred dollars for the crowning achievements of my parents' careers? I would have hoped you'd at least made more money."

Val wants to crawl into a hole. The way everyone is looking at her is exactly why, once she sobered up and realized the repercussions of what she had done, she had done everything she could to cover up her mistake. This was why she didn't want anyone to ever discover this ugly part of her.

And now, despite of the thousands of dollars she sent to some blackmailer, Val was still paying the price. Whoever was behind it had milked her for at least twenty grand over the years.

When she was flat broke and couldn't pay cash, Val had to fork over sentimental pieces of jewelry: a gold cameo from her grandmother, a Cartier bracelet she bought herself after her first big gig, and a distinctive Art Deco diamond pendant her mother had given her before she passed away.

The necklace was the hardest to give up. Val had worn the piece nearly every day since her mother died, even hiding it under her shirt while filming the show. Giving it up had been horrible, but she had no other choice.

Val knows she messed up badly, but she has paid for it. Over and over again. Until she felt like she had been bled dry. When would it ever be enough?

"Wow," Mason swipes his hand across his face. "I have to say, I didn't see this coming. I know how hard the theft was for you and your family, Tate."

No one knew more about how vulnerable and exposed they had felt. The blame they all shared, wondering who had been responsible for the break-in.

Paige shakes her head, avoiding eye contact with Val. "I'm sorry, Tate."

Val knows that after the awards incident, Tate's parents had started fighting. His mom accused his father of throwing too many parties and letting in random strangers. His father told his mother that she was too caught up in her career. There must have been other factors, but the truth was that Tate's parents separated less than six months later.

Val had no idea that stealing a few trophies would cause so much damage. At the time, she'd justified not confessing to what she'd done. It had been a stupid mistake. She'd even tried to contact the shop to see where the awards had gone, but the guy who answered the phone feigned ignorance and hung up on her.

Eventually, Val shelved it all in the back of her mind. Tate's parents got replacement statues, didn't they? They must have.

Val successfully convinced herself it never happened–until she began getting the blackmail letters. Even living in a dodgy apartment in Washington and bartending, she couldn't escape her past.

Tate stands. "I can't even be in the same room with you."

"Tate, please …" Val begs, but doesn't get a response.

He walks out, slamming the door behind him.

"Give him some space," Paige advises. "That was a lot for him to process."

"What do I do now?" Val asks. "He's never going to forgive me."

Jo looks over at her. "I think it's too soon to even think about forgiveness. Just because you confessed doesn't mean everything is okay."

She looks at Paige as she's talking. Paige flushes and looks down at her feet.

"It's going to take a while," Mason agrees. "That was a hell of a shitty thing to do."

Val can't argue with that. Breaking into his parents' room, stealing the symbols of their career, and then making money off it. "I have no excuse for it."

"You really don't. Honestly, Val, this is next-level." Josie crosses her arms. "No one knew? You never told a soul you did this?"

"Never. Not even my mom."

"I wonder who's blackmailing you then." Josie looks around. "My odds are on Justin."

"He's more the 'out in the open type', though," Mason muses. "He'd tell you he knew to your face and then use it whenever he needed a favor."

"True," Josie paces the room. "He's too likely a suspect. But wow, Valerie. I still can't get over this."

Her friends are definitely disappointed in her, but none are as angry as Tate was. Hesitantly, Val asks, "What do you think I can do to get Tate to forgive me?"

"Give it some time," Paige offers. "We've all done some shitty things we aren't proud of. It doesn't mean you can't make up for it." She looks at Josie. The tension between them is thick.

"You're way too kind," Mason says drily. "I'm going to be honest and say that he's never going to let this go. But fuck it. We need to figure out who's blackmailing you."

Val collapses on the bed next to Paige, who squeezes her hand in comfort. Val and Paige are in the same boat. They're both feeling guilty about what they did so many years ago.

Ironically, Val feels a little better now that she's shown her worst colors. The shame and guilt had never gone away, no matter what she did. It tangled up her personal life, made her pop pills she didn't need. She'd worked a dead-end job all this time because she wanted to hide away.

And she feels hopeful about her future with Xavier. For the first time, Val feels like she might be worth more than being a one-night stand or a part-time bartender at a dive bar. She might as well stop hiding and start living.

"If Tate asks me to stay away, I will," Val announces. "Whatever it takes to get him to forgive me."

"We'll talk to him," Josie offers.

"Oh, one more thing you should know," Mason says innocently, and Val can tell she's not going to like what he's about to say next. "Tate's parents are here."

Chapter 44

Josie, August 3

Getting ready for the red carpet can be a hassle, but it can also be fun. And tonight, Josie is determined to enjoy it.

She chose a silver sequined jumpsuit with a plunging back and thick, strappy heels. She blow-dried her full mane of wavy, blonde hair, then put it in rollers to create big movie star curls. She finished the look with large diamond hoop earrings.

Josie is going all out. Because this is it. She doesn't see another *Shallows* reunion ever happening again. Not with what a disaster this one has been.

Val's revelations tug at her heart. Josie doesn't blame Val for what she did as a teen. Val has always been more vulnerable than the rest of them. Her skin had been just a little too thin. The comments and insecurities hit her harder than anyone else. She'd made dumb decisions, but they weren't unforgivable.

Josie is more annoyed at Paige than at Val. What Val did was stupid, but it wasn't deliberate. It had been a spur-of-the-moment decision that she'd been paying for (literally) for years.

Paige, on the other hand, had conducted a full-on offense to break Josie and Tate up and kick Josie off the show. All because Paige didn't want Josie getting all the attention. So, she'd blown up Josie's life instead.

How could Josie ever forgive Paige?

She'll put it aside for tonight. Josie knows there is too much good in the world to dwell on the bad parts. And one of those surprising bright spots is about to show up soon.

As soon as she thinks about Quinn, there's a knock on her door.

Jo pulls it open, and there he is. A surprise addition to her life who made her laugh.

Quinn looks at Josie appreciatively. "Look at you all glammed up. And here I was going to ask if you wanted to stay in and get room service."

"Not on your life. We're going out."

He's made an effort for tonight, too. Quinn is wearing a dark, slim suit that shows off his tall frame. His face is clean-cut and shaven, and his hair, which is a bit longer in the back, is slightly damp from the shower. It's her favorite spot to touch when she's kissing him.

Josie is planning on doing a lot of that tonight. What will happen with Quinn next month, or even next week? She doesn't know. But she's going to enjoy the ride.

"Want a drink?" Josie heads to the minibar. The Reeds is nicely equipped with a mini fridge and snacks. She was lucky to snag a room with a balcony overlooking the Shelter Haven Harbor. It's definitely not a hardship waking up to the sunrise as it glints off the water.

"I'd love one," Quinn says.

She makes him a Manhattan using the same whiskey he had at his apartment on their date night.

Quinn's mouth curves in a grin. "You remembered."

"Of course."

"Can you please stop being my dream girl?" he asks. "Just for a second?"

"I can't promise."

Quinn crosses over to her, lifting her off her feet for a slow kiss. "I could get used to having you as my personal bartender."

"I think I could get used to being one." The unspoken promise hangs in the air. Will there be more dates when she goes back to her regular life?

She hopes so. Lambertville and Avalon are only a few hours apart.

"Josie, I'm not kidding. I want to get to know you better." His face, usually grinning, looks serious for once. "I'm not on security guard duty tonight. I convinced another guy from the fire department to fill in for my shift. That makes me all yours for the next 24 hours." He kisses her neck, and she shivers.

How could she say no? "I'd like that too."

Even with all the chaos of this weekend, something good has come out of it. Something potentially great. Unexpected and surprising, but extremely promising.

"Let's finish these drinks and head over," Josie tells Quinn.

The event is being held at Fourth & Bay, one of Stone Harbor's biggest and most fabulous spots for parties.

"I was at the opening party for Fourth & Bay a few years ago," Quinn tells her. "It's where I first met the owners, Kyle and Ryan. They were the heroes of the Festival of Lights Parade a few years ago."

"I remember seeing something about that in the news, but I can't remember what happened."

"They saved dozens of boats from crashing into the 96th Street Bridge. Roger's daughter tried to lock the drawbridge so the boats would crash into it. They came to the rescue."

"Roger's daughter? Where is she now?"

"She went to jail. She did a few other things, too, like breaking into a beach house and trashing it. That's why Roger offered the cast the use of his mansion. A lot of the town's council members didn't want this reunion during the summer. He's always trying to get them back."

"I'll try not to get on his bad side," Josie laughs.

They finish their drinks and head to the party, which is just down the street from their hotel.

It's already packed. A red velvet rope blocks off the crowds of fans and press from the main entrance.

Crowds of people are yelling, trying to get their attention.

"Eve! Eve!!"

"Over here!"

"Who are you with?"

Cameras flash, the lights strobing in their faces. Even though Quinn has been with them all week, Josie can tell he's caught off guard by the press of attention.

"You really are famous," Quinn says.

Josie shrugs. "Just with fans. There are lots of people who have never watched the show. They have no idea who I am."

He still looks a little taken aback by people pressing against them. She guesses it doesn't help that everyone keeps shouting at her to get a good shot.

Wait until tomorrow, when Quinn is sure to be one of the stories across thousands of fan pages, who will be trying to track down the guy Josie Remington brought as her date to the wrap party. They might even become a meme.

Kyle and Ryan are waiting to greet them at the entrance. "Eve and Quinn, together? Are you *kidding*?" They clasp their hands excitedly.

Josie doesn't correct them with her actual name. She isn't sure which owner is which, but they're both equally friendly and affectionate. Even though she's never met them, they greet her with huge, affectionate hugs.

"We love BOTH of you two!!" Ryan gushes. "Are you really an item? This is too fabulous."

They take photos in front of the restaurant's hot pink sign. More cameras flash, trapping them with their long lenses as they push closer.

"Go ahead," Kyle tells them. "We've got to stay here and keep greeting the guests."

Inside, there's a two-story foyer with swings—*real swings*—dangling from the ceiling. Glittering disco balls hang from the ceiling. There's a wall of fire blazing around the banquet tables and a cascading waterfall with fish bobbing around in the pool below.

It's gorgeous and fun, and just a little bit gaudy, just like the owners.

"Are you on social media? Instagram, TikTok?" Josie asks Quinn.

"Yeah, but I don't check it that often. Usually at the firehouse when we have downtime."

"Is your profile set to private?"

"I don't think so."

"We're going to need to fix that," Josie says with a chuckle. She reaches out and takes his hand. "Ready?"

"As I'll ever be."

They walk into the wrap party together, hand in hand.

Chapter 45

"Stand up for yourself. You're such a pushover."
- Eve to Hazel, Season 1, Episode 2

Paige, August 3

Paige sips champagne as she watches the action on the first floor of Fourth & Bay from the balcony above. It's a hell of a party.

A champagne tower greets guests on arrival. On the first floor, cocktail waitresses dressed in "Duffy Beach Patrol" outfits serve guests trays of boardwalk fries and funnel cake in brightly striped paper cones. The opening credits of the show had been a montage of the six friends hanging out next to a Duffy Beach lifeguard stand.

Under the dangling disco balls, a lazy river is stocked with neon fish matching the color scheme of the show (bright green and hot pink). The event organizers really thought of everything.

From the second-floor balcony, Paige watches sequined burlesque dancers gyrate on platforms while bubbles float around them. Rays of neon lights arc around the room as a celebrity DJ plays remixes of the most popular songs from the past decade.

The guest list is a stellar mix of VIP celebrities and influencers, and now that Tate's famous parents are here, nearly every major celebrity gossip outlet is covering the party. Of course, with news about the fight at the hotel, everyone's trying to find out what caused it. Rumors are flying. If only they knew what Val had done! That would be a story.

Tate is standing by the bar with his family and his business partner, Squeaks. She met her at Sage and Simon's wedding. It's hard to tell—are they just friends or dating?

She won't ask him. She's officially retired. Done messing with people's lives, especially Tate's and Josie's. Paige knows she can't change the past, but she wishes she could make up for what she's done.

Josie still won't talk to her, unless it's absolutely necessary. Paige is certain she's blown up every chance of being close with her again. At least she has Mason and Val on her side. They haven't turned against her, even knowing what she did.

She doesn't think anyone else knows, yet. Simon and Sage acted friendly when she greeted them. Same for Bryce, although that will change as soon as he hears what she did. He's often been quoted as saying *The Shallows* had been his favorite series to direct.

Sage is near the front entrance, mingling with some of the former set and production team members. It's been so long that Paige doesn't remember their names, but she recognizes most of them.

Paige wanders over to join their circle. "Hey, guys. Long time no see!"

"Paige!"

"You look fantastic."

They all greet her warmly.

"Looking gorgeous as always, Sage." Paige hugs the adorable newlywed. Sage looks like a pixie, with her long curls and fringed lashes. She's wearing a floating sleeveless maxi dress that Paige tags as either from Farm Rio or Anthropologie, with a long, retro necklace that matches Sage's bohemian vibe.

Sage leans in for a peck on the cheek. "Same goes, Paige." She looks around. "Isn't this amazing? I wish we had these kinds of parties on the set of *The Shallows*."

Paige nods in agreement. "Seriously." She looks at Sage again. There's something familiar, something she can't pin down. What is it about Sage that's capturing her attention?

It's almost there—she's trying to figure out what it is—then Justin sidles next to her and Paige loses the thread.

Paige offers a polite smile. "Didn't think you'd feel comfortable showing your face around."

Justin flashes his teeth. "I never feel uncomfortable, Paige. It's one of the reasons I'm such a good agent."

She bites her tongue. It's their last night all together. She's going to avoid the drama if it kills her. "Have you seen Val? Or Josie?"

Justin shakes his head. "Sorry, kid."

Simon crosses the room to join their circle, carrying two flutes of champagne. He hands Sage a cocktail and turns to the crowd. "What did I miss?"

Paige stifles a laugh. How could she even begin to explain what's happened over the past few days?

She's pretty sure all he saw was Marty's fistfight. "Nothing much."

"It's great to see everyone here at once," he smiles nostalgically. "Man, we had a good time, didn't we?"

Sage looks up at her husband. "We certainly did." She brushes her hair away from her neck. It sets off bells in Paige's mind. The necklace she's wearing —why does it look so familiar? Paige is certain she's seen it before.

"I wish we could go back and do it again," she says wistfully. It really was the happiest time of her life, before she screwed it all up. Her stomach clenches at the thought, and she grabs a piece of her hair to calm down. Without realizing what she's doing, she starts pulling.

She spots Josie across the room, all cozied up to the hot security guard/firefighter. Of course she is. Everyone wants to be with Josie.

Paige tries not to feel the same grudge she always does whenever she's next to Josie. Because Paige was always second-best. The sidekick, not the golden girl.

Always the bridesmaid, never the bride.

Josie looks gorgeous, per usual. What isn't usual for them is the cold look of dismissal she gives Paige as she glides past them.

"Ouch, that was harsh," Simon says.

"I'm going to go talk to her," Paige tells the group. She can't wait to be finished with this stupid reunion before anything else goes wrong, or she ends up needing a wig from yanking out all this hair.

Paige takes a deep breath and makes her way over to Josie and Quinn. "Can I talk to you for a sec?" she asks.

Josie shakes her head. "Listen, I'm not going to get into it with you right now. I just don't have the bandwidth for long explanations and selfish excuses."

Paige knows it isn't going to be easy to gain her forgiveness. "I really am sorry, Jo."

"We'll get into it later. I do have one thing to ask you."

"Anything." Paige means it with every fiber in her body.

"You need to tell everyone what you did." Except that.

"Josie, no … "

"Yes. That's the deal. The only way I'll consider forgiving you is if you're honest about how you ruined the show. Take it or leave it."

Paige knows what will happen when she tells everyone. The same people who greeted her so warmly will never look at her with trust and affection again. This is exactly what she's been dreading all these years. Losing all of them in her life, and never getting to spend time with everyone again.

She grabs a piece of her hair and pulls. Paige knows she deserves it.

It's time for her to face the music. What other choice does she have?

"I'll tell them." The thought makes her stomach churn, but she doesn't complain to Josie. She earned this punishment.

Josie nods, then sets her glass down. "You should know that some of them already know. Let's get this weekend over with, and we can do our soul searching later."

Paige has had to do worse things in recovery. She just hopes it will help. "I will."

Quinn gives her a sympathetic look, but he doesn't say anything. This is between the two of them.

Jo flicks her eyes at Paige. "I'm still pissed at you, but I love you like a sister. I'm trying to reconcile the two." She looks at Quinn. "Let's go."

They turn and walk away, leaving Paige alone. Once again.

Chapter 46

"You need to start listening to your parents.
We know what we're talking about."
- Mr. Mattson to Josie and Hazel, Season 3, Episode 7

Tate, August 3

"How have you been, darling? You're awfully quiet."

Tate shakes his head. Some things never change. "I'm perfectly fine, Mom. Everything's great."

"And your insulin?" she says, patting his arm. "You're keeping everything level?"

He sighs. "Yes, Mom. I'm on top of it."

"Fantastic. I'm so glad to hear it. Are things going well with your old friends?"

"We're all playing nicely." No matter how happy Tate is when he sees his parents, after a few hours, he can't help getting annoyed with them. His mom reverts back to treating him like a child and hounding him to make sure his diabetes is in check.

He's well aware he's their only child, and of course, they're going to worry about him. But he's also 32 years old. Don't they think it's time they stopped swooping in to save the day?

240

"You know I'm glad you're here, but I don't know how you even heard about the reunion." It's not something he brought up because he knows how they feel about what went down with him and Josie before.

"I told them about it." Squeaks shrugs. "They knew it was coming up anyway, as soon as they saw all those press items about you and Val."

Of course, they saw that. "That was just made up by somebody's agent looking for free publicity," Tate says. He doesn't mention Justin's name. His father knows Justin and would definitely say something to him, inevitably causing even more drama. He can fight his own battles.

"We knew that, darling. Squeaks said you were handling everything just fine," Kate assures him. "But we still wanted to check on you. And she said you were done with your last project, so we figured it was a good time."

"I understand. And honestly, everything has been fine." They've always been *so* protective. When Tate got diagnosed with diabetes, it only got worse. They baby him more now than they did when he was a kid.

Squeaks looks around at the wrap party. "This is some place. I'm going to grab a drink, and I'll be right back." She saunters off, drawing attention as she moves through the crowd.

"She's really something," Crew says, shaking his head. "I'm glad she's in your corner."

"Squeaks is the best." His partner is extremely intuitive. She's likely giving them space to talk.

Tate isn't ready to tell them about Val's confession. He's still trying to process it himself. He can't help but feel guilty that it was one of his co-stars, and that he was the one to give access to his family's belongings. Tate had never even questioned whether it had been one of them. He'd always figured it was some fan who had a crazy obsession with one of his parents.

Tate gazes at his parents. "So, how about you guys?" They aren't looking too angry with each other right now. In fact, they could be considered downright cozy. "You look pretty comfortable with each other. Anything I should know?"

His mom chuckles, the throaty Kate Noble voice she's famous for. "Nothing to worry about, darling." She beams at Crew. This is so odd. He's not used to seeing them get along, much less in the same room.

"Did you two come together?" Tate presses.

"We did," Kate answers. She leans in and plants a kiss on his forehead. "We wanted to come support you."

He never would have guessed they even communicated with each other.

For a few years, Tate couldn't even say the other person's name in front of the other person without an explosion. He's glad that phase is over. "I'm fine. Good. But I do need to talk to you."

Tate decides he will tell them about what happened, but not until much later. He's not going to press charges after all these years, and he'll encourage his parents not to, either. He's not even sure what the statute of limitations is on this sort of thing.

At this point, it feels like Val has already paid the price for a dumb mistake, dreading the letter that arrived asking for money. Knowing someone out there was aware of what she'd done, threatening her, and wasn't afraid to spill it.

"We're staying another night." Kate smiles as Squeaks comes back with drinks in her hands. "Let's all meet for brunch in the morning."

"I got you a glass of champagne," she says to his mom, handing her a glass.

"Thanks, darling." Squeaks and his mom appear to be on close terms.

What was going on? If his parents are staying another night, does that mean that they're staying together? Tate can't even begin to process this right now.

"We're proud of you, son," Crew says, and gently takes his ex-wife's hand. They turn to greet a few guests who have been patiently waiting to talk to them.

"What the hell is going on? Are my parents getting back together?"

Her arms crossed, Squeaks shoots him a look that says he's a moron. "All signs point to yes."

Tate looks back at Squeaks. She's wearing a delicate dress with strappy sandals, something he's never seen her in before. She looks stunning in the pale green color that sets off the dark tones of her skin. Large hoops dangle from her ears.

Tate has never had any doubt that Squeaks was gorgeous, but they're business partners. He's never gone there.

Maybe it's time he did. "Want to dance?" Tate asks. The celebrity DJ is finally playing a slow song.

Squeaks flashes a mega-watt smile. "Thought you'd never ask."

Chapter 47

"She is the kind of girl who shares desserts at a work dinner. Ugh."
- Francesca to Chase, Season 3, Episode 9

Sage, August 3

Pressed against Simon, Sage sways to the music. The DJ has slowed down his playlist from old school rap and pop songs to classic R&B ballads. It suits the mood.

"How Sweet It Is" has just ended, with Marvin Gaye wailing about being loved, and Frank Sinatra is now singing about "The Way You Look Tonight."

Could it get any better? She floats in Simon's arms as they slide from side to side. His glasses tip down his nose as he looks at her from above. The messy hair she adores, which no amount of gel can contain, is sweaty from all their dancing.

"I love you, hubby." Simon smiles in response, his honest amber eyes letting her know he returns the feeling. One of her favorite things about Simon is how easy it is to tell what he's thinking.

She remembers meeting Simon on their first day of filming the show. As an Art PA, she worked alongside the writers to ensure each setting matched the scripts they were writing.

Simon was so quiet that she didn't notice him at first. A lot of the other crew members were louder, funnier, and more exciting. Simon was ten years older, but he didn't seem more experienced than she. If anything, she felt older than him at certain things: how to handle aggressive people, navigate a party, or even balance a budget.

They were different in other ways, too. Simon grew up in San Francisco and had gone to private school before graduating from Berkeley with a bachelor's degree in Film & Media.

One night, Simon was in a trailer going over script revisions, and Sage came in to drop off props. They started talking—both were from the West Coast (well, she said she was), and bonded over the differences from working on the East—and after that, they sought each other out when they weren't working. Grabbing a sandwich from Wawa, having drinks at the Icona, and taking trips to the beach.

When Simon first kissed her, she was more than ready for it. From the moment they went out, they were a couple. Everyone on set said their name together, *Simon & Sage*, as if it was a done deal. A complete set. And that's how she felt. She finally fit.

Five years later, Simon proposed. They didn't have much money, but they were happy. She wanted to wait to save money for the wedding she'd always dreamed of.

It's been exhilarating, getting married and attending the reunion as a guest moderator. A VIP. It's something she's been looking forward to for months and months.

Now that all the planning and waiting are over, Sage wonders what she and Simon will have to look forward to.

"I can't believe this is our last night," Sage whispers to her new hubby. "I wonder if they'll ever do another *Shallows* reunion."

"We'll be too old by then," Simon jokes. "This isn't *Star Wars*. No one will remember who we are."

"True." Content, Sage sways from side to side. "Maybe that's not a bad thing."

They pass Josie and her adorable firefighter. There's Tate and his friend Squeaks, who she met a few minutes ago. They all look happy. Just look at them, paired up with new dance partners, when she always thought of them together.

They glide by Val and Xavier, the former stuntman who decked Marty in front of all those people. Even after working in show biz, reality is stranger than fiction.

Sage flashes a smile at Val, who returns it with one of her own. She can't help feeling smug.

Poor Val. The girl has no idea that Sage is the one who's been blackmailing her all these years. She's literally dangling hints that she's the one behind it, and Val has been too oblivious to notice what she was wearing.

What a sucker.

Sage plans to continue doing so. It paid for her wedding, didn't it? Everyone said it was absolutely stunning. If only they knew how she got the money for it. She has felt bad about it at times, but a girl's got to do what a girl's got to do. She never took more than they could afford. They were all famous, weren't they?

And now that she and Simon are planning on having a baby, she's going to need funds for the nursery. Kids aren't cheap.

Wrapping her arms around her new husband, Sage leans in. "I've never been so happy." She gives him a kiss on his sweet, trusting mouth.

She finally has everything she's always wanted.

Chapter 48

"Can you believe they're together? Give me a break."
- Francesca to Shea, Season 3, Episode 9

Mason, August 3

This party is one of the best that Mason has ever been to, and that's saying a lot. The event organizers have pulled out all the stops.

He nods at familiar faces as he and Kit work the crowd. "Great to see you," he repeats over and over, shaking hands and moving through the crowd.

This will be the last night before they head out of town tomorrow. He can't believe it's almost over. In some ways, it's the most excitement he's had for years. In others, he's ready to go home with Kit and the girls. They could all use some family time.

Together, they make their way to the main bar, where Ryan, ever the perfect host, is standing. He's wearing a sequined tuxedo jacket with a bright bow tie. "You look dazzling," he tells Ryan.

"Aw, thanks, Mason," Ryan preens. "Can I get you two a drink? Shot?"

Mason nods. "I could use a shot."

He looks at Kit, who smiles and says, "Just one. I have to leave soon to relieve the babysitter."

"Only one," Mason agrees, then turns to wave their crew over.

"Josie, get your ass over here! Paige! Get here, pronto. That means you, Val." Mason turns and points to his best friend. "Tate, I see you and your gorgeous partner. Sage, Simon, buckle up!"

In less than ten minutes, he's gathered all of them around him. Tonight, he's not taking no for an answer. "We're going to party," Mason orders.

"What a great idea." Ryan nods to a bartender, and a bottle of top-shelf tequila and slices of lime magically appear at the bar. "Let's go!" he shouts.

The drinks are soon flowing. Everyone is talking at the top of their lungs, shouting to be heard over the DJ.

They're all together. The whole crew: Mason and Kit, Tate and Squeaks, Josie and Paige, Val and Xavier, Sage and Simon. They're downing shots of booze and citrus, laughing and hugging, and it's exhilarating. The music is perfect, and right now, no more grudges are being held. Everything suddenly feels so much better.

Mason puts his arm around Ryan. "Your place is amazing!"

"I can't believe you're all here!" Ryan beams, and the bartender pours another round. "I'm your biggest fan!"

Even the grumpy hotel owner comes over to their spot. Roger always rubs him the wrong way, with his superiority and smug attitude, but he did give them a place to stay all week.

Mason decides to be cordial. "Have a drink," he offers, handing him a shot glass.

"Thanks, man." Roger takes it out of his hand and tips it back.

They form a smaller circle consisting of Val, Simon, Sage, Mason, and Roger. All of them are dancing, arms slung over shoulders in camaraderie.

Sage takes another shot of tequila. She doesn't seem to be handling her alcohol well. It's probably hit her harder. Sage is smaller than the rest of them, with her thin frame.

"You okay?" Simon asks her. "You look a little wobbly."

She shakes her head, turning down the next one that Mason offers. "I need water." She waves to the bartender.

It's a smart move. Mason approves, but he does another round of shots, anyway.

Three shots within twenty minutes. It might be a new record.

"Let's slow down," Val yells in his ear. "We have a long night ahead of us."

"Yes, darling," he promises. She gives him a quick kiss on the cheek.

It's probably a good idea. Kit is giving him the side eye from a few feet over as he catches up with Tate.

Everyone is getting a little loopy as they begin to feel the effects of the alcohol.

"You look just like Ariana Grande!" Roger shouts to Sage.

Mason is impressed that he knows who the singer is. "You know what, you really do!" he agrees, as Val laughs next to him.

"Thank you!" She yells back as she reaches for her glass of water on the bar. "I love Wicked!" She's so little that she has to stand on a rung of her stool to get a better reach. As she leans over, the neckline of her maxi dress gapes open.

Val gasps out loud. "What the fuck?"

"What?" Mason asks. "Did I bump into you?"

But Val isn't looking at him. She's staring at Sage with narrowed eyes, and the look on her face is terrifying. If looks could kill, Sage would be dead by now.

"Is that what I think it is?" she screams, grabbing hold of a long necklace that's peeking out of her dress.

"Let go!" Sage shouts as she tries to hold on to it. But she's no match for Val, who yanks it hard enough to pull Sage closer.

"Ouch!" Sage says as red marks begin to appear around her neck.

Val grabs around her and pulls until the long chain snaps. Clutching the pendant in her hand, Val stares at it almost in disbelief.

"What the hell is going on?" Roger asks.

Mason can only stare. He has no clue.

"It was you?" she yells. "You?" She's nearly choking with anger.

It's a pretty piece. A long silver chain with a filigree diamond and emerald pendant. It looks vintage—maybe Art Deco? Mason can't figure out why she's so angry about it, though.

Val looks like she's about to hit Sage.

Mason twists around. "I need some help here!" This is more than he can handle, especially when he's already a little drunk.

Simon is right behind him, looking confused. "What happened?" he asks. "Val, why did you take her necklace? She got that from her mom."

"Are you kidding me?!? It's mine!!!!" Val screams at the top of her lungs. Other guests begin to notice, their heads swiveling to see what's going on. Even with the loud music, they're drawing attention.

Mason tries to step in. "Let's all take a second … " he begins, trying to control the situation.

He doesn't get a chance to finish. Val smacks his arm as he attempts to hold her back.

Sage grabs the hem of her maxi dress and makes a quick dash for the exit. She isn't waiting around. She flies past the wall of glittering decorations, around the river of flowing water, and out the main entrance.

For such a small person, she moves fast.

Simon races after her.

Val doesn't give chase. She just stands there, completely frozen, clutching the diamond pendant in her hand.

"Are you okay?" he asks. "What should I do?" Mason doesn't know who to call. It's all happening so fast.

Tate and Kit rush over to help.

"Where did they go?" Kit asks. "We were just talking and all hell broke loose."

Tate puts his arm around Val, who's still staring blankly at the necklace in her hands.

"Val?"

"It was Sage," she says softly. "The whole time. It was Sage."

Chapter 49

"I didn't see that one coming."
- Francesca to Chase, Season 4, Episode 9
(the Infamous Prom Episode)

Val, August 3

They're still at Fourth & Bay, trying to figure out what the hell happened.

There's no freaking way that the person who's been blackmailing her is Sage. It couldn't be true. It's literally not possible.

Val is so worked up that she can barely focus. She glances at the empty shot glasses and the bottle left on the bar, then shakes her head. She needs to sober up and get to the bottom of what just happened.

"Sweet Sage doesn't have a mean bone in her body," Mason defends Sage.

"Oh, really? Because she just showed us that she does." Val will never forget the nasty, petty notes that taunted her, threatening to ruin her life.

Time to pay up, Valerie! Or I'm telling TMZ you're the proud owner of an Oscar ... from Crew Masters. Five grand. By Monday.

Thought I forgot about you? I haven't. Three grand in five days. Or else.

Such a pretty Grammy. Think Kate misses it? Pay up.

Over and over again, those notes had come. Piling into her mailbox. Filling her with anxiety. Threatening her sanity.

But it must be Sage. Look at how she took off! The girl had fled as soon as Val grabbed her necklace. Val's mother had given it to her on her 18th birthday. It had been in her family for generations … until she had to give it over as payment to the blackmailer.

It's still hard to believe that Sage was capable of being so cruel to one of her good friends. To threaten someone she knew so well. *Who she invited to her own wedding.* How had she even come to find out what Val had done? The secret she never told anyone?

It doesn't make any sense.

Simon comes back from chasing Sage and joins them at the bar. "I couldn't find her. She's gone." His mouth is wide open in shock.

"Did you know?" Val asks, her chest heaving in hurt and anger, making it hard for her to breathe. "Simon, did you know?"

"I'm not even sure what I'm supposed to know, or not know," Simon responds. He leans his arms on the bar, looking deflated. "I don't know."

Of course, Simon would answer without really answering. Why is Val surprised? He's a writer. He knows more than anyone how to manipulate words.

She might not be a Harvard grad, but Val isn't dumb. "That she's been blackmailing me for years," she responds. "That she took all my money. And anything I held of value, including that necklace." Just saying it out loud enrages Val more.

"But really, Sage? She wouldn't hurt a fly. We all know that."

"She certainly did. She blackmailed me." She swipes her hand under her eyes, brushing away tears. "Terrible letters. For years."

"Why did you go along with it?"

"I paid her so she didn't expose what I did."

"I had no idea. I thought you were accusing her of stealing from you. I figured it must have been some mistake if it was your necklace. Like, she must have found the necklace on set and picked it up by accident." Simon looks around for help. It's obvious he's out of his element. "Just a misunderstanding," he whispers.

Tate comes to the rescue, as always. Even though Val's secret has broken his family. "We're going to figure it out, Val." He puts his arm around her shoulder. "The first thing we need to do is find Sage."

Simon is looking at his phone. "She's not picking up. Or answering any of my texts." He looks like the floor has opened up under him. Or that he hopes it will swallow him. "I just don't understand."

"She's going to answer me. As soon as I find her." Val is going to make her pay for the double betrayal of pretending to be her friend while siphoning her money at the same time.

"What could she even have blackmailed you for?" Simon asks.

Val pauses. This is where it's going to get dicey. But what the hell, Tate and Mason already know. Paige and Josie heard her confession yesterday, and they're all still here. Standing next to her.

It's time to pay the piper. "I stole Tate's parents' awards from their house." It's easier to say the second time around.

"The Oscar?" Val knows that Simon has always wanted to win an Emmy. He's been nominated twice, but lost out both times. Not for *The Shallows*. That never won anything.

"Yeah. And a Grammy. And a couple of others." Val's shoulders slump. "I regretted it as soon as I did it, but they're long gone."

"Where did they go?"

"I pawned them. I guess someone has them, somewhere."

"Jesus. And you're saying Sage blackmailed you about it? How would she even know?"

"I have no idea. But I gave that necklace to the person blackmailing me when I didn't have any more money to pay. It was the last thing I had of value. My mother gave it to me! And tonight, Sage is wearing it."

Simon nods slowly, trying to figure it all out. If anyone can, it's Simon Hartwick. The man's brain could give AI a run for its money.

"How did you do it?"

"There was a locker at the train station. They gave me a combination. And before you ask, yes, I tried to find out who rented it. But there was no way to find out. I would leave things there."

"Seriously?"

Val notices people are staring at them, deep in conversation, mid-party. They're starting to draw attention.

It can't be helped, and she frankly doesn't give a damn.

Val's world just shifted. She still can't believe the blackmailer was someone she knew. All this time, she thought it was a random guy who must have seen her selling the statues. But it was Sage. Not just someone she knew casually, but her friend.

There's a sudden swell in noise as partygoers begin to whisper. Val can tell it's not about their little cast making waves.

It's something else. Something that outshines their little group. The A-list couple made of international rock and movie star royalty is making their way over to them.

"How is everyone?" Kate beams. "It's so great to see all of you together."

Val can't believe how beautiful she is in person, with her long, wavy hair and that distinctive gap in her front teeth. Kate Noble, live and in person. A legendary rock star is greeting them like she knows their names. Actually considers them to be in the same *orbit* that she travels in.

It's still crazy to think she's Tate's mom.

And right next to her, still just as handsome in his 50s as he'd been in his 20s, is Crew Masters, Oscar winner. She feels guilty just looking at them, imagining the trauma she dealt their family by sneaking in and stealing their awards.

She's such an asshole.

"You guys know my mom and dad," Tate says as he introduces everyone.

"Of course! So nice to see you!" Mason flashes a friendly smile.

"Mr. and Mrs. Masters … I have something I need to tell you," Val swallows a knot in her throat. "Could we talk in private?"

After all this time, she's ready to give a full confession. She wonders what the statute of limitations is for theft.

"Can we meet up tomorrow morning? We'll come to your place," Tate tells his parents.

Val shoots Tate a grateful look for her stay of execution. Tate Masters, coming to the rescue once again. Everyone's hero.

"Sounds like a plan," Crew answers.

Simon is still staring at his phone. "I need to find her," he announces to the group, anxiously shoving his hand through his hair. "I'll be back when I do."

Val watches him make his way out of the bar to find his new wife, the extortionist. She's not going to even try to look for Sage. Let her sweat it out, wondering what they're doing to locate her.

Josie comes over with Quinn in tow. Even with all this messy drama, Val can tell that they're good for each other. They look happy.

"Mr. and Mrs. Masters! Great to see you." She gives them each a hug. "What did I miss?"

Val barks out a laugh. "You have no idea."

Chapter 50

"Everything finally makes sense ... in hindsight."
- Eve to Jack, Season 1, Episode 5

Josie, August 4

Josie walks down the main drag of 96th Street. She passes Fred's Tavern, The Reeds Hotel, the Stone Harbor Bar & Grill, Watering Hull, The Fudge Shop, the ice cream stores and clothing boutiques, Hoy's 5 and 10.

Picking up her pace, she crosses Second Avenue by the Stone Harbor Water Tower. In the summer months, they play live music and host farmers' markets in the expansive parking lot. Today, it's empty.

Josie walks past the post office and two-story library, the tennis and basketball courts open to the public. She travels past the Fire Department, the Beach Tag Office, and the row of three-story oceanfront homes before making her way to the wooden steps at the end of the road. Then, her bare feet are on the sand.

The ocean spreads out before her, the line of the horizon hard to discern in the morning fog. The waves crash and roll back, crash and roll back, in a steady rhythm.

Seagulls squawk as they try to steal food from distracted sunbathers, aggressively trying to find someone who might have left a tasty bite unattended. One grabs a potato chip from the hands of an unsuspecting child, who screams out loud.

Josie smells the salt of the ocean and feels the heat of the warm sand on her bare feet. It makes everything instantly better. She loves the water, how the tide comes in and out every day, creating a different beach as the sun rises and sets. You can't ever control it—it just happens. The surf comes in and leaves on its own terms. She needs to learn to do that, too.

Josie spots Tate the instant he steps onto the beach.

His lanky frame and lean, tan legs are easy to spot. Both hands are shoved deep in his pockets, and he's wearing the same baseball cap he used to sport most days on location, a Suncatcher original from Mimi's. His curly hair, slightly longer on the bottom, sticks out of the back of his hat.

Tate Masters. The beautiful face that launched a million crushes and was plastered across the walls of teens around the world.

Josie marvels that no one else seems to realize it's him. Everyone on the beach is so busy doing their own thing that they don't pay either of them any mind.

He makes his way over and stands next to Josie. They don't embrace, just take each other in.

Josie breaks the silence. "Want to go for a walk?" she asks, and Tate nods.

Side by side, they wander down the stretch of beach, neither one of them saying a word. When the silence feels like it's gone on too long, Josie tries to think of something to say.

"I never asked, how did you choose to move to Philly? You were always on the West Coast."

Tate looks grateful for the gentle opening. "It's close to New York and DC, a quick flight to the West Coast. I liked that it's more laid back than some other cities. And I've always been an Eagles fan."

"Ever since you watched Invincible," Josie remembers.

"Dick Vermeil is the GOAT."

She laughs. "He is. So, you're happy there? On the East Coast?"

"I am." Tate pauses, as if realizing what he's just said is true. "Really happy. I've got the recording studio and my partner."

"So, things are good."

"They really are. I'm lucky." He pauses again. "I am really happy with my life, working with Squeaks."

Josie feels a quick twinge of sadness in her belly. She doesn't know anything about him anymore, not the details you share when you're so close to each other that you know what your partner ate for breakfast. They're practically strangers.

"It's crazy how we ended up on these new paths," she muses. "You're a music producer, and I'm a commercial photographer. Who would have thought?"

"Yeah," Tate says and pauses with a sigh. "Josie, you've never been big on small talk. Why don't you tell me why you asked me to come here this morning?"

He's also never been one to play games. "It's our final day in town. I guess I wanted to make amends."

"For what?"

"For not believing in us," Josie says simply. "I didn't trust you enough. I was so caught up that I didn't realize what was happening."

Tate gazes out over the horizon. "I get it. What we experienced was so different from what most people will ever go through. Being so young and in the glow of a global spotlight. We had *way* too much attention on us. It made it hard to grow up."

"It did. And if I say that, people think I'm being a thankless brat." Josie shakes her head.

"I'm glad we had the *Shallows*, but it was a lot to go through. So many people take advantage of our fame as a platform for their own."

"It was," she agrees.

"A lot of it was bullshit, but what we had?" Tate turns to look directly at Josie. She doesn't know if she's ready to hear what he has to say. "It was real. I wouldn't trade it for anything."

Tate Masters. Her first love. Her first everything. Something in her that's been wrapped tight since she got the wedding invitation finally loosens. "I loved you so much."

"Same. We'll always have that. Duffy Beach." Tate squeezes her hand. "And if you ever need me, I'll be there. Just call."

"I will." She was glad she'd chosen him and experienced her teen years with him. But they've outgrown each other, and they both realize it.

"And if it doesn't go through, send me an email," Tate says. "Someone could be messing with my phone."

Josie chuckles ruefully, then turns thoughtful, "Will you ever forgive Paige for breaking us up?" She hadn't thought she could ever talk to Paige again, but walking here, along the beach, she wonders what would be the point of holding onto grudges. It only hurts yourself.

"Since we don't see each other every day, it's not like I have to look her in the face for a long time. I figure it's easier to let it go."

"And Val? She broke up your family."

Tate shrugs. "I don't think it was her stealing the awards that did it. There were other problems there long before she took those statues."

She can't believe he's being so forgiving. "So you're going to give them both a hall pass?"

"There's no point in us always looking back. You saw what it did to Val, never letting go of her past. Living in fear. From now on, she gets a new slate. And hopefully, we can all move on."

"With that stunt double." It's so crazy. Josie heard he was out on bail and cozied up with Val.

Tate reaches out to take her hand, and they stop walking. Josie looks into his face, that gorgeous face that always made her pulse quicken. To be honest, it still does.

"I'll always have a piece of my heart for you, Josie Remington," Tate says.

Is this closure? After all this time?

Josie leans closer and presses her mouth to his. Their song plays in her head. *The memory of all that ... no, no they can't take that away from me ...*

It's not a romantic kiss. It's a nostalgic one. He still tastes the same, of cherry Ludens and mint toothpaste.

"Love you too, Tate Masters." They turn to start walking back the way they came, past the beachfront homes and snack shacks on the sand.

After a while, Tate pauses. "This is my stop. I've got to get back to the house and pack up."

"Tell your parents I said hi."

"I will. You know, I think they're getting back together? And they hired a private investigator to track down the owner of that pawn shop. Maybe we'll get lucky and get the trophies back."

"That would be amazing."

"Hit me up if you're ever in Philly. Squeaks and I will take you out."

"I'd love that."

Tate gives her one more long look, then a brief smile. "See you, Jo Jo."

Josie watches him walk away. She decides to keep walking–she needs a few more minutes to herself to process everything. For better or for worse, she's glad she came to the reunion. She reconnected with her past. And now, she might be pursuing a new future going forward.

Maybe there's something there with Quinn. They still have a lot to figure out, but it's not a long drive to get back to Avalon from Lambertville on weekends or her days off.

It wouldn't be hard to see each other if she and Quinn both decide they want to pursue something more. Josie hopes they do.

Chapter 51

"If you see me at the Farmer's Market on a Sunday, please don't say hello. It might be just enough to kill me."
- Chase, Season 3, Episode 8

Mason, August 4

Mason wakes up early, full of excitement and ready to talk to Kit about everything that's happened during this crazy reunion. He's only been gone a few days, but so much has happened. Kit isn't even going to believe everything that took place behind the scenes. He might already know the big things, but not the messy details.

But first, they need to mend their relationship. Then, Mason can get to all the gossip. He gives him a not-so-subtle shove to wake him up.

"You know, you owe me an apology," Mason tells Kit, then snuggles up to him. It's only 6 am, but he needs his husband's full attention.

"Is that right? For leaving in a huff?" Kit opens his eyes. "Did you also want to apologize for taking off like a bat out of hell? The girls were so upset they didn't get to say goodbye to you."

He props himself up on a pillow and gives Mason a stare he knows all too well. The kind Kit gives when he's about to scold the girls for

"

behaving badly. It's not one Mason is used to being on the receiving end of.

"Well, I am sorry for that. But I had to be here. If I weren't, nothing would have been resolved! I take responsibility for all of it."

"The fake relationship, blackmail, and show cancellation? You fixed all of it?"

The problem with Kit, as much as Mason loves him, is that he doesn't take *The Shallows* very seriously. To Kit, it was just a fluffy teen drama. For everyone else who lived it, it WAS Duffy Beach. The center of everything.

"Let's just say, you'd be proud of me for helping manage it all," Mason replies. "I was VERY discreet."

"I'll bet."

"And I did miss you and the girls. But not Alex. She's pure evil."

"True," Kit concedes.

"I am sorry for taking off without talking it through. The good news is, it made me realize how much I adore you guys."

Kit softens. "We do too. It was so quiet without you around."

"Funny, funny. I do wish we didn't need to start packing up." Mason doesn't want to pop their little bubble together, but it's almost time for all of them to head home.

Today is the final day. There are no conference events on the calendar, except for a going-away brunch at the Avalon Yacht Club. Mason thinks it will be non-eventful, but who can tell? This weekend has been full of surprises.

He promises himself that he'll be more present with Kit when they go back home to Unionville. More flexible with the girls. Nicer to Alex. Well, maybe two out of three.

He's not a saint, after all.

They pack up their things and head downstairs. The kitchen is filled with guests grabbing cups of coffee and helping themselves to pastries from High Dune Baking Company, one of the best bakeries on the island.

Tate and Squeaks are sitting at the island, looking cozy. "Good morning," he says, and plants a kiss on top of Squeaks' head.

Mason notices that when one of them looks away, the other sneaks an opportunity to look at them.

Interesting. He has a feeling something is happening there.

And then there are Tate's parents, looking equally smitten right next to them. They must have come clean to Tate about getting back together because they're holding hands as they sit on the bar stools at the counter.

It might be strange for Tate to see, but Mason personally finds it adorable.

"Man, you guys took all the sticky buns. You're sick bastards," Mason announces to the kitchen.

He grabs a couple of scones and a glazed donut before anyone else can snag them. "These are mine. It's an apocalyptic world, and you're scavengers. Every one of you."

Val joins him at the counter and smacks his hand. "Stop taking all the glazed donuts."

"Kit likes them," Mason says. "Stop being a bitch."

"Look who's talking. And Xavier wants some, too."

"They didn't have any donuts at the police station?" Mason feigns.

That earns him a laugh. "You're such an asshole."

"So, this thing with the hunky stunt double. Is it good? Because if not, I'll fight him. I'd lose, but I'd fight him."

"It's good. Really good. And thanks."

"Cool. Just for the record, I'm here. Always."

Val's face softens. "I love you, Mason."

"Love you too. Come see us."

Kit nods in agreement. "Anytime."

"I will." Val hands Mason a sticky bun from her plate. "It was the last one, but now I'm granting it to you."

They look up as Paige walks in. She looks hesitant, as if she's not sure she's welcome. She gives a tentative smile as she wanders over to the coffee pot.

"Maybe I'll give this to Paige," Mason tells Val.

"The sticky bun of forgiveness."

"Exactly."

Paige joins them at the island and scans the baskets of breakfast muffins and pastries. Mason hands her the sticky bun.

"Behold, the sticky bun of forgiveness," he says.

Val tries to control her laughter.

"What the hell? Stop, Mason," Paige tells him. She looks at the sticky bun with distaste. "I'm not in the mood for jokes."

He pushes it into her face. "EAT it!" Mason yells.

"Mason!! Are you kidding me?" Paige's face has cinnamon icing all over it.

Paige grabs a glazed donut and smooshes the entire thing into Val's face.

"Holy shit, Paige!" Val screams. "Why did you do that?"

"Because it's fun? Get over it."

Instantly, it evolves into chaos. Tate picks up a piece of blueberry muffin and tosses it at his dad, Crew. The Oscar-winning actor, with crumbs all over his shirt, picks up one of the larger pieces and throws it back to his son.

"I can't believe you did that!" Kate is laughing when suddenly, she's hit in the face with a Boston cream donut. Her face looks incredulous. "Are you looking for a beating?" she yells to her son.

"I'm sorry," he tells her, with remorse on his face. "That was meant for Mason."

"I got lucky." Mason had bent down to pull Val off Paige from wrestling on the floor, and ducked just in time for the donut to fly over his shoulder.

Maeve and Ivy walk into the kitchen, rubbing sleep from their eyes. Adorable in their brightly patterned pajamas, they look delighted by the all the food flying around.

"Is this what you do when you're working, Daddy-O?" Ivy asks.

"Very funny, kid." Mason lobs a Danish in her direction, which she ducks.

"Food fight!" Maeve shouts. Crumbs fly everywhere. Sprinkles and frosting are smeared all over the cabinets.

Mason looks around. Kate Noble has cream on the side of her face, which is funny but scary at the same time. She *is* rock nobility. And now she's covered in chocolate icing.

Should Mason clean it off her? Nah. She looks like she can handle herself. Which she does seconds later, plopping a donut on her ex-husband's head.

Mason watches as Squeaks manages to get a whole raspberry scone down the back of Tate's shirt. He decides he is re-nicknaming her Sneaks.

The place is a freaking disaster. No donuts left behind.

Mason has so many crumbs and pieces of food in his mustache that he might need to shave it off.

They're finally acting like themselves. No longer pretending that everything is fine. Being honest about who they are. He loves to see it. Because life is messy, and you never know what's around the corner.

Like a flying donut. And you better be able to clean it up and move forward, picking up the pieces to start all over again.

"I really missed you," Kit tells Mason, leaning in to wipe a smear of frosting off his ear.

He's never been happier.

Chapter 52

"Trust me, you wouldn't believe me. Even if I told you everything."
- Francesca to Chase, Season 4, Episode 3

Paige, August 4

As soon as she cleans herself up from the food fight, Paige drives down to the police station. She's on a mission.

Marty has fled town, which isn't surprising, all things considered. The actor checked out of his hotel suite and simply vanished. None of the cast and crew members has any idea where he is.

Paige is about to change that.

"I still can't believe I'm doing this," Detective Nate Shroud sighs. She's getting the feeling that he's about to hit the limit of his patience with her.

He's been quietly sitting while she shows him all the data she's mined online, but now he gets up from his seat. She stops, waiting to see what he says. There's a good chance that he's about to usher her out of his office.

"Here are mutual acquaintances I found," she presses. "I'm telling you, she's not from Oregon."

"We already verified that," he tells her. "We checked her school records. She's from South Jersey."

"Oh." That makes her pause. Well, you know I can still help," Paige assures him. "I've known Sage for years. I can find her trail."

She is in desperate need of redemption. Every single person from the show thinks she's a piece of shit. Paige might actually have a shot at being forgiven, or at least tolerated, if she finds out where Sage is hiding.

And she can do it. If she's honest, there is no one as street savvy. Until this weekend, there wasn't a single person who knew that she got an entire show canceled!

"I was making calls and searching articles all night. I tracked down all of the productions that Sage Domingo has been a part of since *The Shallows*. See this? I created a timeline of her career."

Paige fans out the spreadsheets across the desk. She's listed all the people Sage has crossed paths with professionally, highlighting the actors she's worked with multiple times.

She has a hunch. Valerie told them that she's been paying off Sage for years, but Paige doesn't think that she made enough money to throw such an expensive wedding. The bride must have spent hundreds of thousands of dollars to host such an elaborate rehearsal dinner and wedding. To do that, she would have needed more victims.

"I bet that Sage has been milking other actors, too. Not just Val."

"How are you going to prove it?" Nate asks. He still looks annoyed, but she's got his attention again. He sits back down in his chair.

"With your help, of course," she beams at him. He groans, swiping his hand across his forehead. "Seriously?"

Paige needs him in order to succeed. He has far more access to data than she does, even if the officer is reluctant to work with her.

Even if the money is long gone, Sage should still be held accountable for causing so much turmoil in other people's lives. She took their biggest secrets and drained them for years.

The problem with finding the other victims is that Paige doesn't know what they did (or else they obviously wouldn't be paying to keep it silent), so it's impossible to predict which one has secrets worth hiding. She has a hypothesis that Marty Lawson might be one of Sage's casualties. He took off as soon as they found out about him and Valerie. Who else could he have taken advantage of?

He's not going to respond to a plea from Paige, but he will if he's called in for questioning by a police officer. She just has to convince Detective Nate to be the one to do it.

He balks at her suggestion. "This is all extremely circumspect," he tells Paige. "I have no reason to believe that Sage Domingo is blackmailing Marty Lawson. All I have is Valerie Worth's statement that the necklace is the same one she used to own."

"But she took off," Paige reminds him. "Who runs if they're innocent? She and Marty are both missing."

"Ms. Domingo hasn't had a chance to defend herself, though. I can't get a search warrant off so little evidence."

"That's why I'm trying to find it. Can't we call Marty in to talk? Off the record."

"He's long gone. There's no way he's in town anymore. He told us he was planning on leaving when he came in to say he wasn't pressing assault charges."

"Can you try him anyway?"

Another sigh. "I'll humor you. But I can't promise anything will come out of it."

He makes a call to Marty. It goes right to voicemail.

"I'll let you know when he calls back," Detective Nate promises.

Paige gives him her saddest puppy dog eyes. The ones that booked her countless auditions as a kid. It's highly effective. "Isn't there anything else we can do?" she pleads.

The detective scratches his chin. "I guess we could put out an APB.

Nothing serious, but just to let people know we're looking for him."

"You're brilliant," Paige tells him.

Nate flushes. "It's not usual, but there's no harm in doing it. Mr. Lawson hasn't responded to multiple calls. That's reason enough to put one out."

He starts putting together the electronic paperwork to send to dispatch. She sits across from him, scrolling through her phone and making notes on common acquaintances. They work together in silent companionship, neither one of them talking for a while.

The silence is interrupted by the ring of Paige's phone. It's her mother. Paige wouldn't ordinarily pick up—her mom can be long-winded—but but Jean was always so keen on show business, dragging her to every audition. She knows the name of nearly every talent scout and director in town. Would she have any insight?

"Hi, Mom." Paige answers the phone. She probably took her mother by surprise. They don't talk to her often. Jean wasn't the most nurturing parent, always pushing her to audition, even when Paige was burnt out. But, she is her mom. She's learned to accept that Jean isn't going to change.

"Hi, darling. Just calling to check on you. How is the reunion going? I'm sure you're attracting a lot of press."

"It's definitely been eventful," she answers truthfully. "I actually wanted to run something by you. Show business stuff."

"Of course. You know I'm always here."

That was a laugh. Paige rolls her eyes. "Did you ever hear rumors about Marty Lawson coming on to young women?"

Jean barks. "Who didn't? Everyone knew that he had an eye for teenagers."

"It would have been nice if you had mentioned that while I was a teen *filming a show* with him," Paige says. "You were the one who introduced us on set."

"I'm sorry, I guess I never thought about that."

Paige wonders if she ever worried about her. And why that still hurts. "A little warning would have come in handy," she says wryly. "I had no idea to be careful about him."

"I'm sorry," Jean says with a huff. "Why are you asking now, though? Did he get in trouble?"

"We're still working that out. Do you know the names of any of the girls he seduced? Were any of them underage?"

"I'd have to think about it, but I think he was careful that they were legal. Barely, but enough."

"If you can text me some names, that would be really helpful."

"I will. How is everything else?"

"Good, Mom. Thanks for calling. I gotta run."

The detective has been sitting there silently, listening to her call. "I think I might have something," he tells her. "Marty is listed as the father on the birth certificate of a baby girl in Wilmington, Delaware. It's from nine years ago."

"Really? Would I know the mother's name?"

"Rebecca Radcliffe."

"Becky? Holy shit."

"Who's Becky?" Shroud has obviously never watched *The Shallows.*

"She played Josie's little sister, Hazel, on the show. She didn't come to the reunion. I'm not sure why."

"This means Marty Lawson may have had a relationship with Valerie Worth *and* Rebecca Radcliffe."

"Ewww. He was supposed to be her dad. That's disgusting."

"You wouldn't believe some of the things I've seen," Nate responds. "And I've only been on the force for six years."

"I don't want to know," she mutters. A thought occurs to her. "Was she over eighteen?"

Nate stares at the computer and does a quick calculation. "In 2015, yes. It looks like she was around 19 and a half years old. Although that doesn't mean she wasn't underage when they first got together, just that she was when she had the baby."

"I didn't even know she was pregnant."

"It looks like she gave the baby up for adoption."

Paige pauses to reflect on the situation. Years ago, Becky had a baby in secret. With Marty, who was supposed to be her FATHER on the show. Her freaking Dad.

There's no doubt that the public would see it as incest – even if they're not technically related, everyone has watched them interact as the Mattson family on TV.

Paige can barely wrap her own head around it. It's a huge secret to keep. Absolutely devastating.

It also explains why Becky took off and never kept in contact with any of her fellow cast mates after the show. She must have had the baby soon after the series ended. How hard that must have been for her.

"Can we call her? Ask if she was ever blackmailed about it?" Paige asks.

Nate shakes his head. "I don't think so. This is her personal business. If no one knew about it, she must have had her reasons."

"I can't imagine how she must have felt," Paige muses. She wishes she had known. She would have tried to help her, or at least helped support her decision."

"Let's respect her privacy. There's no need to contact her at this point."

Paige has to agree. "You're right. Especially considering how hard she worked to keep the secret."

"What I *can* do is ask Marty if he knew anything about it when he calls me back," Nate says. "That's reasonable."

"Let's do that."

"Sounds good," Nate responds, then pauses before adding, "You did a nice job."

Paige realizes that she hasn't pulled at her hair all day. She takes his hat off his desk and plants it on her head. "I think I have a real knack for this," she beams.

Chapter 53

"Bro, I can't believe we won the championship!
This is the best day of my life!"
- Chase to Jack, Season 3, Episode 9

Tate, August 4

"Be honest with me. You guys are really back together?" Tate asks his parents.

Tate, his parents, and Squeaks gather together in the family room after cleaning themselves up from the food fight. The house is pretty quiet. Most of the other guests have wandered off to pack and get ready to leave the island.

"Would you be okay with it if we were?" his dad responds. He's sitting right next to Tate's mom on the couch, his arm slung over the back.

It's been an unusual weekend. Tate hasn't seen them this close to each other in years.

"Of course," Tate assures him. "It would be great if we could all get together, like we used to. It would be a lot easier than always splitting up for holidays and events."

"Then yes, we are," Kate says, looking at her ex. "At least, we're dating. It's not official, like we're not getting remarried."

"Not yet," Crew butts in.

She gives him a look, exasperated but affectionate. "But we are enjoying spending time together. Going out."

"A lot," his dad takes his mom's hand and holds it in his.

"I don't need all the details." Tate covers his ears. "Just give me a heads up when you're getting busy. I don't want to walk in on you guys."

"*Tate!*" Squeaks squeaks, horrified.

"Was that a squeak?" Tate asks. "Is that how you got your name?" She has never told him how she got her nickname. She won't even give him a hint.

Squeaks punches him in the arm. "Shut up."

"It totally was. You sound like a mouse." Tate doubles over laughing.

"You keep going with this, and it's going to get ugly," she warns.

"A squeaker. Holy shit," Tate is still cracking up. He can't help it. His tough partner.

Squeaks crosses her arms. "Payback is a bitch, Tate Masters. We have a long ride home," she warns.

His parents are scheduled to leave this afternoon. They're catching a red eye back to the West Coast.

Tate and Squeaks are driving back to Philly after they attend the going away brunch this morning. They're planning on taking the scenic route back, stopping at roadside farm stands and local wineries before they rejoin city life.

Tate has never felt more at peace. He closed the chapter on his past with Josie, made amends with what happened with Val, learned his parents are dating, and is excited to see if there's more to his friendship with Squeaks than he realized.

"So, I heard the Covington Five might even be reuniting," Tate says. "Our lead singer went to sex rehab and came out a new man."

Squeaks rolls her eyes. "Or at least, his girlfriend and the lead guitarist think so."

Tate isn't sure what will happen, but he's confident that the release of the band's new album is going to put his and Squeaks' recording studio on the map.

Life is crazy. Who knows what's going to happen? You just have to play the cards you're dealt and hope you have a good hand. And if you don't have a solid one, to know when to fold and move on.

"I'm so glad we did this," Tate tells his parents and Squeaks. "This reunion was more than I hoped for."

This part of his life is over. He's changed and can move on with the right frame of mind to pursue new opportunities. Try new things.

They grab their bags and start making their way outside. There's a car waiting to take his parents to the airport. He gives each of them a hug.

"You take good care of him," Kate tells Squeaks as she kisses her cheek.

They watch them drive away.

"What are you thinking?" Squeaks grabs his hand. Tate realizes he's been staring off into space.

"How lucky I am." He squeezes her hand. "I'm wondering if you want to go out with me. On a date." Maybe one day, he might even start calling her Sasha.

"About time you realized that."

The Avalon Yacht Club is hosting a goodbye brunch for everyone who was involved in the reunion. It will be their last time to all be in the room together. Tate and Squeaks aren't not staying long, just enough to say quick goodbyes and get on the road.

He doesn't plan on losing touch with the crew again. That had been a mistake. They had all shared in something special together, something uniquely their own. Tate plans to keep in contact with all of them from now on. Even Josie.

He opens the car door for Squeaks and walks over to the driver's side.

He's going to miss this coastal beach town. "Maybe we should rent a place here next summer?"

"I would do that," Squeaks answers with a smile.

A year later, Tate will write Squeaks a ukulele love song to commemorate their anniversary. It will become a huge hit, skyrocketing to the Top Ten on the Billboard charts.

Tate will even win a few industry awards for it. But not a Grammy.

Chapter 54

"I'm looking for someone who will stick. Someone I can count on."
- Shea to Chase, Season 4, Episode 9

Val, August 4

Xavier hands Val a mimosa. From their spot overlooking the bayside, they watch seagulls fly across the marsh channels, honking loudly. An osprey perches on a wooden pier, carefully observing.

"Knock, Knock."

She grins at him. "Honestly?"

"Knock, Knock," he repeats.

"Okay, I'll play. Who's there?"

"A herd."

"A herd who?"

"A herd you were here, so I came over."

It's so corny it's cute. "Damn it, don't make me laugh," she warns.

"I can't help it. You look tense. Don't worry. Everyone here is on your side."

"*Everyone* here is too busy gossiping about me."

"Let them," Xavier tells her. "It's their problem, not yours. You have nothing to hide."

Not anymore, now that everyone knows her secret; and about what Sage was blackmailing her. Val guesses that's one blessing to come out of all of this. She no longer needs to conceal what she did anymore.

She's still anxious about seeing people, wondering if anyone is going to give her a hard time about it. "Just stick by me, okay?" she asks. "I need your support."

"I'm not going anywhere."

She knows he means it. Val might not be perfect—*who is?*—but Xavier makes her feel pretty damn close to it. She's so glad that he's with her again after being released from the police station without any charges.

The Avalon Yacht Club overlooks one of the many inlets along the bay area. Docks leased by club members secure the sailboats and motorboats. Today is bright and sunny, as sailboats and motorboats cut through the water.

She spots a lot of familiar faces as they wander the outskirts of the crowd. There are still no signs of Marty. That's starting to look more and more suspicious. Maybe he's involved with more than they realized?

Detective Nate had told her, without using so many words, that he could see why Xavier went after Marty. "Just don't let him do it again," he'd said when she was picking Xavier up from the station.

By now, everyone knows or will know what happened between her and Marty, TV's favorite dad. It hurts to think he did it to other girls as well.

Paige had told Val in confidence about Marty's affair with Becky and the baby they had together. She swore Val to secrecy. "The only reason I'm sharing Becky's secret is that you were both taken advantage of by Marty at the same time," Paige told Val.

Val did search (just a little bit!) online, but Becky has no trail. She hasn't acted in anything since their show, she's not on social media, and there are no recent articles about her. It's like she completely vanished.

Val's not going to tell anyone else. She'd tried to reach out to Becky, but she also understands about letting secrets lie buried. It's pretty clear now why Becky dropped off their radar and didn't stay in touch with any of them. She wanted to leave the whole *Shallows* drama of her life behind.

Val looks across the covered deck spanning the club's marina. She may have worked it out with the cast after their food fight, but there's someone else that Val still needs to talk to. She needs to make amends to the couple she stole the trophies from.

Tate's parents are here, standing at a high-top table with Tate and Squeaks. It's now or never.

Val squares her shoulders and tries to muster all of her courage. "Will you walk over there with me?" She looks up at Xavier.

He nods. "You're ready to do this?" She told him everything. No more secrets.

Val walks over to them. She knows she'll never get the chance to talk to them again. Even if they never forgive her, at least she tried.

Tate looks wary. "Val." He starts to rise, but she motions for him to sit back down.

"Morning," Val answers, then looks towards his parents. "Mr. and Mrs. Masters. Do you mind if I talk to you for a second? I promise it won't take long."

"Go ahead," Tate's mom responds, waving her hand at her. Kate Noble isn't exactly cold, but she's not very friendly either.

"I owe you a huge apology." Val's throat clenches. It's hard to get the words out, but she forces herself to keep going. There's no backing out now. "I never should have taken your awards. I've regretted it every day since."

"Tate told us what happened." She doesn't elaborate.

This isn't going to be easy. Val forges ahead. "I will do anything I can to make up for what I did. I can go public about it, if you'd like. Tell the press what I did." She tucks her arms under her shoulders, suddenly so nervous she can barely stand there any longer.

"Val," Tate starts, but he's cut off by his father.

"No, don't do that," Crew Masters says. "It's over and done with. We can't change it."

"I just wish we had known it was a mistake by a friend of our teenager," Kate adds. "We thought it might have been malicious, someone doing it to personally hurt us. That worried me."

"That doesn't make it any more right. I should have told you a long time ago. I was just so scared." Val shakes her head, tears welling in her eyes. "I'm such an idiot."

Kate nods. "You were. But you're not the first and won't be the last to make a mistake. No one else here can judge. We've all done things we regret."

This is her cue to go. "I wanted to say just how incredibly sorry I am. Thank you for speaking with me. You didn't have to do that." Val takes Xavier's hand and turns to walk away.

She's finally ready to let down her guard. It's time to let people in. Start trusting again.

"I really want to see you after this," she tells Xavier.

"Did you think I was letting you go?" he says with a chuckle. "No one else likes my knock-knock jokes."

Chapter 55

"What am I going to do with the rest of my life?
I don't even know what I'm going to do after graduation."
- Francesca, Season 4, Episode 8

Josie, August 4

Josie and Quinn escape the brunch for a view of the water, where they watch Quinn's best friend, Tyson, bending over a row of sailboats docked in the marina.

"Why are you back here messing with the boats? I want you to meet Josie," Quinn yells across the water.

Tyson doesn't even look up from attaching a piece of rope from a buoy to the front of a boat. It looks important.

"This isn't even your yacht club!" Quinn shouts again. "Get a life."

"It's totally okay," Josie assures him. "We can meet later."

"The guy never stops. He thinks he's the only one who knows boats. My job is fighting fires, and do you hear me complain?" he yells over.

Tyson doesn't turn around, but he answers his friend just as loudly. "I hate meeting new people. You know that."

"She's right here, buddy."

"Oh." Tyson looks up from the roping with a sheepish smile. "Sorry about that. I couldn't hear much, with Quinn doing all the shouting."

He secures the rest of the rope and heads toward them. "You must be Josie." He holds out his hand to shake hers.

"It's nice to meet you. I've heard a lot about you and your fiancé."

"Tyson met Margo in kindergarten at Stone Harbor Elementary," Quinn says. "It only took him 20 years to ask her out."

"Good things take a while." Josie tries to keep the peace. They obviously enjoy ribbing each other.

"I like her already." Tyson playfully slaps the back of Quinn's head. "Margo is running late. She said she'll try to make it over by noon."

"I hope she can. Come inside and meet everyone from the show," Quinn tells him.

They walk around the steps to the main entrance.

Mason and Kit are standing in the front lobby with their daughters. Mason is leaning over the younger girl's head, mumbling something about finding donut crumbs, but Josie isn't sure why she'd have them in her hair.

"This is Tyson, who basically runs anything here that has to do with sailing or boating," Quinn says as he makes introductions. "Tyson, this is Mason and Kit. They live in the Philly suburbs."

"We're in Chadds Ford. We run a landscaping business." Mason looks back and forth between Tyson and Quinn. "Wow. You guys really should have been on the show."

"I was away at college," Tyson offers. "Came back after it ended."

"Our loss."

Kit smacks Mason on the shoulder. "Leave this poor guy alone." He turns to the girls. "Do you guys want to get some Shirley Temples?" They answer yes excitedly, and Kit leads Maeve and Ivy toward the bar.

"How about you, Josie? Where do you live?" Tyson asks. He's a lot different than his buddy Quinn. He's much quieter, more mellow.

Shy, even. But she can tell he's someone Quinn relies on. She isn't surprised that he manages the entire fleet of boats at the club himself.

"I'm in Lambertville, New Jersey. It's along the Delaware River. A couple of hours away."

"I've heard of it. They have shad fishing, right?"

She's surprised he knows about it. "Yes, they do. They're known for it, actually."

"They have that festival." Tyson looks like he's actually interested, not just being polite. "I've always wanted to go."

Josie laughs. "You guys are welcome to come up for it and stay at my place. It's called Shad Fest."

"I'd love to."

"Anything with fish is going to interest Tyson," Quinn announces to the group.

"What the hell are shad?" Mason asks.

"Sorry," Quinn laughs. "They're fish that migrate like salmon? They go from saltwater to freshwater to have their babies. They call it the Shad Run."

"It happens every year along the Delaware River, so they have a festival that keeps growing bigger. It's actually a lot of fun," Josie adds.

"It's right next door to New Hope, which we know and love," Mason adds.

"That's it. We have lots of art stores and restaurants."

"We'll come to the fest, but not to fish. We'd be happy to watch," Mason says. "Kit and I are also willing to lie if you want to tell everyone how big the fish you caught was."

Quinn rolls his eyes good-naturedly. "Count us in. I guess that means you have to keep dealing with us townies, Josie. Doesn't the festival take place in the spring?"

"It does. It will give us something to look forward to." Are she and Quinn making future plans? For the first time in a long time, she wants to live a little. Time is going by way too fast. Josie is done trying to lie low, covering herself up to keep from attracting attention.

"Another reunion," Mason says happily. "We're so there." He squeezes Josie's shoulder. "I'm going to find Kit and the girls."

Quinn eyes her intently. "Do you have to leave today?"

"Not necessarily," she says. "But my hotel room is up. I have to check out by noon."

"Then stay with me. Stay as long as you'd like."

Josie cocks her head, considering his offer. "I could be persuaded to stay a little longer."

"We could go fishing when Margo gets here," Tyson offers. "See what's biting out on the water."

"Maybe later. I have plans to keep us busy for a while," Quinn says. "Buzz off, Tyson."

Chapter 56

*"You know that saying, 'If someone tells you who they
are the first time, believe them?' That's you."*
- Eve to Francesca, Season 1, Episode 9

Paige, August 4

Paige is standing next to Quinn at the brunch buffet line when he gets
an urgent call for emergency assistance.

He picks up right away. "This is Quinn."

"We're calling all available units. A call came in that someone is
scaring children at the park on 39th and Dune. They said he's pacing
wildly and acting erratically, threatening to hurt himself."

Paige is so close that she can hear everything the dispatcher is saying.

"Do you have a description of the subject?" Quinn asks.

"I do. It looks like he matches the APB that was put out by the Avalon
Police Department. For a Marty Lawson, of Los Angeles."

"I'll be right there," Quinn promises, and puts his phone back in his
pocket. She watches him dash over to tell Josie that he's leaving.

This is a huge opportunity! She can't believe Marty surfaced. Where
has he been hiding?

Paige drops her plate on the buffet table and calls Detective Nate right away.

"I know. I was already notified," he says. "I'm en route. Just stay put."

"Let me come with you," she begs. "I worked with Marty for years. I can help."

"Absolutely not. You're an actress, not a first responder," the detective tells her. "You cannot be a part of this." He hangs up.

"Whatever." She's going anyway. Paige hurries out of the club, chasing after Quinn.

"Hey Quinn, wait up!" She yells across the parking lot. "Detective Shroud said I should tag along."

If Quinn is surprised, he doesn't show it. "Hop in. We need to hurry."

They rush down 7th Street and up Ocean Drive. Quinn's emergency lights are flashing as he flies past cars pulling over to the side. They run every stoplight.

Paige loves every second. She feels like she's in a Law *& Order* episode!

What should have taken ten minutes takes less than five.

Quinn pulls up to the park. "Don't say anything," he tells Paige as they approach the scene. A group of Avalon and Stone Harbor Police Department cars are parked around the perimeter of the park, blocking traffic.

Paige spots Marty. He's standing next to the open door of a blue Mustang convertible in the parking lot.

The actor looks disheveled, with wrinkled clothing. His usual immaculate hair, perfectly coiffed, is flopping all over his face. In one hand, Marty holds a bottle of vodka, while the other is waving wildly at the officers.

The playground, usually crowded with children playing on the equipment, has completely emptied. They probably scattered when they spotted the erratic man wandering around the parking lot. Who could blame them?

Paige and Quinn join the group of first responders who are standing back, waiting to approach Marty.

"I have the name of the person who placed a 911 call," one of the officers tells them. "The first responder did a great job tying the description of him with the ABP that was put out."

"The dispatcher said he keeps telling them not to come closer," Quinn says. "Do me a favor and don't say anything to him yet."

Detective Shroud is there, too. He looks at Paige. "What are you doing here?" he barks at her. "I told you to stay out of it. That was an order!"

"She said you told her to come." Quinn looks at her in disbelief. "I fell for it."

"I was acting," Paige tells Quinn proudly. "Aren't I good?"

Shroud shakes his head. "Just don't say anything," he tells her, pushing her behind the police barricade. Across the street, the crowds keep growing, with more people stopping as they pass by.

"Everyone keeps telling me that." Paige just wants to watch.

"We don't know if he's armed," Shroud updates them. "He won't answer our questions, so we haven't approached him. We don't need to get any closer."

A few people stand on the sidewalk, gawking at the police standoff taking place in a family vacation town. They're looking at Marty in disbelief.

It's no wonder. She's never seen the guy look worse. Marty's signature long hair, which she now realizes is a comb over, is flopping back and forth on top of his head. It looks like he's been wearing the same clothes for days, and his face is red from sunburn.

Quinn grabs a megaphone that's on top of one of the patrol cars. "Marty, my name is Quinn Kearney. I met you at the reunion. We just want to help," he says calmly.

"Then go away! I keep telling everyone. Just leave me alone!" He looks manic.

"You know we can't do that," Quinn answers. "Can you tell me what's wrong?"

"You know what happened! You all do! I'm being framed!"

"No one is accusing you of anything."

Marty takes a long drink from the bottle he's holding. "Give me a break. My career is over. My reputation is shredded. I'll never work again."

"What about everyone else who loves you? You're America's dad," Quinn says. "A legend."

"Not anymore. I'm getting all these questions from the police. Accusing me of doing things with young women. It's not my fault! They all wanted it!"

"I don't know anything about that," Quinn answers. "I just want you to be safe."

"Safe!" Marty scoffs. "I'm under attack! They're all coming after me, now."

"That's not what I'm worried about. Why don't we talk about all of this in private?"

Marty shakes his head, his hair flapping around from the wind. "I'm not going anywhere."

"I can't let you drive right now. Let's go someplace and talk."

Marty turns around, as if noticing the car he's been leaning against the whole time. "I slept in it," he says off-handedly. He puts one leg inside, then starts bending to sit in the driver's seat.

Paige doesn't even realize it, but Quinn has been moving slowly— monumentally slowly—towards Marty. Seeing his chance while Marty's distracted, he starts walking faster.

Marty notices right away. "Go away!" he shouts.

"Don't do this," Quinn tells him.

"There's no other way," Marty says sadly. "Time to pay the piper."

Paige recognizes the look on his face. It's the same expression he used as the solid TV dad he always played, the one doling out sage advice. Telling the kids what to do when they got caught cheating on a test or were in a fight with their best friend.

He turns around and jumps in the Mustang, revving the engine. The crowd of people begins to back away.

"Damn it," Shroud mutters. He runs to his patrol car.

Marty peels out of the parking lot, evading a parked police car and making a hard left on Dune Drive to make a quick getaway.

Paige whips around to see him take off down the street.

The Mustang is a sports car, made to pick up speed quickly. Plumes of smoke come off the tires.

Is he going to make a mad dash out of town? Create a police chase? He's going fast enough to give himself a decent lead over the police officers who are jumping in their cars. They start turning the cruisers around to go after him, but they're all jammed up.

Marty doesn't get far.

Parked cars are blocking his exit. Without a lane to travel in, he swerves across the grass median, into two lanes of oncoming traffic.

Paige hears horns blaring, and people scream as Marty goes the wrong way on the busy road.

The Mustang weaves as Marty tries to go around them. It doesn't work. He loses control of the car, slamming the 1967 classic Mustang into one of the massive steel legs of the Avalon Water Tower, its basin proudly declaring "Cooler Than a Mile."

The Mustang loses the battle, its fender crumpling on impact. Paige watches in disbelief as Marty's body hits the windshield, which cracks immediately. Shards of glass litter the sidewalk. The engine begins hissing.

Quinn runs down the street to drag him out of the car. Detective

Nate and Paige are close behind. The stench of burnt rubber fills her nose.

Mary is slumped against the steering wheel, unconscious. There's blood trickling down his face. The front of the car is wedged around one of the tower's metal poles.

"Don't move." Paige watches Quinn check Marty's vitals. "Can you say your name?" he asks as he starts to stir.

Marty groans but doesn't answer. His eyes flicker open but stay unfocused. He's silent as they brace his neck and carefully load him into a waiting ambulance to take him to the hospital.

"What's going to happen to him?" Paige asks Detective Shroud quietly.

"The ambulance will take him to Shore Memorial Hospital. They'll do a psych eval and then probably take him to a mental health inpatient center." He sighs. "Damn shame."

"Are you going to press charges? For what he did to Valerie and Rebecca?"

"As far as I know right now, he didn't do anything illegal. They were both of legal age. I'll get a statement from him and verify their ages. But he's getting charged with what happened today."

"Hmm. Val said she was of legal age when it happened," Paige muses. "Young, but an adult. And we know Rebecca was 19 when she gave birth."

"We'll see how it goes, but I don't think they're going to pursue charges at this point. Even if he gets away with it, I'd bet anything that he's right that his career as America's dad is over. He's never going to act again."

"Oh yeah, he's done," Paige agrees.

"This isn't his car, either. I have a feeling he'll get hit with charges for theft of a motor vehicle and fleeing the scene of an incident."

"That's fair. He's such a creep. He needs to pay for what he did. But what about Becky? Are you going to tell him about the baby?"

"There's no reason to. It's her secret, and one she took pains to conceal. Giving a baby up for adoption can never be easy. I say we let it go."

"Agreed."

"I've got to make a call," Detective Shroud says.

"To who?" Paige asks.

"Roger Elliot, to tell him that his car is a total loss."

"Yikes."

Despite the drama, Paige has to admit she likes police work. Maybe she should try out for a detective series. She can totally see herself as another Mariska Hargitay. Helping those in need, advocating for the victims, and showing up in court to testify against the bad guys.

Crazier things have happened, right?

Chapter 57

"It's okay, it's okay. I'm here. I won't leave you."
- Shea to Francesca, Season 4, Episode 3

Sage, August 9

Sage has been hiding out at her mom's house when she hears a knock at her door. She peeks out of the keyhole. Simon is standing outside.

How did he find her? She's always worked so hard to cover where she's from, but here he is on her doorstep on a Friday morning, in less than a week since she fled the party.

She has nowhere else to run, so she opens the door, a little anxious but also excited to see him.

"Simon," Sage breathes. She knows she looks different than how he usually sees her. She's wearing faded sweats and an old T-shirt from a Horde Festival she attended 15 years ago. She found them in a drawer in her former bedroom.

Sage didn't have many options. She didn't bring any of her clothes with her when she fled Avalon.

"Can I come in?" Simon looks exhausted. Even with his glasses on, she can see dark circles under his eyes.

"Of course. I'm the only one home." Sage steps back for him to walk in.

Sage's mother, Maria, had already left for work, so there's no one else around to hear what Simon has to say.

Maria had been so supportive when Sage showed up on the doorstep, crying her eyes out and seeking a place to hide. Sage had shared everything with her mother, who hadn't even given her a hard time about hiding their family from her husband.

Maria just looked sad and a little embarrassed that her daughter had tried so hard to erase the reality of their family. "Honey, I wish you had told me … "

What can she say? She knows she's acted like a piece of shit. And now everyone else knows, too. "I ruined everything. I tried so hard to be one of them that I stole from them. I lied to everyone."

Maria hugged Sage tightly. "Nothing is ever final," she told her daughter. "Have you talked to Simon?"

"No, I took off when Val was yelling at me. I ran a few blocks, and then I called an Uber to get here. I left everything behind. I don't even have my luggage."

"Just stay here for a few days. It will all blow over," Maria reassured her.

A few days have turned into five, and she has no plans to go anywhere. It was surprisingly nice to be back home, getting taken care of by her mother. Spending time with Maria and the rest of their family. She had been so caught up in her new life that she hadn't even realized how much she had missed them.

Sage steps aside to let Simon in, watching him take in the scene in front of him. It's a small house, but it's cozy. There's a shabby, threadbare couch with two faded side chairs and a side table covered with plants. Photos of her and her cousins line the walls.

"I didn't even know you were from Alloway," Simon says, looking around the room. He doesn't look angry, just confused. "You told me you were from Oregon. I went through your entire list of online friends until I figured it out."

"I know." She looks down at her feet. "I lied to you. About a lot of things."

He snorts, pushing his glasses back. "That's an understatement."

"Does everyone hate me?"

"No, Sage," he says softly. He finally looks directly at her. "But they don't understand it. How could you do that to Valerie? She was a good friend."

"You don't know what it's like to grow up like this. Always trying to get out. I just wanted to belong. To have a glamorous life." She shrugs. "To do that, I needed money."

Simon shakes his head. "I didn't care how much money you had. And when we got together, you know everything of mine became yours."

Sage knows that Simon doesn't understand. How could he? He's never dealt with the embarrassment of wearing second-hand clothes that never fit, or were never the right trend. To always want to feel pretty, but learn to make do with what she had- self haircuts, dying her own hair, and shopping at thrift stores.

Maria was already aware of how much her daughter tried to hide her roots. When she first came to visit Sage in California, Sage made sure her mom only wore the outfits Sage had pre-approved or bought for her.

Sage had even instructed her mother not to talk much about her job as a receptionist at a concrete firm, the town she grew up in, or her lack of a degree. Maria had dropped out of high school when she became pregnant with Sage.

Eventually, Maria stopped coming to visit ... until the distance between them grew so big they couldn't bridge it.

Sage knows she's a terrible person to be so ashamed of her mother, who did so much for her. And now, everyone Sage cares about has found out exactly what she's been doing to fund the lifestyle she always craved.

She had thought she was so clever, but in the end, don't secrets always come out? Who was she fooling?

Sage swallows. "There's more," she says. And Sage finally tells him everything. How she found out that Val stole the statues because she was at the same pawn store, selling the Alloway High School graduation ring her mother had gifted her.

Maria had been so proud that her daughter had graduated from high school when she'd had to drop out. And Sage had pawned it for a quick buck.

Val never even noticed Sage at the store. Why would she? She wasn't used to looking at other people. She was used to being the center of attention, herself.

It started as an idea at the back of Sage's head, something crazy, until she started justifying it. Why should Val get away with it? After all, she hadn't stolen the statues. Val did.

One day, she sent the first letter. When it worked, and Val paid, she just kept sending them.

Then, it happened again. Finding out about something she could use for leverage.

She was walking along the beach one night when she happened upon Marty Lawson and Rebecca Radcliff. They were naked in the dunes. She quickly turned and left them alone. They'd been too busy to notice her.

It was so gross. He was playing a TV dad, and he was having sex with one of the teenagers from the show. He had to have been at least 20 or 25 years older than Rebecca.

She tucked that secret in her back pocket until she needed it. Especially when she noticed that Becky had gotten really quiet … and gained some weight around the middle.

Was she the only one who realized Becky was pregnant?

All it took was one letter, and Marty quickly paid up. He was her biggest source of income. The reason she was able to fund so much of her new lifestyle as the soon-to-be Mrs. Simon Hartwick. Someone glamorous. Someone special.

Once she felt that way, it was impossible to go back to being the poor, quiet nobody of Sage Domingo.

Sage explains all of this to Simon. Why not? He's her husband now. She has no secrets left. She's probably going to jail for what she did, anyway.

"Why did you wear the necklace you blackmailed from Val?" Simon asks.

"I don't know," she confesses. "I had it for so many years that it felt like mine. And I think maybe I was trying to get caught. I think I was done hiding everything."

Simon looks at her sadly. "But then why didn't you tell me? We could have found a way out of this."

"I don't know. It started to weigh on me, but I couldn't figure out how to end it. It was like I was obsessed with the show, but I also hated what it made me become. How hard I tried to catch up."

"I can see how that could happen," he muses. "But we can't keep these secrets from each other."

"I realize that. I've realized a lot of things."

"Did you ever try to find out where the statues went?" Simon asks.

"I did go back to see if I could buy back the ring," Sage says. "It was gone, just like the statues. The owner said he sold the trophies to a collector from Brentwood. He couldn't even remember selling my ring. It had been worth so little to him."

"Would he give you the name of who bought them?"

"No, and I didn't press him. Do you think I'm going to get arrested?"

Simon shakes his head. "Here's what I think. If we can fix this. If we can get the statues back, and you agree to pay her back, I think I can convince Val not to turn you in. Maybe."

"Really? That's more than I'd hoped."

"Yeah. And Marty doesn't know it was you blackmailing him. Besides, he's in a mental health ward right now. He's got his own problems to deal with."

Not to mention, learning he's a dad to a ten-year-old kid, she thinks. Sage isn't going to be the one who tells him.

"We will need to deal with it eventually, though," Simon says. "I'm done with keeping secrets."

"Okay," Sage sighs. She hopes that's a long way off.

"If you can believe it, Paige has been working with the detective from Stone Harbor Police," Simon says. "Why don't we go talk to her and figure out what she knows?"

He's being so understanding—more than she ever could have expected. "You and me?"

Simon smiles. "Of course. We're a team. I meant it when I said those vows." He looks down at his hands, then back up at her. "We will need to go to couples counseling."

She'd agree to anything. "Absolutely."

"I still can't believe you hid all this from me."

Sage's nerves are shot, but she takes a deep breath and plunges ahead. "I'd really like you to come back here when this is done. To meet the rest of my family."

"I thought you didn't have any family?"

"It's huge. Tons of cousins," Sage admits sheepishly. "I didn't invite them to the wedding. But I'd like you to meet them."

"Sounds like a plan." He tugs her hand to pull her closer. Sage wraps her arms around his neck.

"I love you."

"Love you too." They kiss, and Sage realizes how close she came to losing him. *How dumb I was to risk losing all this*, Sage thinks.

Sage sends her mom a quick text to let her know that Simon is with her. And that she's okay.

Suddenly, things don't seem as bleak anymore. Even though she might be facing charges for blackmail and extortion. If she has Simon in her corner, she can get through anything.

"Oh." She turns to Simon. "You should probably know, my real name isn't Sage."

Chapter 58

"Don't you wish we could do it all again?"
- Chase, Season 4, Episode 9 (Series Finale)

Josie, August 12

"I'm really glad we were able to connect before we leave," Josie tells Paige as they're seated at their table. As the only ones left in Avalon, they decided to meet up for lunch at the Icona.

"Me too," agrees Paige. "Thanks for joining me. I can't believe I'm going to say this, but I miss everyone. It seems quiet without them."

"It does," Josie agrees.

It's a perfectly sunny beach day. From their table on the second floor, they have a full view of the ocean stretched out before them. Families drag beach chairs and gear up the wooden walkways, making their way to the sand.

"I can't stay too long." Josie takes a sip of her iced tea. "I'm meeting up with Quinn later." She was talked into staying for another week by a very persuasive Quinn.

Tate and Squeaks left for Philly, and Mason and Kit are already back home in Chadds Ford with Maeve and Ivy.

Val had to get back to Washington, DC, a few days ago. Bryce and

Justin flew back to California on a private plane out of Atlantic City.

"I know. You're the only one here for me to update about the trophies," Paige responds. She's gotten deep into her role as an amateur sleuth, playing detective with Nate Shroud.

"That's right. So, what's going on with it?" Josie asks. She knew that Tate's parents had hired private investigators to follow leads from that time, but the pawn shop closed, and they hit dead ends.

Paige was the one to find a connection. She'd called Justin and asked if he had any names of big collectors in the LA area.

"Surprisingly, Justin has been a huge asset." Paige waves her fork. "He's been relentless, asking around, and visiting local pawn shops in Los Angeles."

"Who would have thought? Stranger things have happened."

"I think he feels a little guilty about messing with our lives," Paige shrugs. "And who knows, maybe he needs a hobby. But it actually paid off, and we got a name: Sam Holman."

"Who's that?"

"A big collector of awards and things like that. And he's from Brentwood, the town Sage mentioned the pawn shop told us about. It fits. I guess he's also a huge Kate Crew fan."

"It sounds like that could be the guy," Josie looks out at the view.

"Yeah. Nate is calling Leo today." Paige's eyes darken. "I'm not allowed to be on the call."

"Give it a rest, Detective Paige," Josie teases her. "You've done enough."

"How about you? Are you planning on staying long?" Paige leans over the table. "Quinn is so dreamy," she whispers.

Josie grins."He is, right? I'm not sure yet. I need to get back, but I like being here. And I like spending time with Quinn."

There's more to it than that, but Josie has learned to keep some things to herself. She will always love Paige, but she'll never really be able to fully trust her again.

They talk about other things, catching up on stories from previous times. Soon enough, they're finishing their lunches and splitting the bill.

"So, this is it? Will you come visit me again?" Paige asks.

"I'm going to be in New York in September. Let's meet up then." Josie opens her arms, and they lean in for a big hug. Despite everything, she knows Paige will always be part of her life.

Later, Josie will get a text from Paige with an update: it's confirmed that the purchaser was Sam Holman. He's offered to give it all back, as long as Kate Crew is there when he makes the hand off. She's happy to comply, offering to give him a personal photo opportunity and a signed guitar as well.

Leo is thrilled.

So are Tate's parents. They may have had the trophies replaced by the academies after the theft, but they aren't the same as the actual ones they held in their hands when they were on stage to receive the honors.

A couple of hours later, Tate calls to thank Josie. He told her that his parents have even moved back in with each other.

"They're acting like teenagers," he says. "Staying out all night, making out in corners, whispering and giggling. I can't handle it."

"That's crazy," Josie laughs.

It's good to hear from him. They've come to a solid place with each other. Old friends with a shared past.

Later, she'll meet up with Quinn at their special spot on the 92nd Street beach.

"How did your lunch with Paige go?" Quinn asks from where he's sitting cross-legged on a picnic blanket. He looks gorgeous in a navy polo and striped board shorts, with a baseball cap turned backward.

The sun streaks across the clouds, gradually dimming as it makes its exit. Hot pink and orange bands color the sky. They'll begin to fade as night approaches.

"I got a lot of updates. She said that Detective Shroud told her Marty Lawson broke four bones in his face." Josie sighs. "It should be fixed by a good plastic surgeon, but we think he'll be blacklisted from Hollywood for life."

Quinn nods, waiting for her to continue.

"Val and Xavier are setting off on a cross-country trip in Xavier's Sprinter van. They're hitting all the national parks and documenting it on a blog that's getting a lot of attention."

"Good for them," he says.

"She also said Val isn't going to press any charges. Detective Shroud still hasn't decided if he'll get an arrest warrant for extortion."

"Ouch. Isn't Sage on a payment plan to pay Val back?"

"Yeah," Josie says with a laugh. "She has ten years to go."

Quinn grins. "Better than nothing."

Josie looks down, then back up. "I also heard from Tate. They found the guy who has his parents' trophies."

"That's great. I'm glad they're getting them back." There's no jealousy in his voice. Quinn is unlike anyone she's ever dated. She trusts him enough to tell him anything.

"Oh, and Mason and Kit are coming to Shad Fest."

"Don't forget, Tyson and Margo said they want to come, too. We'll make it a party."

Josie moves over to his spot on the blanket. She rests her back against his chest, content and at peace.

"Stone Harbor has the best sunsets in the world," Quinn had told her last week, while they sat on a dock off the bay. "It's a fact."

He's been trying to prove it to her ever since.

"So, you get to do this every day?" Josie asks, swirling the wine in her glass. "Walk to the ocean and watch the sun set?"

"If you're asking if I want to do it with you, I can promise I will," Quinn answers. "As long as I'm not on call at the firehouse, I'm here." He leans down to kiss her softly, brushing his mouth against her cheek.

"That sounds like a pretty good plan."

Josie watches a group of teen girls walk by. Their heads are down, giggling to each other. She sees them walk past, then stop and turn around.

"Are you Josie Remington from that TV show, *The Shallows*?" one of the girls asks shyly.

Josie nods. "I am," she says proudly. She doesn't even wish for a hat to hide herself. After all this time, she realizes she can be Josie Remington, AKA Eve Mattson. They're both a part of her, as halves and the whole.

"Can we take a selfie?"

About the Author

Erica Reilly was born in New Jersey and raised all over the East Coast. She lives in West Chester, PA, with her husband, Brett, and four children. Their extended family has been going to Stone Harbor for three generations.

You can connect with me on:

http://www.ericamreilly.com

https://www.facebook.com/erica.reilly.writes

Also by Erica M. Reilly

The Swells of Stone Harbor
What's the difference between a Swell, a Benny, and a Shoobie?

Margo St. James can tell you. As a third-generation Stone Harbor native and local artist, she watches the town's population balloon from 800 to over 20,000 as soon as Memorial Day Weekend arrives.

But this summer is different. Someone in town is sinking sailboats, targeting businesses, stealing town property, and breaking into beach homes. Who's behind it and what are their reasons for wreaking havoc on 7 Mile Island?

www.ingramcontent.com/pod-product-compliance
Lightning Source LLC
Chambersburg PA
CBHW032002150726
47990CB00005B/1812